ACHRON KINDNESS

by

Algerine Onyx

TELEMACHUS PRESS

Cover designed by Telemachus Press, LLC

Cover art:
Copyright © iStockPhoto/513303342/aopsan
Copyright © iStockPhoto/514176585/powerofforever
Copyright © iStockPhoto/518281556/PeopleImages
Copyright © iStockPhoto/621385748/4x6

Published by:
Telemachus Press, LLC
7652 Sawmill Road, Suite 304
Dublin, Ohio 43016
http://www.telemachuspress.com

Visit the author website:
http://www.algerineonyx.com

You can contact the author or its representative at:
TCalr@protonmail.com

FICTION / Science Fiction / Alien Contact

ISBN: 978-1-945330-73-5 (eBook)
ISBN: 978-1-945330-74-2 (Paperback)

Version 2019.05.10

A NOTE FROM THE AUTHOR'S REPRESENTATIVE

This book consists of "speculative fiction." Well, kind of ….

It's a story told by an alien entity (not "another nationality" but rather a "not-human" type alien). It (the alien) has taken the *nom de plume* "Algerine Onyx" (for reasons of its own; I only know what it tells me). It's also known by its instantiation number, which is simply "#5." I'm not totally clear what the deal is on instantiation, but I presume that Onyx will explain when (and if) it feels like it.

Algerine Onyx—aka "#5"—is a "transitioned intelligence" or "TI" for short. It is apparently one of several hundred currently loose in our world (remember, I only know what it tells me). Since Achrons in their biologic form don't reflect sexual dimorphism, neither do their TI's (my limited understanding is that in their original habitat they reproduced by some form of vegetative reproduction, possibly budding or fragmentation).

Thus, Achron TI's are often referred to in the story as "it," at least when they haven't taken the form of a human or other animal (no, they're not "body snatchers"). Algerine, who told me about the Achron lack of sexual polarity, approves of the use of the pronoun "it." But when an Achron has taken human form, we decided to use normal gender-references for normal human males and females.

In their original form Achrons are a species living in a star system not too far from the Pleiades Cluster, over 400 light years from Earth. The Achron TI's on Earth no longer have their original form, of course, but they still identify as "Achrons" (kind of like how we humans continue to identify with our hometown sports teams even after we've moved away).

This book? #5 decided it wanted to be a storyteller-to-humans, and contacted me to inquire about representation and assistance. That's how I became an "ALR" or "Alien Literary Representative" (the first and only one on Earth to my knowledge).

Why doesn't Algerine do its own publishing? I think it wants its stories to be filtered through a human perspective, for one thing (even though some would say I'm a lawyer, not a human). Otherwise I really don't know. Achron TI's have their own reasons (they sometimes act so …

alien), but I do believe that #5 just simply enjoys the old-fashioned human pastime of storytelling.

There's another thing that's cool about Achrons: They're quite funny (as in "ha-ha!" not *"odd"* ... although they're that too). They seem to have one hell of a sense of humor, and Algerine seems to enjoy high-level humor as much as it likes telling stories. (Like I say, Achrons are kind of ... *alien*.)

What follows is the result of a collaboration with #5, aka Algerine Onyx. The story belongs to it ... I just help in various ways, including doing the literary representing.

Algerine says it hopes you like the story. But if you don't, then it wants you to know "you're a xenophobic humano-normative chauvinist." (I didn't want to say that, but I have a duty to render communications from my client as accurately as possible. Sorry about that.)

So ... *enjoy the story*, human readers!

Timothy Condon, ALR (Alien Literary Representative)
The Gorham Arcology, Gorham, New Hampshire 03581
TCalr@protonmail.com

NOTE: The contents of this book are intended solely for the human and alien reader, and may contain confidential and/or legally privileged human or alien information. If you are not a human or alien, or if this message is addressed to you in error, you can alert the author by sending an email to its representative below.

Visit the author's web page at:
www.algerineonyx.com

You can contact the author or its representative at:
TCalr@protonmail.com

TABLE OF CONTENTS

ACHRON KINDNESS

CHAPTER 1
Suburban Bliss: A Lemonade Stand.

The scene? Norman Rockwell all the way. Nice neighborhood, tree-lined street, and a little girl with a lemonade stand. Behind the girl is a black dog with some white patches lying in the grass.

Add in a folding table and chair, some paper cups, a pitcher and a misspelled cardboard sign—*"Lemoade! 25cents"*—and there you have it: Suburban bliss in the heartland city of Winston, Pennsylvania. *It could be anywhere!*

Now add in two police cars with lights flashing, an ambulance blocking the road, and the little girl fighting back tears. She faces Officer Kenny McKinney, one of Winston's finest. As a local cop he's no better and no worse than many others.

Think about it: You get a job as a cop, maybe because you like to tussle. You might do some good too, even if it's only incidental. In the beginning at least. Then it starts to eat away at you. And after a few years, you begin to see humanity as the unmitigated pool of shit it is.

Oh well.

McKinney didn't particularly like busting up the kid's lemonade stand. But rules were rules. The kid couldn't ignore them. Especially when a neighbor rushed to call the police after spotting the lemonade stand. Mrs. Harriman Newton the Third ... she was on it immediately, loudly indignant that "a business" was being set up on her street. *Right there in her neighborhood!*

Orders are orders too, even when they result from an old busybody calling the cops about nothing. *Jesus*. Officer McKinney could see the house from where he was standing. It was two blocks down the street. *Lady must have eyes like an eagle*, he thought. *Old bag*.

So the sergeant downtown tells McKinney, "The chief says go out there and shut it down. Little girls don't vote."

Officer McKinney walked up to Sarah McLaughlin's lemonade stand. Another cruiser arrived, bored on a Saturday morning, looking for some fun at McKinney's expense.

"I'm sorry, honey, but you can't have a lemonade stand here," he said to the girl.

Two other cops wandered up. It was Art Smith and Jase Crandon from the south side. McKinney turned to them: "You guys got nothing better to do?"

"Figured you might need some *backup*," said Smith, grinning widely. McKinney turned back to the little girl. The "*Lemoade 25cents*" sign hung down from the front of the table.

"Look," said McKinney to the girl, "you're not allowed to sell lemonade unless you have a city license." He paused. *Damn this sucks*. "Do you have a city license to sell lemonade?" *Of course she doesn't. The city doesn't allow licenses for kids' lemonade stands*.

The little girl was angry, despite fighting back tears. Sarah McLaughlin was 7 years old. She'd just finished first grade. It was summer. "Why can't I?" she said with as much defiance as she could muster. "I'm not doing anything wrong." Her lips were trembling, tears filling her eyes.

McKinney could hear Smith and Crandon snickering behind him. *Sigh*. "You can't because it's against the law," he said tiredly. "I'm sorry kid, but you have to take it down. You can't sell lemonade unless you've got a city license."

Sarah tried another angle. She held up a cup of lemonade. "Here," she said. "Try it. You'll like it." She was almost pleading.

McKinney took another breath. "I can't do that," he said. "Look, you have to take down your lemonade stand. I'm sorry." He didn't take the cup of lemonade from Sarah McLaughlin, and didn't feel so good about himself this morning. Especially with the two smirking cops behind him.

"What seems to be the problem here?" asked a voice from one side.

McKinney turned his head to look. A homeless bum, disheveled and dirty, had shuffled up. He stopped behind the lemonade stand pushing a grocery cart with a few ragged possessions. An old guy, maybe in his 70s from the look of him. Bushy white hair flowed out from under a grimy baseball cap while a large white beard made the old guy look like some kind of skinny Santa Claus. He stood leaning on an old cane.

Officer McKinney reacted immediately: *"This is not your business sir!"* he snarled in his command voice. *"Please move on now sir!"*

Sarah was fighting back tears, looking back and forth between the police and the bum.

"Oh I think it *is* my business officer," said the old man. "Are you some kind of strange pedophile? Bothering this little girl today? Budding entrepreneur that she is?"

McKinney began grinding his teeth. *I deal with this shit too much. Old bastard's asking for an ass-whipping.* He could feel Smith and Crandon move up behind him in support. They may have been ragging him a minute before but no one—*no one*—challenged police authority in Winston, Pennsylvania. Especially some dirty old bum shuffling down the street.

The old man turned to Sarah and spoke in a kindly voice: "What gave you the idea to sell lemonade today, young lady?"

McKinney cut in: *"I told you to move along, mister.* I won't say it again. *Get outta here!"*

Sarah looked back and forth between the two, her eyes fearful. "I want to buy a doll," she said in a small voice. "It's special. I saw it in a window at the Bailey Mall." She was choking out the words, still holding back tears.

"How much money do you think you'd make if you sold *alllll* your lemonade today?" asked the old fellow, smiling as he stretched out the word.

Officer McKinney stood there steaming. He clenched his fists. *This guy is going to take a beating if he doesn't get the hell outta here.*

"$15 if I sold it all ... I think," said the girl. She was still looking back and forth between McKinney and the bum. The old man reached into a pocket and pulled out a $100 bill. "Here my dear," he said. "I'll buy *alllll* your lemonade right now ... and then *I* can stay here and sell lemonade!"

The girl hesitated, then reached out and took the outstretched bill.

Officer McKinney noted the $100 bill. *What the hell. Asshole probably stole the money.* He turned his head and keyed a shoulder mic, muttering into it to call for backup. *Good chance for some stick time. Work out some of the kinks. Teach people not to fuck with cops.*

The old bum was talking to the little girl: "Go on home now," he said with some urgency. "Run home fast!" He was still smiling. "I need to talk with these gentlemen. Now take that money for your doll and go fast! You can come back to get your table and chair later."

Sarah didn't hesitate. She was scared. The police were crowding in, looming over the old man. Terrified, she ran down the street as fast as she could. She looked back once as she heard voices rise, but didn't stop or look back again.

The old bum had sat down on Sarah's folding chair. He planted his cane in front of him, resting his chin and hands on a tarnished brass ferrule. "What seems to be the problem here?" he asked rhetorically. "Has it come to this, officers? Harassing kids out of their lemonade stands?"

McKinney stood facing the bum, his rage building. His face was turning red. *Dammit, blood pressure spiking again. Shouldda taken another of those goddamn heart pills this morning.* He kicked out violently and his boot sent the folding table flying along with paper cups and the jug of lemonade. Smith and Crandon stood on either side facing the bum.

The old man didn't even flinch as the table was kicked aside. He seemed unafraid, almost indifferent as he contemplated the police officers facing him.

Backup squad cars screeched up, slamming on their brakes. The shift sergeant arrived. A glance showed the lieutenant's car had pulled up too. *Shit*, thought McKinney. *No backing down now, even if I wanted to.*

McKinney calmed a bit. The sergeant and lieutenant would call the shots. *Not my problem.* He stood looking down at the old fool, wanting to smash his face in. But a thought intruded: *This could go bad ... witnesses around, people looking out their windows. Fuck'all. Leave it to the brass.*

"What's the status?" snapped the lieutenant as he and the sergeant stepped up to join the three cops facing the bum.

Smith spoke up from beside McKinney: "This guy must think he's some kind of privileged character, Lieutenant. He's interfering with McKinney."

"And he's got a weapon," said Crandon from the other side, gesturing at the old man's cane. The bum looked serene. He didn't move. His chin and hands still rested atop the cane.

Lieutenant Jeff Jacobs read the scene. *Could be a PR problem.* The old guy was nothing, an old bum to be disposed of at will. But neighbors were coming out onto their lawns to see what the commotion was. Others were peering out their front windows. *How to play this ... .*

Shit. The lieutenant knew he had to back his guys. He wasn't going to throw away fifteen years of brown-nosing. He *had* to back up the cops no matter what. That was the code. He stepped forward and spoke in his command voice: *"Sir! You must vacate the area immediately!"* There were now five cops facing the bum, seven if you counted the two plainclothes guys who'd arrived and were hanging back.

"Face it," replied the old guy, "you're all acting like assholes. *Just following orders,* right?" He scanned them, turning his head. *"You need to stop pushing people around,"* he said.

The cops glanced at each other. McKinney was the lead street cop present. It would be his call if the lieutenant and sergeant stepped back. McKinney looked sideways at them. They shrugged. The lieutenant nodded. *Take him. We'll deal with any fallout.*

Another voice interrupted. It was both urgent and calming at the same time. *"Wait a minute, wait a minute, just wait a minute would you?"* It was another cop, just arrived.

Fucking Caisson, thought McKinney, *what a pussy.*

CHAPTER 2
Beatdown on a Bum: Very Bad Idea.

The new cop shouldered his way into the tableau. *"Just hold on, would you guys?"*

Buster Caisson had been on the force for a couple of years. He was a decent cop, but still viewed with suspicion by some. In the Winston Police Department, the motto was *hit first and hit hard*. No one—*no one*—challenged the authority of cops in Winston. That's the way the citizens wanted it.

Buster Caisson though, he wasn't so hot on the attitude. For one thing, he wasn't an adrenaline junky like so many other cops, itching for a fight, for the chase, for the gun draw. Buster had seen and done all that in the Marines, especially during his time in the Sandbox Wars in the Mideast. Repeatedly, in fact.

After four years as a Marine grunt, Buster Caisson got an honorable discharge along with a bunch of ribbons on his uniform. Several were for combat action and there was a bronze star with a combat "V" for valor. The bronze star, he said, was for not getting his ass shot off while helping his buddies draw back in a desert ravine and calling in drone strikes. He mustered out and went back home to Indianapolis where he'd grown up and been a high school sports hero (including varsity point guard on the basketball team and quarterback on the football team).

After four years in the Marines, Buster found it easy to move back home into his parents' basement. He kicked around with some old high school buddies and got an associate of arts degree at the local community college. He especially enjoyed civics and history, two areas that interested him. It was an easy time without much direction. Then one of Buster's buddies suggested he try the police academy at the community college. "Hey, it could lead to a decent job as a cop," his friend said.

Buster figured *why not,* and applied to the police academy. Turned out he liked it. He was pretty good at it too. There was also an intangible. Buster didn't talk about it, but he liked the idea of doing something good, doing something like what he'd done in the military. Helping people who were being kicked around. Catching and busting the bad guys. It all appealed to him, and in the Marines he'd been good at it. So the idea of being a cop was a natural fit... or so he thought.

After graduating from the police academy Buster got lucky: He snagged a job with the police department in Winston, Pennsylvania, graduating from the academy at just the right time. He started at the bottom as a rookie patrolman.

Buster liked police work. His basic equanimity helped, but an easygoing nature made some of his fellow cops think he might be weak. So they tested him. He invited two of them out behind the station on a couple of occasions and beat the shit out of both of them. After that, he didn't get tested anymore. It helped that he did martial arts and kept a workout routine in both Jiu-Jitsu and a Japanese style of karate, Shotokan.

One of the cops he beat up behind the station had gotten a broken wrist. Even though it was only a green stick fracture, Buster had felt bad about it and apologized. The wounded cop held a grudge and didn't accept the apology. His name was Kenny McKinney ... but he didn't hassle Buster anymore. If the rookie cop wanted to appear mild-mannered, that was his business.

On the day of the lemonade stand confrontation, Buster Caisson was one of the street cops on duty, and it was in his district. "Would you all just calm down and step back a second?" he said as he walked into the middle of it. He held his arms up, hands out at both the cops facing the bum and the old man himself. "There's no need to go ballistic on this, okay?"

"This ain't your deal, Caisson," snarled McKinney. "Butt the fuck out!"

"Bullshit," said Buster Caisson. "This is in my district and I'm on duty." He looked over at the lieutenant and shift sergeant. They showed studiously blank faces back at him. *Shit.* He ignored McKinney and turned to the old man. Caisson could sound gentle when he wanted to, and now he squatted down in front of the sitting bum. "Look man," he said in a low voice. "We've got to enforce the ordinances in Winston. If the rules don't allow a lemonade stand, we don't have any choice." He slightly shrugged his shoulders.

The old man listened to Buster Caisson with interest, his eyes bright. He even smiled. "My, my," he said in a low voice, "what have we here, a reasonable officer of the law?" The bum held out his hand. "Amos Tucklee."

Buster Caisson shook the old man's hand. "Buster Caisson," he said. "Actually, it's Patrolman Caisson, Winston Police Department. And if you don't mind, I'm trying to keep you from getting hurt here."

"I think I realize that," said Tucklee. "And don't think I don't appreciate it! These so-called *police officers* are acting like hired thugs today." He smiled at Caisson. "Hired *goons,* if you will!" His eyes were crinkling in mirth.

Buster Caisson sighed and stood up. He looked down pensively at the old man. *That's what I get for trying, dammit.* "The girl can't have a lemonade stand," he said flatly.

"She doesn't *have* a lemonade stand," said Tucklee. "Her lemonade stand was the object of a friendly takeover a minute ago. *I* own it now." He grinned widely and gestured behind him with the cane, holding it near the metal head. "I bought her out!"

Caisson was aware of tension, even rage, building behind him as he faced the bum. "Can't you just pick up and leave?" he implored. "So no one gets hurt?"

The old man stood up suddenly and stepped forward facing Caisson. "I do believe I like you," he said. "So I'm going to help you get some distance from what's going to happen here." Even as he spoke his body seemed to *flow,* pivoting impossibly fast. His arms flew around Patrolman Caisson ... who suddenly found himself flying through the air. He landed an impossible 30 feet away on top of a car, then bounced and rolled off the other side, gasping in pain as he hit the ground and felt something give in a shoulder.

The old man had moved in a flash, and ended up sitting back in the chair where he'd started. No one had reacted, it happened so fast. The cops were left open-mouthed. Several looked over to where Caisson had hit the car roof and rolled off the other side.

"Sorry about that, Officer Caisson!" called out the old man. "Please stay down over there!"

What the fuck just happened? thought Buster Caisson as he lay crumpled on the ground behind the car.

Officer McKinney was the first to recover. He leapt at Amos Tucklee, screaming: ***"On the ground right now asshole!"*** He reached out to grab the old man and throw him down but heard a sharp ***crack!*** No one but McKinney had moved. He stopped abruptly, looking curiously at his outstretched right forearm. It was hanging nearly at a 90 degree angle, broken cleanly and completely between the wrist and elbow. He hadn't felt anything, it was so fast. The pain hadn't even started. The old man was motionless. He still sat on the folding chair, his chin again resting atop the cane. He did not appear to have moved.

McKinney stared stupidly at his ruined forearm. *No one moved,* he thought dumbly. He couldn't feel his hand. The old man grinned up at him, eyes squinting in mirth. The cane had moved so fast ... somehow it had lashed out and come instantly back. *Not even in an eye-blink!* It was even faster than that. *He didn't even fucking move,* thought McKinney.

The pain came then, a wave engulfing the stunned policeman. He grabbed his forearm just behind the break and sank to his knees howling, a guttural primal scream rising from a twisted mouth. His eyes bugged out as he stared at the badly broken arm. Several of the other cops pulled out guns and all began screaming commands: ***Put your hands up! Put down the cane! Drop the gun! Hands on your head! Don't move! Get down! Get on your knees! Hands behind your back!***
Amos Tucklee sat motionlessly, observing. His hands and chin were still resting on the tarnished brass ferrule at the end of the cane. In the midst of the screaming cacophony he held a hand up to one ear, cupping it comically: "What are you all *saaaying?*" he said loudly. "I can't *hear youuu!*"

Other units were arriving. A fire truck trundled up while two other police cruisers screeched to a halt beside it. A second ambulance pulled up behind the first one. McKinney was roaring in pain on his knees on the grass, holding his bent forearm in front of him, staring at the break. **"Mother*fucker!*"** he roared.

Amos Tucklee spoke to the wounded officer: "What did you expect, Mr. McKinney? You tried to assault a defenseless old man! You should be *ashamed* of yourself!"

McKinney grimaced hatred at the bum. *"Mother ... **fucker!**"* he howled again.

Amos Tucklee gazed placidly at the cops screaming commands. He had to speak up to be heard: "Well come on and *get* me fellas! Don't just stand there like *cows!* And help your friend while you're at it!" He reached out with the cane and tapped McKinney lightly on the shoulder, laughing.

*The old bastard's **laughing!***

A cop on a huge motorcycle roared up behind the elderly man. Dropping the cycle on its side, he launched himself at Tucklee, aiming a kick at his head with a heavy motorcycle boot ... and again, faster than any eye could see, the cane lashed out, this time behind and to one side, impacting the cop's knee just above his high leather boot. There was another sharp **crack!** this time louder than before. The cop shrieked in pain and fell sprawling on the grass.

The shouting police officers seemed to coalesce and explode into action. Half of them leaped on the old man while others held their guns outward to protect from imaginary foes. Amos Tucklee was immediately knocked off his chair and went down in a tangle of flying knees, fists and nightsticks. Yet even with the truncheons slamming into him, he was able to yell out from the melee: *"Message from outer space assholes! Ollie ollie oxen free! Better stop messing with kids and their lemonade stands!"*

A half dozen more cops joined the fracas thinking **who the fuck IS this guy?** All were kicking, stomping and wailing the hell out of the old man. Lead-weighted clubs rose and fell at the center, thudding loudly into his body. Others stood back with pistols drawn, looking to menace anyone who tried to interfere.

No one did. Tucklee was now prone on the ground and unmoving as the beating continued. Some of the police officers were kicking him in the side and back. Another knelt, grabbed his hair, yanked his head up, and began beating him in the face with a fist. Another stomped repeatedly on his legs.

One of the old man's ankles snapped loudly. Blood spurted as multiple hands hauled him up then slammed him forcefully onto the sidewalk on his face. Two cops drove knees into his back. Another bone broke loudly as his arms were violently yanked back and twisted up behind him. Amos Tucklee appeared unconscious, his body limp and bloodied as the beating continued, when something … happened.

The old man *exploded.*

First there were a dozen cops present … *and then there were not.* Old Amos Tucklee, Kenny McKinney, Jase Crandon, Art Smith, Lt. Jacobs, the shift sergeant, the motorcycle cop, the two detectives and others who had all piled on … in a thousandth of a second, they were *gone.* Every person inside the immediate blast radius appeared to *vaporize.* They just *disappeared.*

Beyond the blast radius, protected behind the vehicle where he had fallen, Buster Caisson was trying to raise himself up on his uninjured arm.

The blast flattened him again.

CHAPTER 3
Strange Facts for Agent Maxim.

The physics of a high-explosive blast are well understood by science ... but science doesn't convey what it's like to be nearby when such an event occurs. The most common cause of casualties from suicide bombers is shrapnel packed in an explosive vest ... but for a few thousandths of a second there's also an over-pressure blast wave.

More than a dozen policemen were involved in beating Amos Tucklee to death or were close by when the blast occurred. Everything at ground zero of the explosion site ... disappeared. The lemonade stand, the chair, the bum, the cops on top of him, the grocery cart ... even the police *motorcycle*. All were simply *gone*. As if vaporized.

There was only a crater in the ground at the spot.

Others nearby were injured. People were thrown down, eardrums were burst, police cars and ambulances were wrecked. Homes and property were damaged. Nearby windows were blown out and doors knocked off hinges.

But at the scene, only the crater remained.

The bomb caused house and car alarms to go off, and sirens were heard racing to the scene almost immediately. The blast was also detected and noted by certain government agencies. Automated alerts went out to the FBI, Homeland Security, the TSA and other federal agencies including the NSA and CIA. National security systems were alerted and preplanned exigencies snicked into place, searching for information, seeking evaluation.

Sarah McLaughlin had made it home and was far down the street when the bomb went off. She and her mother were shaken but unharmed.

The FBI was on the scene within minutes. Within an hour word of a suicide bomb attack spread. In another hour communications were circulating at high levels indicating a problem: There was no shrapnel in evidence at the blast site. Nor were there any bodies or body parts to be found. In another hour whispering began. *There's nothing there but a crater.* No bloody tissue, no debris, no twisted metal. Everything was just ... *eradicated.*

In Washington, DC the President's domestic security adviser took note of an explosion involving a lemonade stand in Pennsylvania, but didn't include it in the daily briefing. He waited for further information. The preliminary consensus was some kind of random terrorist bombing.

The preliminary consensus was wrong.

Local police and FBI on the scene went heavy-handed on the investigation, as usual. The neighborhood was cordoned off and sealed. Residents were taken out of their homes and interrogated. Sarah McLaughlin's parents were arrested and held incommunicado under one of the Patriot Acts. Sarah herself was to be placed with a foster family "for her own safety."

A state bomb-squad forensic team was dispatched to the scene and it wasn't long before there were some unsettling observations: *It wasn't a "normal" terrorist bombing.* In fact, it wasn't a normal explosion. The blast wave propagation damage appeared to be ... abnormal.

The blast forensics team was baffled. For one thing, there was no blood at the site. *None.* There weren't any body parts either. "Goddamn, that doesn't happen," said one team member to an FBI agent. "There's got to be body parts."

But there were none.

Even more odd was the lack of debris. The table? The folding chair? The grocery cart? Okay, they could be blown away, maybe sailing through the air and out of the immediate vicinity. But a motorcycle? An *entire motorcycle?* "That doesn't happen," said the bomb squad guy. "Where the fuck is the motorcycle?"

Searches were ordered in ever-widening circles as more police and FBI agents arrived. *Nothing was found.*

The FBI took control of the investigation and Special Agent Angela Maxim was assigned to run it. She didn't make the decision to clamp down on the entire neighborhood. It had already begun by the time she got on the scene.

Angela Maxim was unusual. Maybe it was because she was an Army veteran, maybe it was because she was a female minority in a male-dominated profession. She wasn't a ball-buster, for one thing. And she tried not to abuse civilians caught up in an investigation. She also got along well with her fellow agents.

Maxim had gone into the Army at age 18, right out of high school. She'd served time in one of the Sandbox Wars, then got out after a few years and went to college on the GI Bill. That got her a degree in accounting with a minor in criminal justice. From there it was easy to take the LSAT and attend law school. After graduating with honors she was snatched up by the FBI looking to boost its political correctness bona fides.

At not quite 30 years old, Angela Maxim found that working in the FBI suited her. Unlike other agents, she wasn't interested in being a gung-ho G-Man. On the contrary, Angela Maxim was cerebral. She specialized in white collar crime, a complex and often convoluted arena involving obscure paper trails and money flows, from Ponzi schemes to drug cartels to corrupt fedgov operators in the Treasury Department and IRS.

That meant that knotty complicated stuff often ended up on Angela's desk, and she welcomed it. Other agents were only too happy to unload such cases on her, and it boosted her popularity considerably.

Angela Maxim was an unusual agent in other ways too: While she'd seen combat in Iraq and Syria, she was comfortable being mild-mannered. Having lived through the fire of military service and combat, she wasn't inclined to bust balls. *Life's hard enough*, she thought, *no reason to make it harder.*

"Oh, I'll *shoot* somebody's ass if I have to," she'd say over a drink at an FBI watering hole after work, "but I'd really rather not. I'm an accountant and a *lawyer*, for god's sake." And she'd leave it at that. The other agents would laugh, but they respected her attitude ... as well as her brains, bravery, and unflappability.

Not only had Angela Maxim survived the Sandbox Wars, she was also a looker. She had fine white skin framed by long, straight, almost-black hair that cascaded over her shoulders when she let it loose. "A remnant from some Spaniard who washed up on an Irish beach," she joked. "I'm part *Black Irish!*" Other than that, her heritage was mostly Celtic.

The brains, easygoing manner and good looks caused more than one agent in the office to ask Angela Maxim out on a date. And she did date a little, but was very careful to keep it light. *Very light.* "Don't get your sex where you get your checks," she'd say, sometimes apologetically at the end of an evening. After all, she did like some of the guys from the office ... but she knew it wouldn't be good policy. For all the well-known reasons.

Besides, there were other things Angela Maxim really enjoyed ... like working out complicated puzzles involving white collar criminality. The toughest ones featured really smart criminals who could put together laby-rinthine scams generating blizzards of paper along with cascades of illicit money. In her own mind she would privately thank them. Then she would unravel the whole thing and burrow down to the nub, finding the weak spots. *And there was always a weak spot.*

Angela admired other people who did what she did. Like the guys at the SEC who'd finally—*"finally"*—gotten a clue about Bernie Madoff back in the 2000s and taken him down. She read books about such cases, picking up tips and thoroughly enjoying the reading. The bottom line was that Angela Maxim couldn't be cowed by complexity or baffled by bullshit ... no matter how smart the perps were. "Thousands of people lose their life savings to these assholes," she'd say. "The least we can do is take 'em down. It's not terrorism and it's not bank robbery ... but it's still bullshit."

Her agent friends agreed. They respected a girl like Angela, but white collar crime wasn't what they signed up for: Like most agents they craved action, cops-and-robbers shit with terrorists spraying AK rounds and trying to bring down airliners. They wanted *adrenalin,* a big high that never got old and was never better than when they were *kicking ass and taking names.*

Problem was, as the fedgov and its agencies got ever more powerful—*including the FBI*—they were also becoming more abusive.

"Power tends to corrupt," thought Angela Maxim, who was comparatively easy-going and cerebral. Originally that made her something of an outsider at the FBI. She was also known to be something of a straight-arrow, rever-ing the foundations of American government ... and she let it be known.

Increasingly, though, such values were honored mainly in their breach ... if at all.

Nonetheless, Maxim refused to cross a line: If something was required by law and by the Constitution, she would not ignore it. She never bent the rules for either convenience or necessity.

"Bad guys can be taken down without *us* breaking the law," she argued. "We've got the tools, and the rule of law is more important than a collar." Other agents looked at her oddly when she talked that way: *Jesus ... a god-damned Tinkerbell.*

"If we can't take 'em down inside the law, we're not the good guys," Angela Maxim insisted. "It's as simple as that!" Her fellow agents thought *jeez, what a straight fuckin' arrow,* but didn't say anything. And they still respected her, even if a little oddly, for her uncompromising outlook. Besides, she would come to the watering hole after work just like anyone else, have a drink and talk ... so she was okay, even if a little straight-laced.

Thus it was somewhat unusual that Special Agent Angela Maxim got put in charge of investigating a terrorist bombing resulting in a number of deaths ... apparently sparked in a dispute over a little girl's lemonade stand. *And where an entire Harley Davidson motorcycle had gone missing.*

"Hold it, hold it," she said to the bomb squad guy. "What do you mean *that doesn't happen?*"

"I mean there's gotta be debris," the guy said. "There's gotta be shit lying around, like blood and guts unless it's a fuckin' A-bomb. Shit doesn't just, like ... *disappear.*"

Agent Maxim thought about that for a second. "How far out do we need to look? The debris has to be somewhere. It could have gotten blown out of the immediate vicinity, right? I mean, if it was a big bomb stuff could be thrown quite a distance, right?"

"Well, yes and no," said the bomb squad guy. "If it was one hell of a big bomb, yes. But to throw everything like that it wouldda had to be bigger than the one that went off. Lots bigger. Vehicles around it wouldda been trashed and flipped. Fronts of houses would've been blown away." He paused. "It wouldda been like the Murrah building bombing in Oklahoma, like a big truck bomb, and that ain't the case here. The crater's not big enough."

"There is a pretty big hole in the ground," she observed.

"Yeah," he said, "but not one big enough to make stuff *disappear*. Not enough to throw a whole fuckin' *motorcycle* out of the neighborhood. No way. If it was that big, the front of some of these houses would be gone." The guy waved his arm in the direction of some of the homes on the street.

In the back of her mind, Maxim felt a hint of alarm. Bells were going off, but she couldn't tell why. "Look," she said, "the stuff has to be around here somewhere. I'll expand the search area."

A city police captain was standing nearby. He'd come up to liaise with the FBI. She turned to him: "You heard the bomb squad guy?" The police captain nodded. "Let's get all the people here we can," she said, "and widen the search pattern. How many city cops can you get here?"

"Probably 40 or 50," he said. "How about the feds?"

"Most of my people are interviewing witnesses and neighbors," said Angela. "But I'll tell them to see you soon as they get free. You tell 'em what sectors to cover. I want 100 yards out in all directions. Hell, some of the stuff could have been thrown *over* these houses. Who knows ...."

The police captain nodded again.

"Let's see if we can find some of it before the day's out," she said.

"I'll get it started," said the cop. He strode away to talk to a group of police waiting nearby.

Maxim pulled out her cell phone and called the office. A female voice answered. "Marge, I'm at the blast site from this morning. I'm getting some strange reports from the local bomb guys. I think we're going to need an explosives team out of DC to look at this. And I need more manpower. There's a motorcycle gone missing at the blast site."

"A what?" said Marge.

"A motorcycle," she said. "A full-sized Harley Davidson has gone missing, and there aren't any body parts here like there should be. Something's weird. Call up the county sheriff and get the local town departments to send some people. We're going to need to cover this place out to a pretty good distance. Ask Murphy to send an agent to collect all the dash cams and electronic stuff here too."

"Will do," said Marge.

"ASAP please," said Angela.

"Always," came back the response.

Angela Maxim signed off. Tendrils of uneasiness crept up her back. Something was ... *wrong*. She didn't care if she usually did white-collar crime investigation. She knew "not right" when she saw it. And this was not right.

Something's going on, she thought ... *something not ordinary*.

Her unease persisted as the chill up her back crept into her mind.

CHAPTER 4
Mrs. Harriman Newton III Loses a Hand.

The police quickly cordoned off the Wilding Oaks neighborhood as government agents converged from multiple police departments and the FBI. Sarah McLaughlin's mother and father, Dave and Meghan McLaughlin, were arrested for allowing their daughter to set up an unauthorized lemonade stand and therefore causing the tragedy.

Sarah's father David was a local contractor, while her mother Meghan worked for an insurance agency. A quick check by the authorities revealed that Dave McLaughlin had been politically active in local politics as a member of a Tea Party type group fighting against rising city and county taxes.

Sarah was taken downtown and held until the police chief met with the local district attorney, Nick Alabattis. Also present at the meeting was the publisher of the local Winston newspaper. Possible narratives were discussed before it was agreed that the explosion would be called domestic terrorism, with Sarah's parents characterized as dangerous right-wing activists and possibly neo-Nazis for their Tea Party activism.

Nick Alabattis nodded at the agreement. As an elected local politician he knew there was opportunity in the tragedy. *No crisis should go to waste*, he thought, especially when it came to local citizen groups fighting against taxes. The local media that served the Winston political structure called them "selfish" and "greedy", as did the public employee unions whose benefits and pay raises came from ever-increasing local taxing and spending.

The anti-Tea Party narrative could be expanded now. *Anyone* who protested bigger local government could be characterized as far-right dangers to society ... and even potential terrorists. After all, higher taxes were necessary to fund the many public projects that always enriched well-connected local insiders.

"Government doesn't shrink and it shouldn't shrink," said Alabattis in his election campaign. "Our city and county governments need to grow so they can do more good. Higher taxes are necessary to provide essential services demanded by the public!"

It was all bullshit, of course, and Nick Alabattis, like any politician, knew it. But with the police department and local media in his corner, the public ate it up. So on this day he directed that Sarah McLaughlin be put in a foster home for the time being. "Use the standard abuse and neglect charges," he said. "Get Child Protective Services to come get her."

Sarah McLaughlin's whereabouts would not be disclosed to her parents. Nor would they be allowed to talk to her. *That's one hell of a lever*, thought Alabattis, reflecting that it would also help his re-election campaign the following year. *Just doing the right thing, protecting a little girl from her dangerous and abusive parents.*

Sarah McLaughlin ended up in a filthy foster home with eight other children, some of whom had been subject to *real* abuse and neglect. Some of the kids in the house were also mentally ill and violent on occasion. The foster parents were a homosexual couple who were paid $75 a week for each child in their charge. Both were alcoholic drug-users, so most of the money went for booze and drugs.

In the meantime every resident in Wilding Oaks was being interviewed by investigators, including Mrs. Harriman Newton III, who was visited by an FBI agent at her home where she had lived for many years. Childless, she and her husband had decided early-on that life would be better without children.

All that money, they reasoned, *would be better spent on us and our interests than on unnecessary children.* But Mrs. Harriman's husband had died, leaving her alone, but "quite comfortable and financially independent" as she was quick to point out.

With no husband, no children, and no grandchildren, Mrs. Newton had little to do. She took up the slack by meddling in the affairs of others in her neighborhood. Thus it was no surprise that police were called by her that morning as soon as she spotted Sarah McLaughlin's "Lemoade stand".

When a police cruiser showed up, Mrs. Newton was happy to point out the "illegal business" two blocks away. After the explosion, other law enforcement agents visited, which also made her feel important as she explained how she had promptly reported the illegal lemonade stand.

A day later, while the Wilding Oaks neighborhood was still cordoned off by the authorities, Mrs. Newton was thrilled to be visited by a second FBI agent. She quickly answered when the doorbell rang, seeing that it was another investigator at her door. The explosion, deaths, and excitement had alleviated her boredom and loneliness, giving her a sense of *importance*. After all, she had called in the violation, insisting that the law be enforced. *It's too bad about the dead people,* she thought, *but we all have an obligation to obey the rules.*

At the door was a young man in a dark suit. *Very official-looking,* she thought approvingly. He had short brown hair, black-rimmed glasses, and carried a notebook with a clipboard. Mrs. Newton barely looked when he proffered his identification. She invited him in, eager to talk about her important part in the recent events. She led him to a chair in the living room and they both sat down. She asked if he would like coffee or tea.

"Thank you Mrs. Newton, but that won't be necessary," he said. "My name is Steven Antonelli, and I have been designated to be your contact with some federal authorities in this matter."

"But wasn't that an FBI agent I talked to yesterday afternoon?" she queried.

"Yes ma'am," said Mr. Antonelli. "But there are different departments, and I like to interview important witnesses personally rather than relying on reports." Mrs. Newton sat up straighter, happy for the attention.

The investigator continued: "My understanding is that you called in the complaint on Saturday morning, is that correct?"

"Oh yes," she said. "Just as soon as I noticed it."

"What did you see exactly, ma'am?"

"Well, the child was down the street. She had set up some kind of ... *roadside stand* in the middle of our neighborhood. I was afraid she would be blocking traffic, making things dangerous."

"Did you know that setting up a roadside lemonade stand was illegal?"

"Well ... not exactly," said Mrs. Newton. "Not at the time, but it seemed obvious that such a thing should not be allowed. I've lived in this neighborhood for many years. I knew immediately it was probably in violation of some rule. And in addition to the traffic problems, the girl was also blocking people from using the sidewalk."

"Yes ma'am," said Antonelli, jotting notes on his pad. "Did you see anyone prevented from using the sidewalk?"

"No I did not," she said proudly. "I was able to report the obstruction the very first thing in the morning, before it became a problem."

"Did you see any problem with vehicular traffic at the location when you noticed the lemonade stand?"

"Not at all," she answered. "As I said, I reported it early in the morning as soon as I saw it. There was no opportunity for traffic flow to be impaired."

"Then how is it that you knew there would be a problem with street or sidewalk traffic?"

Mrs. Newton was nonplussed. "I have lived in this neighborhood for many years ..." she began.

"I understand that," said Antonelli. "So you are familiar with that intersection, correct?"

"Quite right," said Mrs. Newton. "And as such, I feel it is my special obligation to ensure the orderly safety of this neighborhood. All rules, laws, regulations, and ordinances must be complied with, or we would have anarchy you know."

The agent nodded his head as he jotted more notes. "If a car had stopped to buy lemonade, ma'am, could another car have gone around it?"

Mrs. Newton looked perplexed again. This wasn't going the way she expected. "Well ... yes, probably. Our streets are quite wide in Wilding Oaks."

"And as you said, you didn't actually *see* any traffic being impeded, correct?" Antonelli put the tip of his pen to his lips and gazed at Mrs. Newton.

"Well that's not really the question," she said. "That's not the point at all! While it is true that we have very little traffic in our neighborhood, the fact is that the girl was breaking the law."

"Yes ma'am," he said. "Did you know that she was trying to make money to buy a special doll for herself?"

Mrs. Newton was becoming agitated. She knew that a dozen police officers had died, she'd read about it in the paper that morning. But if that was the price of preventing people from doing whatever they wanted, then it was a price well-paid. "Now see here," she said. "I have no idea what the child may or may not have been trying to do ...."

Steven Antonelli interrupted her conversationally: "She was trying to sell cups of lemonade."

"Well yes, of course," she responded, "but it's the principle of the thing! I have always felt that rules are put in place for a reason. We can't have everyone just doing whatever they please whenever they want to!"

Antonelli had the pen up to his lips again; he held it there and talked through it, which looked odd: "So while you didn't know that Sarah McLaughlin's lemonade stand was illegal at the time, you still chose to call the police about it?"

Mrs. Newton sounded put-upon: "Yes," she snapped. "I did my duty as a responsible member of society and property-owner in this neighborhood!"

"If you had known that your call would result in the death of a dozen people, would you still have made it?"

Mrs. Newton frowned at him. "Well of course!" she said petulantly. "I told you, we have to uphold the rules, I don't want anarchy and neither do you or your employer the FBI!"

Steven Antonelli regarded Mrs. Newton levelly from where he sat, as if examining a laboratory specimen. "I didn't actually say I was from the FBI ...."

Mrs. Newton was getting more agitated. "Then it may be time for you to leave, especially if you don't believe in upholding the law!" She moved to get up.

Antonelli leaned forward across the table and matter-of-factly put a hand on Mrs. Newton's chest and shoved her back down into her chair. "I'm not through interviewing you," he said.

"Young man you will unhand me right now and leave immediately!" she demanded.

"I have not completed my investigation," he said. "In fact, I'm trying to understand what motivates you ... and people like you. What makes you do the things that you do? Will you humor me?"

Mrs. Newton was terrified, her eyes wide. She didn't respond.

"You see," said the investigator, "I'm something of an anthropologist. I study people. I try to understand why they act the way they do. You have just caused the death of a dozen human beings. Yet you seem unconcerned with that fact ... even proud of it. I am trying to understand why."

Mrs. Newton's voice was quavering. "Please leave my house immediately! I don't know who you are or why you are here, but I do not want your presence here. I will call the police!"

The man's voice was gentle, still conversational: "I don't think so, Mrs. Newton, because if you try get up out of that chair I will stop you with force. And force is what we're discussing here, isn't it? By calling and complaining to the police about Sarah McLaughlin's lemonade stand, you wanted them to use force against the girl, didn't you ... to stop her from selling cups of lemonade."

He smiled across the table at Mrs. Newton and continued: "Essentially you wanted help from people with more power than you ... to impose your will on Sarah McLaughlin on your behalf. Is that a fair statement?" He raised his eyebrows questioningly.

Terrified, the older woman shrank away from him in her chair. "Please, I don't know what you're talking about. You can have whatever you want. Please just take it and leave."

"Thank you for the offer, Mrs. Newton, but I'm still trying to understand what motivates you. Why did you do what you did? A dozen people were killed as a result of your public-spirited phone call. Sarah's mother and father have been taken into custody by the police. Sarah herself has been taken from them and put into a foster home where she is subject to extensive abuse from two alcoholic caretakers and several truly abused children, some of whom are mentally ill and violent. Can you explain to me in your own words why that is a desirable outcome?"

"I don't know!" wailed Mrs. Newton. She was holding her hands over her face, crying and terrified. "It was the normal thing to do! It was ... it was something to do. I didn't know this would happen."

"No," responded Antonelli, "of course you didn't anticipate the cascade of events you caused. How could you? We know you humans rarely consider the consequences of your viciousness until it boomerangs."

Mrs. Newton stopped rocking and removed her hands from her face. *"We?"* she asked quizzically. Then, *"You humans?* You said, *you humans?"*

Antonelli nodded his head. "Yes *we* ... and yes, *you humans"* He paused and sighed. "What an ugly reality you live in, with your pervasive lies, violence, injustice, wars, coercion ... even genocide." He paused again. "We intend to help."

Mrs. Newton stared at him now, bug-eyed. She could hardly breathe. She was faced by a lunatic.

"I'm going to let you think about it," Antonelli continued. "Let's call it a *proof of concept*." He held his hand out across the table. "Here. Please take my hand."

"What ... what do you mean?" she said fearfully. The man was holding his hand out, inviting her to shake hands as he reached inside his jacket to retrieve something.

Mrs. Newton held out her right hand hesitantly. "Please go away," she said again.

Steven Antonelli grasped her hand as his other came out of his jacket holding a plastic quick-tie. He pulled the older woman's hand toward him and smiled. It was an odd, twisted, open-mouthed smile, showing bright white teeth nicely aligned.

Mrs. Newton was looking at his face as her hand came off, severed cleanly at the wrist ... which was now spouting arterial blood. Antonelli grabbed the severed hand and held it in his teeth as he seized the stump of the elderly woman's forearm and squeezed it to shut off the spurting blood. He deftly slipped the plastic quick-tie over the stump and yanked it tight.

It occurred so fast that the older woman sat transfixed. She was looking at the young man's handsome face and his oddly open-mouthed smile ...

and then at the end of her forearm was a bleeding stump! Her mouth hung open, gaping. She would soon be screaming, turning white and going into shock.

A cell phone appeared in the man's hand as he held up her forearm, her severed hand dangling from his teeth. He dialed 911 and the answer was immediate. He spoke around the severed hand, a wizened finger clamped in his teeth.

"We've got a severed hand here," he said. "Address 458 Anson Court in Winston. It's a couple of blocks from the Wilding Oaks explosion site. There's a tourniquet on it, but ... *can you give us a hand?*" He punched the phone off and took the severed hand from his mouth. He waved it at Mrs. Newton who tried to scream, but only squeaks came from her mouth.

"I'm going to take this with me," he said. "You will do without it for a time ... maybe forever. I might give it back to you, or I might not. But I do want you to think about what you have done, and why you did it. *Reflect* upon it. Do you understand?"

Mrs. Newton was in no condition to respond. She was turning white as she tried to scream, her truncated arm still held up in front of her.

"Message from outer space!" he barked at her as he stood up: *"Ollie ollie oxen free. You need to stop fucking with people."* He turned and walked through the front door without closing it, swinging the severed hand as he strode out.

In less than a minute a police cruiser slammed to a stop in front of Mrs. Newton's home. Two uniformed police rushed through the open front door, their hands on their holstered pistols. She was still sitting, screaming weakly, staring at the stump of her forearm held up in front of her.

Within a few more minutes FBI special agent Angela Maxim was on the scene. An immediate search for Mrs. Newton's severed hand was mounted, but nothing was found.

The hand had simply ... *disappeared.* As had Steven Antonelli.

CHAPTER 5
Psychiatrist-Time for Agent Maxim?

Special agent Angela Maxim stood in front of Mrs. Harriman Newton III's home. She turned slowly, looking up and down the street, then circled the house, nosing into bushes, testing windows, looking for something, *anything*, out of place.

Damn! Maxim thought. She was back in the front yard again. She looked across the street, then in both directions slowly turning her head, taking in everything. Her initial uneasiness had been magnified.

It wasn't just Mrs. Newton's missing hand. There were other things. There was the surviving police officer, Buster Caisson ... what he had told her. Or rather what the suicide bomber had done to him before the bomb went off. Then there were the suicide bomber's last words, what he'd yelled out before everyone present had died.

Angela Maxim, like any cop at any level, was used to seeing *odd* ... but this was beyond odd. The missing bodies, the missing blood, the missing debris ... an entire *motorcycle* missing for god's sake. All ... *gone*.

And now this. She was still in front of Mrs. Newton's house, standing silently, unmoving. *Something is wrong here*.

An FBI forensic team had been called and was inside the house. Mrs. Newton had been evacuated to the hospital, complaining bitterly to the EMT crew about her missing hand, demanding that they find and reattach it. The forensic team in the house was clad in white isolation suits, deploying DNA sniffers and small vacuums. Photographers would follow to record the scene.

Angela Maxim noticed a dog running loose on the sidewalk. It trotted toward her unattended and in violation of the city's strict leash law. *That's odd*, thought Maxim. *No owner. Must be a stray.* But no, the dog was no stray. It appeared well fed and had a sleek black coat and a collar around its neck. It looked to be 30 or 40 pounds and had a few white spots on its otherwise all-black coat. It seemed to be interested in agent Maxim as it trotted toward her.

The FBI agent turned away. *No time for stray dogs.* She was facing the front of Mrs. Newton's house again. The front door was partly open. She could see the white-suited FBI team moving about inside.

It wasn't clear whether she heard it first or felt it. Maybe both at the same time. As Angela Maxim stood in front of Mrs. Newton's home she realized the dog was right next to her ... urinating on her low-heeled black shoes. "Shit!" she said, jumping to one side.

She put out a foot to shove the dog away. *I don't want to KICK the pooch,* she thought. *I love dogs as much as anyone else, but ... the damned thing pissed on my shoes!*

She considered giving the dog a swift kick as it looked up at her baring its teeth. It wasn't growling. The hair on its back wasn't standing up. It was ... *grinning* at her. *What the hell, what's so damned funny?* thought agent Maxim. She stepped back a couple of paces. The dog followed her, still baring its teeth in a "submission smile," the kind seen in countless adorable online dog videos.

The dog stayed in front of her, still grinning up. Maxim glanced around to see if anyone was looking. The dog moved to a position to pee on her shoes again. Maxim jumped away. "What the hell, dog!" she yelled. "Get outta here! Go piss on someone else's shoes!" She waved a hand at the dog to shoo it away. "Go on!" she said. "Go away!"

The dog turned to face her again and sat down. It was still looking up with that stupid grin on its muzzle.

Maxim looked around again. *This could be embarrassing.* But no one was present except for the team inside the house. She heard a child's high-pitched voice speak: "Doctor Maxim, I presume, har, har, har ...."

Angela looked around. She had clearly heard a child's voice. The dog still sat in front of her, looking up at her intently. She spun around sharply, looking for where the voice had come from.

It came again: "You won't find anyone, Agent Maxim. It's me ... *down here.*"

Maxim raised her voice, still turning and looking: "Hello? Where are you? And who just said *it's me?*"

One of the hazmat guys came out the front door pulling off his hood. It was Ed Rendell. Maxim had known him for several years; he was part of the quick-reaction team they used to seal off crime scenes. "What?" he asked. "What's up Angela?"

"Did you or one of your guys just say something to me?"

"Not us," he said. "But we're wrapping up in there. You can tell the photogs to come on down. We'll be out in a few minutes. Lab results will take a day or two." He put his hood back on and turned to re-enter the house.

"Thanks!" said Maxim, a little too loudly. She turned entirely around again, looking for where the voice had come from, scanning trees and bushes where some kid had to be hiding. The dog still sat at her feet looking up. It was motionless.

"You won't find one," the dog said in a childlike voice. "Sorry to twist your view of reality Angela, but eventually you're going to have to come to grips with it. With me, that is."

Maxim looked down at the dog: *"Did you just speak?"* she said very slowly.

Ed Rendell turned around on the front porch. "Angela, you okay? Who're you talking to?"

"Calm down," said the dog in a lower volume, "or you're going to be taken to a looney ward. Yes, I did just speak. It's me. The dog. The one at your feet." It still had that stupid grin on its face.

"Nobody, Ed," she called out to Rendell on the porch. "Just talking to myself again." He shrugged and went back into the house.

Maxim stared down at the dog and said one word: "No."

"Oh yes," said the dog, "and we need to talk. Privately. Unless you want to be talking to docs in a mental ward. How about you come with me, so we can chat."

FBI special agent Angela Maxim stood transfixed, staring down at the dog.

"Woof!" said the dog as it looked up at her. But it wasn't a normal dog's bark. It was a *child's voice* saying the word "woof".

"Fuck this shit," said Maxim. She was starting to sweat. She could feel it on her lower back.

"Now, now," said the dog soothingly. "That's bad language, Agent Maxim. Now come on, you know you want to talk to me, no matter how crazy it is. So humor me ... and follow me."

"Wha ... " was all Angela Maxim could get out. She stooped down to examine the dog more closely.

It spoke to her in its childlike voice: "Look, I may just look like a dog, but I've still got a pretty good vocabulary." It barked playfully at her and jumped back a couple of feet, this time with "real" dog barks, the kind that say *"Come on! Let's play!"* The pooch backed up some more, squatting down on its front legs.

Ed Rendell was back on the porch putting some equipment into a box.

"Hey Ed," said Maxim, "I'm going down the street to check things. Anyone needs me, tell 'em I'll be right back."

"Will do," said Rendell, not looking up from what he was doing.

The dog jumped around happily at Maxim's feet as she strode purposefully down the street. She didn't look at the dog jumping around at her feet. She looked at the houses, the trees, the street ... *anywhere but at the damned mutt!*

"Good stuff, Angela!" said the dog when they were some distance away and nearing a corner. He walked alongside her now, looking up. "Don't you want to know who I am?"

Maxim answered out of the side of her mouth as she walked. She didn't want anyone to see her talking.

"This. Is. Not. Happening. " she said slowly and deliberately. "And you're not a talking dog. There's something going on ... in my head."

She heard a child's peal of laughter. *"Okaaaay,"* said the dog. "If you *saaaay* so." It laughed again in the high-pitched child's voice, giggling: *"Move along, move along, nothing to see here except your own neuroses!"*

Maxim came to the corner and looked down. The dog had stopped and was leering up at her. *That stupid shit-eating grin again.* They turned left and followed the sidewalk for a way. There was no one in view and no street traffic.

Maxim knew that if she started talking to a dog and someone saw her ... *not good.* She stopped, scanning the area. This part of the neighborhood was empty. It was far enough away from the twin excitements of a suicide bomb and an elderly lady with an amputated hand. No one was around.

"Okay dog," she said, sounding resigned. "Talk to me."

"Ask me who I am first," said the dog. It sounded querulous, almost indignant. The child's laughter came up to her again. The dog was *joshing* her. "Go on," it said. "Ask me. We must maintain the niceties, after all. Good manners are always called for!"

Angela Maxim stared down. The dog was sitting on its haunches and smiling up at her with that irritating grin. *Those eyes are aware,* she thought. *Well, what the hell.* "My name is Angela Maxim," she said. "What's yours?"

The dog's muzzle opened and it licked its chops. *"Bond,"* it said in a slowly exaggerated voice. *"James Bond."* It let out another peal of child's laughter. Maxim looked around again. *Still no one watching. Good.* She'd heard the dog crack a joke, and its laughter. *It's coming from the damned dog!*

"Am I having some kind of a psychotic event?" Maxim asked to no one in particular

"Not at all," said the dog in its high-pitched voice. "But you can be excused if you think you're going a little nuts. After all, it's not often you get to meet a dog clearly enunciating the English language, not to mention utilizing proper syntax and grammar. I have a hell of a good vocabulary too! Glad to meet you, by the way."

The dog's mouth wasn't moving as if it were talking. It was just open, although not that widely. The voice was coming from *inside* the dog's mouth. It raised a paw to shake with Maxim. The FBI agent looked around again furtively.

"Oh come on," said the dog. "If anyone saw you they'd just think you're being nice to a stray." It was still holding its paw up. *No one around,* thought Maxim. Feeling like a fool, she reached down and shook the dog's paw.

"See?" said the dog in that flat little voice. "That wasn't so bad was it?"

Maxim was stunned speechless. She just stared.

"Oh, incidentally, my name's not *really* James Bond," said the dog. "That was a joke. You know, the great line from the movie? *Doctor No?* One of the great movie lines in history?" It *woofed* again, like a normal dog. "You've got to admit, that line by Sean Connery is a cultural marker, no matter how old the movie is!"

"Rosebud," said the FBI agent looking down at the dog. She couldn't help it. It just popped out.

"Oh yes," said the dog from the sidewalk. "That one too. *Citizen Kane.* Orson Welles. But I think Connery's line surpasses it, don't you?"

FBI Agent Angela Maxim felt dizzy. She abruptly squatted down, putting a hand out on the sidewalk to steady herself. Then she sat all the way down and put a hand to her forehead. The dog regarded her from a few feet away. Maxim stared back at it. The dog turned his head quizzically, as dogs will do when they show perplexity, but said nothing.

Maxim pulled out her cell phone and hit 911. "This is FBI Agent Angela Maxim. I'm in the Wilding Oaks neighborhood. I'm down from where the blast occurred. I need a squad car immediately."

"Sorry, Angela," said the dog. "Time for me to make my exit. If I'm still here you all might try to catch me. And while I do enjoy a good chase, I've got other stuff to tend to. I'll be back in touch though! Count on it!"

Maxim lunged, trying to grab the dog but it easily dodged and jumped away. It loped down the street, entered a side-yard through a hedge, and disappeared.

Within seconds a city police squad car slammed to a halt where Maxim sat on the sidewalk. The cop jumped out and hurried over to her. "You okay ma'am?"

Agent Maxim wearily waved her cell phone at him and struggled to her feet. The cop helped her up. "Momentary dizziness," she said. "Thanks for coming. I think I'm good now." She thanked the cop, then turned and walked back to the corner. She turned right and stood silently looking down the street toward the home of Mrs. Harriman Newton III.

~~~~

A couple of days later Angela Maxim met with an FBI psychiatrist. At her request. She'd met the psych and talked to him before at agency events, but she'd never asked for a formal meeting. The psychiatrist performed an evaluation and found her well-oriented as to time, place, person, and other indicia of mental stability. She didn't mention her conversation with a talking dog, but did talk about the bomb blast, the many dead, and the trauma involving the elderly woman's severed hand.

Then she sidled up to the idea of "hearing voices." Without being specific. *Just in theory.* The psychiatrist told her as far as he could tell she was quite normal, but probably overstressed. He offered a prescription, but she declined.

Later, Angela Maxim talked to the police officer who had come to help her that day. She asked if he'd seen a black dog running around at the time. The cop said dogs never ran loose in Wilding Oaks. It didn't happen. If one did a dozen busybodies would instantly call in complaints. The cop knew the neighborhood well. It was in his district. He knew many of the people who lived there personally.

The psychiatrist had asked Angela if she wanted to be transferred off the case. She demurred, but wondered in her own mind if the dog had been real.

"I'll stay on it," she told the psych. *Besides, what connection could a damned talking dog have with a suicide bombing ... or maiming an elderly lady?* Even if the dog *was* real ... *which it wasn't.*

Agent Maxim decided she needed to talk to Mrs. Newton directly. About what had happened.

And about how her hand had ... gone missing.

CHAPTER 6
Agent Maxim and Mrs. Newton.

She's one tough old bat, thought Angela Maxim as she sat in Mrs. Harriman Newton III's living room. *Damn. Not a week since the old battle-axe lost her hand.*

"Yes ma'am, I am definitely from the local FBI office. Here is my card," she had told Mrs. Newton at the front door of the elderly woman's home. Mrs. Newton had started to reach for the card with her heavily bandaged right arm, but remembered she no longer had a hand at the end of it. She'd taken the card with her left hand.

"You can call the local FBI office to check on my identity if you wish," said Angela Maxim helpfully.

"I most certainly will, young woman," said Mrs. Newton. She shut the front door, leaving Maxim standing alone. After closely scrutinizing the business card, she picked up an old telephone handset with her left hand, laid it on the table, and laboriously punched in the FBI office number.

Maxim had been escorted to Mrs. Newton's home by two uniformed police officers in a marked squad car. Mrs. Newton had seen the officers when she looked out her front door and was greeted by the FBI agent. One of them had waved as Angela stood patiently.

"I was already interviewed by that young man who said he was from the FBI!" Mrs. Newton snapped at her. "And look what it got me!" She'd actually held the stump of her right forearm up and shaken it in Angela Maxim's face. *I swear to God,* thought Maxim, *she's downright proud of it. It's like a war wound or something.*

Mrs. Newton held the old phone receiver to her ear while it rang. "Hello, this is Mrs. Harriman Newton the Third calling from the Wilding Oaks community neighborhood. I have a woman here at my front door who *says* she is from your office." She paused, listening, then snapped, "I don't care if you can or cannot give out information about who works there young lady! I demand to know if she is telling the truth!"

There was a further pause as Mrs. Newton waited. Presently someone came on the phone at the FBI office. "Yes, as I said, this is Mrs. Harriman Newton the Third in the Wilding Oaks neighborhood where a bomb was recently set off. There is a woman here claiming to be from your office." She paused again, listening. "Well *course* I don't know for sure what her name is," she snapped. "I only know whom she represents herself to be!"

She listened some more, then spoke again. "Yes, she was accompanied by two city policemen, but I demand confirmation from your office. She represents herself as—she paused, looking at the business card again— "Special Agent Angela Maxim of the Federal Bureau of Investigation. You *are* the Federal Bureau of Investigation, are you not?" She listened. "Very well. Thank you." She preemptively hung up the phone, then went back to the front door.

Opening the door and standing aside, Mrs. Newton told Angela Maxim, "you may proceed young lady."

"Yes ma'am," said Angela. She entered the house, feeling beads of sweat forming in the middle of her back. The elderly woman indicated a chair for Maxim to sit, and sat herself in another chair across a coffee table.

Mrs. Newton regarded the FBI agent with a mixture of contempt and hostility. She was resigned to dealing with a nonentity who clearly did not belong in an upper-class neighborhood and doubtless would never have the wherewithal to become so ... unless she married up of course.

"I'm sorry to bother you ... " began Angela Maxim.

"I'm sure you are," said Mrs. Newton acidly.

" ... but I need to know precisely what occurred here between you and that intruder several days ago."

"I have already told the story, over and over!" snapped the old woman.

"Yes ma'am," said Maxim, "but that was the local police department you spoke to, and the federal government is even more interested in hearing what happened."

"Did the local police officers not share their reports with you?" demanded Mrs. Newton.

"Yes ma'am, they did," said Maxim, "but there may have been some small piece of information or some fact that might have been omitted. I assure you that in order to protect you and the public this is necessary."

Mrs. Newton said nothing. She just stared across the table with a petulant look on her face. "I cannot be bothered to continue saying the same things over and over for public servants who are apparently unable to fully perform their duties." She paused, looking sternly at Angela Maxim. "I will tell you only once what I have already told several people several times."

"Thank you ma'am," said Maxim. "Now first of all, could you tell me what time of the day it was?"

"How would I know?" snapped the elderly woman. "All I can tell you is that it was in the afternoon, after I had fixed and consumed my normal lunch at precisely 12:30 p.m. Then this ... this *monster* came into my home not 30 minutes after I had completed eating!"

"Can you describe the person who came to your door?"

"I have done so already," said Mrs. Newton. "He was very ugly ... a rough, uncouth sort." She looked meaningfully across at Angela Maxim. "He *said* he was from the FBI."

"That is a very serious crime," responded Maxim. "I can assure you that he was not with the Federal Bureau of Investigation, and that he will be arrested and fully prosecuted."

"I should hope so!" exclaimed Mrs. Newton. "It is hard to believe that the FBI would *hire* such a person, much less allow him to interview people. He appeared to be very rough trade indeed."

"He was not from the FBI," repeated Angela Maxim. "Now could you tell me approximately how old he was?"

"How could I *possibly* know his age? I didn't *ask* him, I can assure you that!"

"Well, can you give me an estimate, an opinion from having seen him?"

"Perhaps in his fifties. He had wrinkles on his face and short black hair."

Angela Maxim was jotting down notes as Mrs. Newton spoke.

"He spoke very disrespectfully to me!"

"What exactly did he say, ma'am?"

"He accused me of wrongdoing! When I explained to him how I had performed my duty in reporting an unauthorized commercial business on this very street, he obviously disapproved!"

"Can you tell me what you mean by that, ma'am?"

Mrs. Newton was getting more agitated. "Exactly what I just told you! He seemed to think that it was *I* who had done something wrong by performing my duty as a citizen upholding the law in this neighborhood!"

"What did he say?" Maxim asked again.

"Well, when he became snippy. I told him in no uncertain terms that all laws must be upheld or we will suffer anarchy!"

"Did he respond to that?"

"Yes he did, and in the most uncouth manner, I might add. He asked me if I would have upheld the law knowing that 12 people had been killed as a result. *He said that!*"

Mrs. Newton wasn't abashed, and didn't appear particularly concerned about the deaths. *More than anything,* thought Maxim, *she's pissed off about losing her hand.*

"What was your response, ma'am?"

"I ordered him out of my house forthwith!"

"What happened then?"

"He spoke more gibberish, and revealed to me that he had lied to me, that even though he had said he was from the FBI, he was not! I ordered him out again, but he said he was trying to understand why I notified the police about illegal activity on my street!"

"Was that when ...."

"It most certainly was!" This ... *monster* spoke to me as if he was *questioning my motivations!* It was insulting! I told him in no uncertain terms that I do not want anarchy on my street, and neither would he."

Angela Maxim was scribbling in her notebook. She looked up: "What happened then please?" This was the bad part, where most people would break down. Mrs. Harriman Newton III was far tougher than that. *Beyond tough*, thought Maxim.

"He pulled on my arm and my hand fell off!" she said indignantly. "I didn't feel a thing. It was as if he just pulled on it and it came off! He picked it up from the table right here, not three feet from where you sit."

Shit. She's not even fazed by it. "What did you do then, ma'am?"

"What did I *do*, young lady? What did I *DO?*" Mrs. Harriman Newton III might lose it after all, thought Maxim. "I simply stared. There was no pain. But there was blood, until that ... that *lunatic* pulled out some kind of plastic band and fastened it around my wrist to stop the bleeding. Then he called the police."

"*He* called the police?" asked Maxim. "Right then when it happened?"

"Yes he did," said Mrs. Newton. "He was holding my hand in his mouth. Between his teeth."

Holy shit, thought Angela Maxim, looking across at the old woman. "How long did it take for the police to arrive?" she asked.

"Within a minute or two. It was very fast. They saw that I needed immediate medical attention and I was taken to the hospital. *And now this!*" she exclaimed, waving the stump at the end of her right arm at Maxim again. "How am I going to face my friends at the bridge club? How am I going to be able to attend events at the country club with *this!*"

The elderly woman appeared to be blaming Angela Maxim for her misfortune as she waved her stump across the table. Angela's thoughts were alarming: All she could see in her mind was a man holding a severed hand in his mouth across from Mrs. Newton, the hand with an outstretched finger pointing in her direction. *Geez ....*

"I'm sorry, Mrs. Newton," she said tentatively.

"Well I should *hope so!* Since it was *your office* whom the man was representing!" She clearly blamed the FBI for the trauma, since the intruder had apparently identified himself as being FBI.

"Did this ... man say anything else, or give you any further information that might be of help to us, Mrs. Newton?"

"There was gibberish at the end," she said, still indignant.

Angela Maxim resisted blowing out a breath, and raised her eyebrows at the elderly woman. *Let's hear it you old hag.* "And? What was it that he said?"

"*I told you already,*" Mrs. Newton snapped. "It was gibberish!"

"Could you tell me ... what *kind* of gibberish?"

"He quite clearly said something like *this is a message from outer space*, as if he thought it was some kind of ... *joke!*"

"Anything else?"

"Yes. He said something else that was very strange. He said *ollie, ollie, oxen free!*"

"*Ollie, ollie, oxen free?*" repeated Angela Maxim.

"*Just that!*" said Mrs. Newton. "The man was clearly mentally deranged. And then he said something very ugly."

"What was that, ma'am?"

"I do not wish to repeat it," said Mrs. Harriman stubbornly. "It was ugly language."

"Mrs. Newton," said Maxim, "it is very important that we know every detail of what you heard from this ... this monster. By telling me what he said you are assisting us in catching him. He will be prosecuted to the fullest extent of the law."

Mrs. Newton doggedly shut her mouth and compressed her lips as she looked across the table at Angela Maxim. "I will not speak those words out loud," she said.

"Can you whisper them in my ear then?" pleaded Angela. "No one else will be able to hear. It will be just our little secret."

Mrs. Newton was softening. She obviously wanted to repeat the words to Maxim. "Well, if you wish, young woman." She leaned across the small table. Angela leaned forward over the table and turned her head to the side so the woman could whisper in her ear.

"He said ... *you need to stock up on fucking people,*" she whispered. Angela Maxim jotted on her pad while still leaning over.

"*Stock up on fucking people?*" Maxim repeated. "As in, going to the grocery store?"

"Not at all!" snapped Mrs. Newton. "He didn't say it like that. I was light-headed, I've already told you. It was those words, or words like them. But he clearly put the emphasis on ... the bad word."

Time to stock up on FUCKING people, thought Maxim. *Huh?*

"Ma'am, I'm sorry, but I'd like you to think very, very hard for me if you will." FBI Special Agent Angela Maxim looked gravely at the elderly woman across the table. "Could the words have been different? Do you have any idea what he might have meant?"

"Well isn't it quite clear?" demanded Mrs. Newton imperiously. "He was ... was *criticizing* me for upholding the law. He asked me if I regretted reporting the lawbreaker on the street. In view of the police officers killed!" She sniffed at Maxim and straightened her back. "I said *of course* I did not regret *anything*. I told him that is the price for avoiding *anarchy.*"

Angela Maxim sat silently, thinking. *Stock up on fucking people? Stock fucking people up? Aha!* "Ma'am, could it be he said it's time to ... to *stop fucking with people?*"

"Yes, of course," Mrs. Newton said. "This is what I have been telling you! And I will thank you not to use that word in my presence young woman."

You need to stop fucking with people. Hmmm ....

Angela Maxim spent little more time with Mrs. Newton. The words spoken by the nutcase had not been disclosed to the Winston Police. There was no indication of any such wording in the police report Maxim had reviewed.

What an imperious bitch, she thought. *I'm here trying to help her and she's chewing me out.* Agent Maxim closed her notebook and thanked Mrs. Newton for her time. She stood up to leave.

"You *will* find this wicked monster will you not?" Mrs. Newton demanded.

"I expect we will ma'am. And when we do I will personally see that we throw the book at him. He is guilty of multiple serious crimes, not the least of which is what he did to you."

"If you do find him," asked Mrs. Newton, "might it be possible to also find my hand? I am told that they are quite good at reattaching hands in hospitals these days."

"I couldn't say, ma'am, but I promise you we'll conduct a thorough search for it everywhere."

"Good," said Mrs. Newton, "because one of the last things the man said before he left was that he might give it back to me."

Maxim paused where she was standing and looked quizzically at the old woman. "I beg your pardon? He said what?"

"Oh yes," said Mrs. Newton. "The lunatic apparently fancied himself to be a doctor. I very clearly remember he said, 'I want you to think about what you did. I might give this back to you.' And then he left with my hand!" Mrs. Newton was more indignant than hopeful.

Really pissed off, thought Maxim, who stood there with her mouth open, gaping at the old woman. *Jesus. What the hell is THAT all about.*

"We'll do everything we can, Mrs. Newton, and we will find this person one way or another." She nodded to the elderly lady who was still sitting in the chair fuming about her lost hand. She did not get up.

Agent Maxim let herself out of the front door and closed it. She stepped down to the front walkway and let out an explosive breath. *That was just bizarre.* She looked up and down the street as she walked out to her car. About a half block away, on the other side of the tree-lined street, a young man was walking a dog.

The dog jumped and tugged at the end of a leash, sniffing here and there as dogs do. It was a medium-sized dog, maybe 30 or 40 pounds. It was black. Well, mostly black. It had some white spots on it.

It has some white spots on it.

FBI Special Agent Angela Maxim crossed the street and strode toward the man with the dog.

CHAPTER 7
Angela Meets Bill. And a Dog Named Spot.

Maxim was walking at an angle, heading directly toward the guy on the other side of the street. The dog was mostly black, but had some white spots on it. Maxim was thinking about Mrs. Newton and her missing hand. *What a tough old battle-axe.*

Angela smiled as she approached the young man and his dog. *Talk about a good-looking guy ... geez.* He was maybe 30 years old, slim but muscular, with tousled blonde hair ... and he was very handsome. *Surfer-boy,* came unbidden to Angela Maxim's mind. *Almost movie star looks.* She reprimanded herself mentally: *Screw that. This is business.*

Maxim said hello as she approached. The guy sported a light beard, not much more than a few days worth of stubble really. Like his hair, the beard was blondish. There was some kind of subtle smell coming off him. He wasn't sweaty, but he was dressed in running shorts and a dark blue T-shirt with "Northwestern" across the front. He wore blue sneakers over low-top white athletic socks. His legs were well-muscled. *Must be a runner,* she thought.

The fellow smiled back at Angela Maxim. "Hello yourself," he said with a grin, then added, "you know, we really should stop meeting like this." He had really nice white teeth.

Maxim smiled in spite of herself but quickly wiped it off. "I'm FBI Agent Angela Maxim," she said in a serious voice. "You live around here?"

"A few streets over," he answered, still smiling.

"We're interviewing people about the excitement the other day," she said.

"Well this is Spot," he responded, gesturing at his dog at his feet. It was well-trained and sat still, looking up at her. "I'm William Hamilton Smith," he said. "Aka Bill." He held out his hand. "Let's maintain the niceties, shall we? Good manners are always called for."

That phrase. Where the hell have I heard those words? Angela Maxim shook hands with the guy. "Mind if I call you Bill?" she asked.

"Feel free!" he said, flashing a thousand-watt smile.

Jesus, she thought, looking at his teeth again.

"But it would be better if we were dating."

Cheeky ... and cocky. She regarded him with a cool frown, showing disapproval. *Damn he's good looking. And that smell coming off him ....* "Where exactly do you live, Mr. Smith?"

"Oh, we live in the next neighborhood over," he said, gesturing in a general direction. "Go over 3 or 4 blocks and take a right. We figured we'd stroll over and see the sights today."

"We? Do you live with someone?" she asked.

"Oh no, just me and Spot," he said easily. The dog heard its name and turned to look at him, then back to Angela Maxim. It appeared to be nothing more than a normal dog.

Maxim looked down at Spot. *Could that be the dog from the other day? Am I going crazy?*

"We thought there would at least be some wreckage to look at," said Smith.

A tiny pinpoint of suspicion lit up in Angela Maxim's mind. "Wreckage?"

"Sure," he said. "You know, busted up cars, broken windows, that kind of thing?" He made it sound like a question. "It sure sounded exciting in the newspaper."

"There's not much to look at," she told him. "Would you tell me your exact address please?" She held her notebook up expectantly.

"Aw shucks," he said. "I'll tell you mine will you tell me yours." He was grinning at her.

She dropped the notebook to her side, feeling a flutter in her chest. *That smell coming off of him.* Then … *what is this shit? Am I a teenager?* "Your name and address sir?" she asked sternly.

"Would that be for investigation, or are you coming on to me?" The grin was still plastered across his face.

Cocky bastard. Anger flared in Maxim's mind. She was mad at herself. *I'm not going to put up with this shit.* "I don't come on to people, Mr. Smith, and the only time you might make that mistake is if I was putting handcuffs on you."

"Sounds exciting," he said, deadpanning. The smile had disappeared, but the hint of a grin still tugged at the edge of his lips. "Fifty *more* shades of gray?"

Bullshit. This is going nowhere. "Your address!" she snapped.

"One last thing, before I tell you," he said. *That smile.* She stepped back, putting some distance between herself and the guy. *Cocky wise ass,* she thought angrily, but … *that cologne, or whatever he's got on him.* "When I tell you my address will you tell me yours?"

"I don't give out my address," she snapped. "What's yours, dammit!"

"2417 W. Elmhurst," he said quickly, then "Will you go out to dinner with me?"

She looked up from her notebook and gave him a long cool stare. She wasn't smiling. "You always ask FBI agents out to dinner?"

"Not up to now," he said. "But then I've never met one before, especially a really pretty one. So thank you for coming over to chat!" The damned grin was back.

Through it all the dog was strangely calm at his feet. *How come it isn't jumping around? Tugging at the leash?* It was hard for Angela Maxim to keep a straight face at the cheeky bastard. In spite of herself she smiled now … but it was a dangerous feral smile. "Very well Mr. William Hamilton Smith. Feel free to call me at my office."

"Have you got a card?" he asked hopefully.

She stared at him. The feral smile was gone. "The office is downtown, Mr. Smith. Look it up. Will you please remain here for a moment?"

"For you? Sure!" He smiled at her, showing beautiful teeth.

Angela Maxim stepped a short distance away, pulled out her cell phone and punched in a single digit to call her office. She watched Smith as she waited for an answer. "Marge, would you look up 2417 West Elmhurst in town right now? Tell me who lives there?"

"Sure," said her assistant. "Stand by." Maxim stood unsmiling, the phone at her ear. She continued to stare coolly at Smith, who squatted down to pet his dog and ruffle its coat. Then he leaned over and made a big show of whispering into the dog's ear. Both of its ears perked up.

Marge came back on the line. "Owned by a single guy," she said. "William H. Smith, IV."

"What's he do?"

"He's a lawyer," said Marge. She paused for a second, then came back. "He's a litigator for Cooney and Ivey downtown. Civil law." Marge paused again. "He's an insurance defense guy." *Aha. A courtroom gunslinger. That's where the cockiness comes from.*

"Thank you Marge," she said. "Would you put a tag on any calls that come in for me over the next few days? I want all incoming numbers logged and any messages tagged and sent to me immediately."

"Will do."

Angela Maxim punched the call off, put the phone back in her jacket pocket and walked over to Smith. He was still squatting down, ruffling the black coat of his dog.

"What was that all about?" he asked.

"I understand you're a lawyer," she said.

"Why, I do believe you've been stalking me!" he said teasingly.

Teasing an FBI agent. Angela Maxim didn't believe this guy. "Not actually," she said. "Just checking things out. The situation here is somewhat tense, as you are doubtless aware. A number of police personnel were killed."

"Can't be too careful!" he said brightly.

She stared at him again, unsmiling. "In the meantime," she said, "I'd like to know ...." But he interrupted her.

"Hey, me first! Dinner? Have we got a deal? Downtown? A nice restaurant? Say *Imbroglio's* after work one day?"

This guy was getting on her nerves. "You'll have to call the office first, Mr. Smith." Then she regretted saying even that. *Fucker.*

"It would give you a chance to *investigate* me a little more," he said, putting a slight but suggestive emphasis on the word.

Angela Maxim stared at Bill Smith unsmiling. *Jesus what a cocky asshole!* She forced herself not to smile.

"You work for Cooney and Ivey downtown, Mr. Smith. I understand they don't put up with sexual harassment in their offices."

"I'm not in the office!" he replied easily. "Besides, how is it sexual harassment to ask a very attractive, very desirable lady out to dinner? I mean, all you have to say is no." He was still squatting down petting the dog, grinning up at her.

Agent Maxim stared down. She wanted to knock his block off. And yet ... *damn he's good-looking. And that ... that smell coming off him.* "Like I said," she said, "feel free to call my office if you want." *That should put an end to this.*

"I'll bet I'll have to get in line, too," he said, standing up. She looked hard at him. Was he getting snotty? No, he wasn't. He was still flirting with her. *Flirting! What IS this bullshit?* She had to hand it to him though ....

"Sure," she said, "get in line."

"Can I cut to the front?" he said hopefully, holding back laughter.

"No one gets an automatic yes," she said. "And some don't get a yes at all, especially cocky litigators." *There. That ought to put him in his place.*

"I'll do it!" he said. "I'll call and wait in line if I have to!"

Oh what the hell. "One other thing, Mr. Smith ...."

"Please, call me Bill!" he said, smiling eagerly.

"How long have you had your dog?"

A look of perplexity came over his face. "How long have I had Spot?" he repeated. He seemed puzzled.

"Yes. How long have you had your dog."

Smith looked down at Spot, then up at Maxim. "Several years, I guess. Since he was a pup. Why do you ask?"

"Where did you get the dog?"

"Still investigating?" Smith said, grinning again.

"Just curious," she said. "He looks like a nice dog."

"Nice indeed!" said Smith. "He can talk too!"

Agent Maxim's mouth formed an "O." She involuntarily moved back one step. "Oh really," she said, trying to project sarcasm.

"Sure," said Smith. He looked down at the dog again. "Spot! Do your talking thing! Go on! Talk to the lady!"

The dog looked at her, then back at its owner. "Go on," he said, gesturing in her direction, "talk for the lady!" The dog looked back at Angela Maxim and started a low howling, the way dogs will howl when they hear a siren. "That's it, that's it!" said Smith, encouraging the dog. He was chuckling as he turned back to her. "See? He talks!"

Angela Maxim smiled in spite of herself, but it was a tight smile.

The dog stopped howling. "Now shake hands with the lady," said Smith, gesturing again at the FBI agent. The dog physically turned toward Maxim, stepped forward a few feet, sat on his haunches, and held a paw up for the FBI agent.

She stood frozen, staring down at the dog. It was exactly like the dog had done that had spoken to her. "Do you talk to people, Spot?" she said. She hadn't meant to say that ... but it just came out of her mouth, automatically.

The dog was still sitting on his haunches, still holding out a paw to be shaken. He moved his paw up and down as if to say, *"Here, shake my paw!"*

"Do you talk like a normal person?" said Maxim, looking down at the dog.

"Only when he wants to," said Bill Smith. "It wouldn't do to talk in public. What would people think?"

Maxim looked back at Smith. "You're very funny Mr. Smith," she said flatly, clearly not amused.

Smith was uncowed. He was grinning again: "Please call me Bill!" he said. "I find a good sense of humor, even in the face of human folly, often makes a guy more attractive to girls. Don't you agree?" He raised his eyebrows at her. It was comical.

He's adorable, she thought. "No comment," she snapped. *Jesus he smells good.*

"Well then maybe I can try again," he said. "When we go out will you agree to laugh at my jokes? Humor is important!"

"I told you, Mr. Smith, get in line." That also just popped out of her mouth. This was getting to be a bit much. She was peeved at herself.

"Thank you for your time," she said, then turned and walked away. She was aware that her butt was swinging in a certain way ... more than it normally did. *GodDAMMIT!* she thought. After walking 15 or 20 feet, she decided *what the hell* and twisted around to see if Bill Smith was ogling her butt.

He wasn't. Instead, he was looking directly into her eyes, as if to say *I knew you were going to do that.* He held up one hand and gave her a little wave, still grinning. She was furious. *I hate him! Cocky bastard! But ... damn he's good looking. And that ....*

She glanced down from Bill Smith's face to look at the dog. It was grinning at her too. It had a stupid, goofy-looking dog-smile on its face ... just like the one she had seen several days before. A chill went down her spine. She turned and stomped away in her practical black FBI service shoes. She didn't look back.

The dog watched her receding back, then looked up at its master. "Think she made me?" it asked in a high-pitched voice.

Bill Smith glanced down, grinning. *"Nah!* You do *canis familiaris* too well," he said.

The dog giggled.

Smith watched Angela Maxim striding away. This time he did ogle her butt. It was very attractive, especially the way it was moving.

Human sexual dimorphism, thought Bill Smith, *is this great or what?*

CHAPTER 8
Hope for Sarah McLaughlin.

When David and Meghan McLaughlin were released from jail two days after being arrested, they knew their daughter Sarah was missing.

Frantic, they called the police and were told that Sarah had been "temporarily" placed in a foster home by the state Division of Child Protective Services "pending investigation." Their further frantic inquiries were met with solid stonewalling from every government representative, including the police department, the district attorney's office, and higher levels of the Division of Child Protective Services all the way up its headquarters in the state capitol.

No one would tell them where their daughter was.

Sarah's mother Meghan was continuously distraught and sobbing after it became clear their daughter would be kept from them. Her husband tried to console her. "We'll have a lawyer file papers immediately," he said, but he didn't know what the process would entail. *This is essentially a kidnapping,* he thought. With a number of dead police officers, the situation looked dire for both them and their daughter. He wondered if his involvement in an anti-tax civic organization would count against him, if his outspoken activism had anything to do with the situation.

Dave and Meghan McLaughlin hired a lawyer who tried, but couldn't pierce the stonewall thrown up by the local authorities. The elected district attorney, Nick Alabattis, was running interference for both the local police and Child Protective Services. The lawyer filed a writ of habeas corpus to find Sarah. The judge refused to set an emergency hearing, saying he was too busy.

But the real reason the judge wouldn't set an emergency hearing was that he worked with the DA's office and the police every day ... and thus was part of the problem. He directed that a hearing be held on the writ of habeas corpus and Sarah McLaughlin's whereabouts after a month and a half. When the McLaughlin's lawyer protested, the judge rebuked him. There were 12 dead cops for one thing, and for another the child's parents were under investigation for both child neglect and abuse.

In the meantime an anonymous tip was said to have been received by both CPS and the DA's office about the McLaughlins. The anonymous allegations were then leaked to the local press, which instantly ran with the storyline that Sarah's parents were abusive and neglectful.

Naturally the police and DA's office refused to reveal who had made the accusations, saying, "All such allegations must be investigated. Let the system work." Then they added, "Initial information suggests there may have been abuse or neglect or both. We are still investigating."

The media ran with that too, and the story became that the McLaughlins' lawyer was trying to put an abused and neglected child put back into the hands of her abusive parents. The judge scowled at the lawyer and ignored all objections.

Thus it was that David and Meghan McLaughlin found themselves alone at their home, frustrated, terrified and impotent. They faced the entire local political power structure, including the Winston Police Department, the district attorney's office, and the local media that served both. Sarah McLaughlin's mother Meghan couldn't sleep and hadn't slept since the day they'd been arrested. She was in tears virtually all the time.

Sarah's father David did his best to comfort and reassure his wife, but there was little to do in the face of the solid stonewall thrown up by the local authorities. There seemed to be no choice other than to wait for the court hearing.

"Unacceptable," said Meghan McLaughlin bitterly. She was sitting stiffly in the kitchen as she ground out the words. Her husband tried to comfort her.

"I don't give a shit what we have to do!" shouted Meghan. *"Dave, they've got our daughter!"*

He felt helpless, lashed by his wife's words, and his heart too was breaking. "Meghan, we're up against the police, the DA, the entire state CPS. I don't know what else we can ....

David McLaughlin was interrupted by the phone ringing. He rushed to answer it, hoping it would be Sarah or word of her whereabouts. It was not. On the line was a male voice that identified himself as Aaron Akron, a lawyer with some kind of organization called the Individual Justice Foundation.

"Is that the organization out of Washington, DC?" asked Dave McLaughlin. He had heard about legal foundations that brought lawsuits all over the country on behalf of powerless citizens abused by various levels of government.

"No sir," Aaron Akron answered on the phone. "That would be the Institute for Justice in Washington or the Individual Rights Foundation in California. We're based in New England."

"I've heard of those others," said Sarah's father.

"We do similar work," said the attorney, "except we're particularly interested in the type of situation you and your wife are facing. We've read the media reports and see that you've already been convicted in the eyes of the public by the local media which serves your local power structure. I understand also that your daughter is being held incommunicado by the state division of Child Protective Services."

"That's right," said Dave McLaughlin grimly. *Not going to beat around the bush.* "It's basically a goddamn legal kidnapping. I don't know what else to call it."

"Well the IJF may be interested in assisting you," said Akron.

"We'd appreciate any help," said McLaughlin. "We do have a lawyer, but it appears he can't get the court system to budge. He wasn't able to get any information about Sarah's whereabouts, and the judge has refused to set a hearing until a month and a half from now. We don't even know if Sarah is being held in Winston." He kept his voice from breaking only with some effort.

"I'd like to fly down and meet with you and your wife immediately," said the lawyer. "Would that be acceptable?"

"Of course," said McLaughlin, hoping against hope. "Where are you coming from?"

"Our headquarters is in New Hampshire," said Akron, "but we do public interest litigation all over the country, particularly in the population centers around Boston and New York."

"Feel free," said McLaughlin. "I don't know if there's anything you'll be able to do, but feel free to come meet with us."

"I'll want to discuss the facts with you and your wife in some detail," Akron said. "Then perhaps meet with the authorities there. If things pan out, the IJF might be able to make a difference."

"Anything that could possibly help us get our daughter back is welcome," said McLaughlin, "and greatly appreciated. Come down immediately, and if you need a place you can stay at our home. We have extra bedrooms."

"Thank you," said Aaron Akron. "I will be there this evening."

"This evening?" said David McLaughlin. "That's certainly quick."

"We work fast when something like this is going on," said the lawyer, "especially when it involves children."

Several hours later the McLaughlins' doorbell rang. The individual at the door was a youngish man, probably in his 30s, and very large. He wore a professional suit with long-sleeved white shirt and a subdued tie. A clean-shaven face was framed by a pair of wire-rimmed glasses, and he carried a brown leather briefcase. "I'm Aaron Akron," he said, holding out a business card.

David McLaughlin took the card. "That was fast," said Meghan McLaughlin, standing behind her husband and looking over his shoulder. David looked at the card closely before inviting the man in. The business card identified him as Aaron Akron, Esq., Chief General Counsel for the Individual Justice Foundation located in Manchester, New Hampshire.

Akron waited patiently. He stood 6-foot 5-inches tall, and at approximately 280 pounds understood himself to be an imposing figure. There was very little fat on his body, and more than one person had said he looked more like a professional wrestler or MMA fighter than a lawyer.

"Do you have other identification?" asked David McLaughlin.

"Of course," said Akron. He set his briefcase down, pulled a billfold from his inside jacket pocket and produced two other plastic cards: "This is my bar card showing I'm a member of the New York state bar association, and here is my New Hampshire driver's license."

McLaughlin examined them. The guy appeared to be what he said he was ... even if he did look like a professional wrestler. Dave McLaughlin smiled as he handed the ID back. "I'm sorry man," he said as he stepped aside and invited the lawyer in. "We're really freaked out, as you an imagine."

Akron smiled. "Under the circumstances, I can't say I blame you at all," he said. "The forces arrayed against you are formidable, and aren't overly concerned with the niceties of complying with the law ... or Sarah's well-being."

The giant lawyer entered the McLaughlin's living room and sat down in a chair where invited. David and Meghan sat together across from him on a couch. "What can we do to find out where Sarah is?" asked Meghan McLaughlin anxiously.

"I'm afraid I can't answer that question yet, Mrs. McLaughlin," he said. "My preliminary inquiries indicate she's been placed in a foster home on the outskirts of Winston."

Meghan McLaughlin brought her hand to her mouth. Tears were coming into her eyes. "How do you know this?" asked Dave McLaughlin.

"As a public interest foundation, we have many friends and many resources," said the lawyer. "Preliminary inquiries were made as soon as your situation was brought to our attention." He did not tell the two distraught parents that he already knew where Sarah was, and that the two foster parents in the home where she was being kept were two middle-aged males, both alcoholics and drug-abusers.

Meghan McLaughlin was now crying openly, her hands clenched in her lap. She sat stiffly upright, her husband's arm around her shoulders.

"Is there anything that can be done now?" asked Sarah's father.

"Yes," said Aaron Akron. "If you give your permission for the Individual Justice Foundation to represent you and legally intervene in this matter on your behalf, we will take certain steps immediately. However, I need to talk to you about the situation."

The discussion lasted for another hour. Aaron Akron probed to see what kind of parents they were, and if any of the media lies about them might be accurate. He was unsurprised to find they were not. Sarah's mother and father answered questions forthrightly, trying to help and occasionally asking questions of their own. There were unspoken queries too, such as, *"Why is this happening to us?"* and *"How can they get away with doing this?"*

Aaron Akron answered their questions as best he could. In the end he paused, then asked a final question of them.

"No," answered Meghan McLaughlin immediately. "Absolutely not. That's not possible. We have jobs here. Sarah has friends both in her school and in this neighborhood. If we moved away, how would we live?"

"I'm sorry to tell you this," responded Akron, "but there may be a move afoot in your neighborhood to ask you to leave."

"What?" asked Meghan McLaughlin, clearly shocked. "But why? Why would anyone do that?" At the same time David McLaughlin asked, *"How would you know that?"*

Akron answered forthrightly: "The *why* of the question is that much of the public automatically believe lies purveyed by the authorities and the media. Since you have been accused and arrested, you must be guilty. The media has amplified that, as they always do. I'm sorry."

He turned to address Sarah McLaughlin's father. "As to how I could know that, there are certain individuals who are discussing the matter through various electronic means in your neighborhood. The IJF has been allowed to listen in ... and some inquiries have been made."

Meghan McLaughlin began sobbing again next to her husband, who sat stone-faced, his mouth set in a frown. "That can't be." He held his wife around her shoulders and looked across at the lawyer. "That can't be," he said again.

"I'm sorry," said the lawyer.

"Do you know if it could have anything to do with my anti-tax political activism?"

"That is almost surely a factor," said Aaron Akron. "The city of Winston, like virtually every city in America, is run by people who are concerned primarily with maximizing their power and wealth. That power and wealth is sought at the expense of the public which is usually helpless against local corruption."

"What other purposes do they serve?" asked Meghan McLaughlin bitterly.

"Destroying potential challengers to their power for one thing," said Akron. "Because of your husband's political activism in fighting to keep taxes low in Winston, you both may have been identified as a threat to business-as-usual. Unfortunately, this could be part of the reason your daughter is being kept from you."

"It's so ... *corrupt,*" said Dave McLaughlin helplessly. "It's so *dishonest.*"

"There are a dozen dead police officers," said Akron. "Politicians sometimes admit that 'no crisis should go to waste'." Dave McLaughlin nodded knowingly. "With so many casualties," continued the lawyer, "the city's power structure is lashing out to show the public that they're '*doing something*', that they're '*effective*'. In order to be effective, they must have victims and scapegoats. The dead are their victims. You and your family, I'm afraid, have been chosen as scapegoats."

Meghan McLaughlin shook her head jerkily from side to side. "No," she said. "I don't believe it. I won't believe it."

"I understand," said Aaron Akron. "In any event, the IJF will bring in an experienced attorney to intervene in the process. We will take certain actions as quickly as possible to get Sarah back to you and out of the environment into which she has been put." He'd been taking occasional notes on a yellow legal pad. Now he put it into his briefcase and stood. "Thank you for having me," he said. "We will be back in touch with you very soon. We'll do what we can."

"*Thank you,*" said David McLaughlin in a shaky voice. Meghan was still crying and shaking her head as her husband stood to shake hands with the giant lawyer, who turned and left through the front door.

"Godspeed," called out Dave McLaughlin grimly.

CHAPTER 9
Angela and Bill Dine Out.

After Angela Maxim stomped away from mister cocky, the co-called *William Hamilton Smith*; she went to her office and told Marge to pull a background check on him.

Something's odd about that guy. He's ... beyond cocky. The dog too. A background on Smith would include detailed information concerning date and place of birth, schools attended, grade point averages, colleges attended, professional and other licenses, criminal history, registered vehicles, and much else. She felt odd asking for it, but ... *dammit, something's not right.*

Maxim wouldn't let herself think the dog with Bill Smith was the same mutt she *thought* she'd met ... before. But her sense of unease persisted.

When Marge shot the report back, it was a comprehensive 30 or 40 pages of information only police agencies could obtain. Born in Dallas, William Hamilton Smith had gone to a private school through the 8th grade, then finished up in a public high school. Played baseball and tennis. Lettered in track and field. Played saxophone in the band. Graduated with a high GPA. One sibling, a twin girl. Mother and father longtime residents of Dallas, solidly upper middle class people. Father an insurance agent, mother had been in real estate sales, both retired now.

In short, a nice middle class family with two kids. Smith had gone on to the University of Texas. He was a Longhorn. *That's funny, the T-shirt said Northwestern.* He'd graduated with a triple major in physics, astronomy, and nanotech engineering. *Triple major?* Then straight to law school where he was on law review and a member of the Order of the Powdered Wig or whatever it was at UT. *Straight into law school? WTF?* Smith was recruited right out of law school by the Cooney & Ivey firm in Winston. Now he was a fifth-year litigator doing insurance defense. Well-liked by the firm members, Smith was apparently doing a good job and on a partnership track.

In sum, the only thing unusual about Bill Smith was that he was smart as hell and was wasting his brains being a lawyer. *And a flack for insurance companies at that. Hmmmm. That's at least part of where the cockiness comes from.*

Angela still felt ... odd about him, but couldn't pin it down. *Something still not quite right.* Was she losing her perspective? Just because some guy had a nice smile and expensive cologne? Then it came to her: *He's too damned normal.*

She hoped he would call.

He did ... within 48 hours. Marge put the call directly through because Angela had warned her ahead of time.

"So," he said, starting right in. "I hope you're not angry at me."

"Should I be?" she asked coolly, turning it back on him.

"Not at all Angela, but sometimes people don't like my brand of ebullient humor."

"Ebullient," she repeated. "You've got a good vocabulary, Mr. Smith." She said it with a smile in her voice, maybe even a little flirtatiously.

"Please, let's test it out!" he said. "Let's go out to dinner this Friday and we can match vocabularies. And so you can start calling me *Bill!*"

"Isn't that rushing things a little?" she said. It was Wednesday, after all.

"Spot doesn't think so," said Bill Smith. "He said he really likes you."

Maxim felt a tingle of nervousness. It sounded ... odd, him saying that. A small bell was ringing at the edge of her consciousness. "Oh yeah," she said sarcastically, *"the talking dog thing again."*

"Hey!" he said mock-hurtfully, "there's no law against talking dogs, is there?"

"Imbroglio's?" she asked, moving the conversation along.

"Yes," he said. "Friday. How about 7:00 p.m.? I can pick you up."

"I don't think so," she said. "Let's make it 6:30. I'll come directly from the office."

"Okay by me," he said. "You work late, you FBI types?"

"Usually," she said.

"Okay, deal! Imbroglio's at 6:30 on Friday. You like wine?"

"Yes, but only a little."

"Red or white?"

"Red."

"I'll make sure we have a nice Cabernet to share when you get there."

"Indeed," she said. "I'll see you Friday evening, Mr. Smith."

"*Please* ... call me Bill," he said. "I'm looking forward to an evening with you." And for once there was no hint of mirth or flirt in his voice.

On Friday Angela left the office early to have her hair done. Then she rushed home to get cleaned up. *What to wear, what to wear ... it can't be flashy, gotta look like something I'd wear coming from work.* She agonized over her wardrobe, settled on a Tahari ASL pantsuit with a notched stand collar and a simple white buttoned shirt. *No necklace.* And no other jewelry except for the small ring her mom had given her when she was a teenager. She twisted and turned in front of the Cheval adjustable mirror in her apartment. *This will work.*

Then ... *shoes.* There was no way she could get away with wearing 5-inch CFM's ... not that she'd want to. Well, not on a first date anyway. *And not coming straight from the office.* She settled on a pair of practical black suede pumps with 3-inch heels.

Make-up. FBI Special Agent Angela Maxim spent more time than usual getting her makeup and lipstick right. *Just right.* At 6:15 she left her apartment carrying a simple Tasha Rhinestone clutch, the one she'd snagged at Macy's. *Simple but elegant.* She jumped into her Beamer and headed out.

The drive to Imbroglios would take about 20 minutes. *Can't get there too soon.*

But what if he thinks I can't be on time? What if he thinks I'm not punctual? She resisted gnawing on a knuckle as she drove. In spite of everything, Angela Maxim felt good. The guy was ... intriguing. *Whether there's something odd about him or not, intriguing is good.*

She thought on it as she drove, and decided it was the dog. A black mutt with some white spots. *And he kept saying the damned dog can talk!* She paused her thinking: *Calm down Angela! This will be a nice, enjoyable, normal dinner date. A chance to get to know him.*

At Imbroglio's Angela gave her BMW to the valet and walked in. It was 6:35. *Perfect. Fashionably late, but not too late.* She was escorted by the concierge to the back of the restaurant where Bill Smith had a cozy table set aside just for two. A candle burned in the center of it. *How romantic.* Bill Smith stood to greet her, took her hand and after a moment's hesitation leaned in to air-kiss her cheek. She let him. *Is that forward? We've only just met.*

Bill stepped up behind her to hold her chair. "I hope this isn't sexist or too old-fashioned," he said with a grin in his voice.

She turned her head back to him. "Not at all!" she said pertly. "I'm *charmed* by your male chauvinism." *Touché, big boy.*

"Well, well," he said, sitting down across from her. "A female cop—an FBI agent no less—who's presumably a glass-ceiling-breaker ...." He paused and lowered his voice conspiratorially: "And you're not a feminist *ball-buster?"* He grinned across at her, then formally held out the wine bottle, bottom down, with the label towards her.

"Would you judge me unmercifully if I was?" she said, mocking him. A sly smile tugged at the edge of her lips. *This could turn out to be fun.*

"Do that to the wine too," he said.

Was that a double entendre? Angela glanced at the wine bottle label. *"Chilean,"* she observed.

"I tend to stay away from the California brands," he said, "and I do like some of the brands from Chile."

She let him pour a dollop of wine for her inspection, then made a show of inspecting and sampling it, then turned her eyes to him and batted her eyelashes: "You may pour ... *Bill.*" He filled her glass to the correct level.

"Why no California wines?" she asked, taking another sip. *Not half bad* ... him *and* the wine.

"California, you know? He said. "And all that it implies? The sooner it collapses, the sooner rebuilding can start."

And awaaay we go! "Political, are we?" she said, gazing over the top of her wine glass at him. *That smell.* It was still coming off him. She could just catch the lightest aroma from across the table. It was the same bewitching cologne she had smelled on him the other day. *I must ask about that.* "Do we have a political radical here?"

Bill Smith poured wine into his own glass, set the bottle down, and sampled it. "Hope it doesn't get me ... *arrested*," he said impishly, "you being FBI and all."

The evening and meal proceeded with them enjoying each other famously, bantering back and forth as they flitted from one subject to another, talking about everything from politics in Patagonia to pork bellies in Peoria. From oceans and ecosystems to music and musk oxen. Angela Maxim relaxed. The conversation was enjoyably alluring ... as if they'd known each other for some time, far longer than they had. No subjects were off limits, and she was surprised to find they had many things in common.

When food came they ordered a second bottle of wine.

"So," she said, "let's talk about college. You're a lawyer. Where'd you go undergrad, and what was your major?" *Bad me*, she thought, *feigning ignorance and all.*

"Majors," he said, taking a bite of his filet mignon. "Three of them."

"Oh really," she said. "Tell me about it."

"I had the most unlawyerly major in the world," he said. "I started out in physics, and that led me into astronomy. It was fascinating. I wanted to see the moons of Jupiter, Saturn ... and *Uranus*."

Angela Maxim narrowed her eyes at him. *He pronounced that last one the wrong way. On purpose? Wine must be getting to me ... or him.*

"The next thing I knew, I segued into—or rather *added on*—nanotech engineering. Physics led me into that too."

"Really," she said, impressed. "So how do you go from a triple-STEM major into law school?"

He grinned across at her at the question.

God he's adorable ....

"Pure avarice," he said. "Or maybe just pragmatism. There's no space program anymore except for the private companies, and it's a hard slog for them, dealing with all the fedgov bureaucracy, meddling and intrusion ... *no offense meant*."

"None taken," she said. "Go on."

He continued: "Plus I didn't like the idea of being cooped up in a lab. I'm a lover, not a thinker!" He sounded plaintive.

Adorable. Angela wanted to hug him right there on the spot. She laughed sharply at his remark: "Hah! Promises, promises, big-boy!" *Did I just say that?*

He grinned at her. "Okay, I'll admit it, I say that to all the girls. But this time I'm serious."

She felt a little hot flash ... down in her tummy, like the wine was starting to encroach. She took a bite out of her steak, eyeing him across the table. *That smell! I swear to god, I must be ovulating.*

"Look," she said, "there is one thing I want to find out about you."

"Anything," he said. "Ask anything, and I'm yours."

"What is that fucking *fragrance* you're wearing?" she swore. *Ouch! Did I just use a bad word?* In the dim light she was blushing.

Bill Smith ignored it: "Fragrance?" he asked.

He wants to play coy. Touché! "Yeah, you know, like ... *cologne?*" She said it with an edge of sarcasm. "Whatever it is, I smelled it on you the other day, and I've got to say it smells pretty damned good. *Provocative* even .... " *I will NOT jump this guy's bones. I will NOT.*

"Boy have I got news for you, Angela .... "

"What?"

"I'm sorry, but I'm not wearing any cologne. That's just what I smell like." He sounded abashed, as if he was admitting to body odor.

Angela Maxim took another sip of wine. *Gotta watch the wine, better start tapering off.* "You're bullshitting me," she said. *Oops! Bad language again!*

"No," he answered. "Honest Native American."

"You mean *honest injun*," she corrected him.

"Yeah ... *honest injun*," he repeated, grinning. He held his wine glass up in front of his lips, tilted the glass slightly, and took a small sip. The tip of his tongue was slightly exposed, exploring the rim of the wine glass. It was almost ... erotic. Angela Maxim watched him like a bird in front of a snake, mesmerized. She felt the warmth in her belly spreading as his eyes delved into hers.

Jesus. It's the wine Angela! It's the wine! Keep it together! She boldly stared back into his eyes. "With an aroma like that, you must have a stable of girls fighting to get at you," she said.

"I haven't been on a date in almost a year," he said, "this is actually the first one in a long time." He looked at her meaningfully. "Even longer since I've met such an engaging and beautiful woman." He was doing that *tongue-thing* again with his glass of wine.

The tongue! It was alarming to Angela Maxim as it peeked out at her, just touching the rim of the glass. She tilted her head to one side. "Bill ... are you doing what I think you are? You trying to seduce me or something?"

A naughty boyish grin came into his eyes: *"Yes."*

Angela felt herself melting, her heart beating in her chest. She was breathing heavier as the warmth she felt spread. A devilish grin came onto her own face. It was reflected in her eyes as she stared boldly back at Bill Smith.

His eyes might be getting a bit unfocused too, she thought. *Good. Good that I'm not the only one ....*

"Yeah, well you need to know one thing," she said mock-sternly: *"I don't seduce that easy."* She paused, then added, "I don't hop into bed with any strange man I meet either."

*Holy shit! Did I just say that? Shut **up**, Angela!*

Bill Smith was still grinning. He put a hand to his chest, proclaiming innocence: *"Oh I assure you Angela, my intentions are purely honorable!"* He paused, resisting laughter. "Besides, I wouldn't want to commit a *peccadillo* on our first date ...."

"*Peccadillo*," she repeated dryly. "Okay, I'll bite ... *what's a peccadillo?*"

He paused for effect, then said, *"That's what you get when you cross a woodpecker with an armadillo."* They both burst into raucous laughter then looked around guiltily to see if they had offended other patrons.

"I'm sorry," said Angela, "but the wine must be getting to me." *It's **gotta** be the damned wine! No more wine for you!*

"Me too," said Smith with a grin, "and that's a *good* thing."

"A good thing indeed," she murmured, watching him. *He's so damned **cute!***

Dinner was over. They'd consumed one bottle of Cabernet and were some of the way through the second. She leaned forward, her thumb tracing the rim of her wine glass. It slid along slowly, experimentally.

Welllll ... " she said tentatively.

"*Welllll*," he answered, echoing her, "would you consider sampling a much better wine, a nightcap? Or some coffee or orange juice? Or a Dr. Pepper? At my palace?"

Maxim was looking down at the table, shaking her head slowly back and forth.

"I take that as a no," he said gently.

Angela glanced up. She didn't fully raise her face, but peeked out at him through her eyelashes, her eyes half-hidden by her hair. *Such a nice night,* she thought. The wine, the candle, the dinner, the fascinating talk and quick, funny repartee ... it had all been perfect. She sighed and shook her head again. "Bill, I can't ...."

"I understand," he said. His eyes were dancing. "I'm glad you survived the evening, anyway ... and I hope it wasn't *too* awful." Angela Maxim began to feel flushed again. His eyes were teasing her, caressing her across the table, as if they could pierce her clothes.

One side of her brain was screaming, *Jesus Christ girl, are you insane? Don't do it!*

But the other side piped up, *Oh big deal! Have a nightcap! Besides ... he's a special guy!* **Really** *special. Why not find out more?*

The other side of her brain cut in: *Yeah, but you don't have to be a slut to "find out more!"*

The other side countered: *Oh buzz off! This man is a gentleman. A very* **desirable** *gentleman ... and he's* **very** *attractive. Smells good too!*

Angela Maxim came to a decision.

CHAPTER 10
Angela and Bill Do More than Dine Out.

Angela Maxim tried to scowl at Bill Smith across the candle lit table. She sternly pointed a finger at him: *"No funny business!"*

He held his hands out in a conciliatory gesture. "None whatsoever!"

"And coffee only," she said, trying to give him a hard look.

"Nothing but coffee," he reassured. "So you won't crash your car driving home!"

"Are you far away?" she asked. She already knew. It wasn't even a 10-minute drive. *More like five at this time of night.*

"Not at all," he said. "You can bring your car or you can leave yours here and we'll go in mine."

She laughed out loud in exasperation: "I can't believe I'm even considering this!"

"I've got two things that will close the deal," he said eagerly.

"Oh boy," she said sarcastically. *"What?"*

"First, I'm driving a Tesla Model S."

"Really!" she exclaimed. "You. Drive. A. *Tesla?* I thought they were all in *museums* now."

"They are!" he said, sounding boyishly proud. "But I have one! And you can ride in it with me! For coffee!"

"What's number two?" she asked.

"Oh! The second thing is that we'll have a chaperon at my place."

"A chaperone?" She was suddenly sounding dubious.

"Yeah," he said brightly, "Spot's there!"

She laughed again. *I really must be ovulating. Jesus. This is just plain nuts.* "Lead on then," she said, nodding assent to him.

Bill Smith lived in a smallish split-level in a nice neighborhood filled with gays, young couples, and young single professionals ... one of which was him. He pulled up to a garage door but left the Tesla outside, then got out, came around, and opened open her door for her.

"You didn't have to do that," she said, pretending to be rummaging in her clutch as she waited to see if he would.

"I know," he said. "But I prefer to. *Sorrrry.*" He made himself sound abashed. To Angela he sounded boyish.

Adorable! Just adorable.

They went into his home, which was small, comfortable and nicely decorated. It was also well-ordered and clean. Angela Maxim looked around, putting her clutch on a kitchen counter. "Tell me, Bill," she said, "are you some kind of neatnik? This place looks too ... *orderly.*" He chuckled at her.

"I mean, you *are* a bachelor," she added defensively.

"I have a maid come in every week or so," he said. "But it's only me and Spot, so I try not to make too much of a mess in between cleanings. So it's not that much work to clean up after me."

"Hmmmm," she answered. Smith stepped to a door in the hallway and opened it. "Hey Spot!" he called out. The black dog bounced out the door and started jumping up and down at Bill's feet, begging to be petted.

"Now watch yourself," he said to the dog, "I've got a friend here ... you remember Angela from the other day?" The dog stopped jumping for a moment and turned to look at Angela. It barked a couple of short dog-yips her way, then turned back to jumping at Bill's feet.

He reached down and petted the dog, scratching behind its ears and ruffling its coat, then went to the kitchen and started up a coffeemaker. He also looked over a wine rack pulled out a bottle of red and flashed the wine bottle at her with a naughty grin.

"Maybe for me," he said, then gestured at several comfortable chairs in the sunken living room. "Please ... get comfortable."

"Maybe some wine for you," she echoed as she sat down on a small couch with a pretty blue corduroy pattern. It wasn't a love seat, but was smaller than a normal couch. Two could sit on it comfortably, if closely. She leaned back, throwing an arm over the back of the couch and crossed her legs as she watched him putter in the kitchen.

While the coffee cooked Smith pulled out a corkscrew and opened the bottle of wine he'd selected. They chatted as he worked: How long had he lived here, how did he like the neighborhood, what's the commute like ... the regular things.

He asked if she took cream or sugar. She said both, and when he came into the living room he was carefully carrying a little platter with a cup of coffee, some sugar and cream ... and two wine glasses on it. The opened wine bottle was in his other hand. The platter went on the coffee table in front of Angela as he sat down at the other end of the couch ... which was still fairly close to her.

"All for you!" he said, gesturing at the platter. They were close enough on the sofa to talk intimately, but not so close as to be touching. *Yet.* Bill Smith reached out to pick up a wine glass and pour some red wine for himself. He held it up and swirled it, then turned to look at Angela. Another naughty grin creased his face as he raised his eyebrows and tilted the glass of wine questioningly in her direction. His eyes were dancing with mirth.

Angela Maxim gave him a long, cool, disapproving look ... and said, "You bastard." She picked up the other wine glass from the table and said accusingly, "You do this with all the girls, don't you."

"Not really," he said as he poured some wine for her, then leaned back comfortably, kicked off his loafers and tucked a leg up under him. He stretched out an arm on the back of the sofa and held up his glass to her. Their arms on the back of the sofa were touching lightly. She held her glass out and they toasted.

"To you," he said in a gentle voice. "This was a wonderful night."

"And to you," she said, lightly touching her glass to his. "You made it wonderful, Bill." She took a sip of wine. "But I am curious," she continued, "are you serious that you haven't had a date in nearly a year? I'd think you'd be beating the girls off with a stick."

"Nah," he said, "who's got time to date anyway? I've been really crazy-busy at the law firm ... and then there's the gym, doing laundry, taking care of Spot, paying bills, *et cetera, et cetera.* Life gets in the way, you know? Too busy! Besides, I haven't run across anyone that I really wanted to get to know ... not for some time." He looked meaningfully toward her. "Not until now."

"*Until now*," she echoed. "*Wellll* then ... I guess you're saying you *like* me, hah?" Her voice was light ... a simple question.

You didn't just say that! she screamed at herself inside.

Bill Smith answered seriously. There was no goofy grin on his face now. He wasn't even smiling. "I'm very glad I met you, Angela ... and from what I see I like you a lot. You're smart, beautiful, interesting and ... compelling." He paused, took a sip of his wine, then added, "*There, dammit! I said it. And I'm sorry but it's true.*"

She felt herself flush. The warmth was coming back into her belly. She was sure she was turning beet red and tried to hide it by taking a sip of wine.

"There is one negative, though," said Bill Smith. It hit her like a punch to the gut.

Jesus! Get a grip girl! "And what's that?" she asked offhandedly.

"Well, you *are* a cop, Angela. And you *are* with the FBI. And that *does* make you a little, uh ... scary and formidable, you know?" He was grinning again, joking.

She leaned toward him on the couch with a smile. Her voice was sultry and low: "I might shoot you if you're a bad boy ... but I don't bite." He leaned in toward her. Their faces were only inches apart. Her eyes were lazy, hooded as he touched his lips to hers ... very, very lightly, and pulled back.

She tilted her head slightly to one side, a smile playing in her eyes. Her lips were slightly parted where he had kissed her. "More?" she murmured. "More of that?"

He answered in a low voice: "You promise not to shoot me?"

"I promise," she said, then closed her eyes. She felt his lips touch hers again and they kissed, slowly and languidly. His tongue tentatively touched her lips, then retreated. She breathed. *More.* His head tilted slightly to one side, and the tentative tongue came again ... curious, questing. She parted her lips, letting him in, touching his tongue with hers. He cupped the side of her cheek with his hand, and she put hers atop his as they continued.

His hand glided to the back of her neck and pulled her against his lips. She scooted up closer to him on the couch. *Ummmmm.* "This is nice," she murmured as his lips caressed hers, then her cheek, then her neck. She slipped an arm behind him and pulled him closer to her. She was breathing heavily and could barely keep from squirming against him.

Bill Smith paused, murmuring in her ear. "Come with me?" he asked in a low voice. She pressed her face into the crook of his shoulder and neck, pausing ... and then nodded silently. He stood up, bent over, and scooped her up off the couch effortlessly. Her arms went around his neck and she held her face against him. *That smell.* She breathed him in deeply. "*Ummmmm ...*" she murmured slowly, "you smell nice."

He held her against his chest as he carried her down the short hallway, then turned into his bedroom. He bent over and put her gently on the bed. *Strong,* she thought. She lay back, her arms splayed out to either side, and closed her eyes as she felt him undress her, his hands and lips caressing her at the same time.

She leaned up to let Bill Smith take her shirt and bra off, then lay back and lifted her hips as he slipped her panties down her legs. *I want this,* she thought. She was sinking into a fugue state, filled with desire for him, one that burned and grew inside of her.

Lying naked on the bed, Angela watched Bill Smith stand up and strip off his own clothes. Their eyes met again as they shared a small knowing smile, and she closed her eyes as he lay down beside her. She let herself sink into the moment as he explored her body, lovingly caressing her.

It went on for a long time, the touching and kissing as they melded together. Several times she felt her body spasm, as if tiny electrical shocks touched her deep inside. She gave herself up to it, sinking into a kind of delirium, pulling him tightly against her as she gasped repeatedly under his touch. It was as if her body was an entirely unknown land ... and he was its explorer.

She felt his lips touch her ear: "Will you merge with me?" he murmured.

"I think I already have," she said in a hooded voice, lost in a reverie of feelings.

"Shall we become one?" he asked in a low voice.

"Oh sure," she murmured back, "why not." She slipped her arms around his lower body and pulled him toward her. He was almost entering her as his hands gripped and guided her legs that had turned to spaghetti.

Bill paused again, his lips touching her ear: "Will you give yourself to me? To merge with me entirely?" he whispered. "The two of us ... together?"

Don't! Don't you dare! screamed a tiny warning voice inside her head. *You don't know him! Don't do it!*

She lay still, and it stilled him too. She held his face in her hands, pushing back slightly as she gazed into his eyes. "Entirely?" she asked in a low voice.

"Yes," he said back to her. "For both of us. It goes both ways."

That's how love works.

She was still holding his face silently, but inside she was crying out for him. *"Yes,"* she breathed, and shifted her body slightly to open herself. Her arms slipped around his back and she pulled him gently, firmly, inexorably toward her until he was fully and completely entered into her. *"Yes to all of it,"* she said, still staring into his eyes. *"Yes to you ... to all of you."*

Angela held Bill Smith tightly against her, moving in a loving embrace as he seemed to expand within her, his very essence linking and joining them to merge their bodies as well as their minds, their spirits ... their *allness.*

Angela Maxim felt her body dissolving into a single, central, perfect point of ecstasy, flowing into an indescribable oneness with him. It bordered on delirium. She felt as if he had not only entered her fully, but unspeakably suffused his very consciousness and essence throughout her body. She felt herself merging with him, and in the end surrendered herself entirely and willingly, in a way she had never, ever done before. She felt love ... it was pouring into and around and over her in a slowly building wave.

I've never felt anything like this, she thought, drifting inward toward a type of ... *centeredness,* like she had never felt before. She was a star in space, pouring her light down upon him, and Bill Smith was a planet encircling, caressing and devoting itself to her, enthralled with her very existence.

Wave upon wave of perfection engulfed Angela Maxim at a very specific point in space, time, and consciousness. It washed over her, rippling through her mind and body until at the end she cried out, her body thrashing as her entire universe *burst* ... into a thousand billion scintillating particles of ecstasy.

She bit hard into Bill Smith's shoulder as she cried out, drawing and tasting his blood even as her consciousness disintegrated and she felt him expand inside of her as his strong, loving, protective arms held her tightly.

Don't give a shit, was one of her last thoughts as she drifted toward sleep, her head on his chest. *Slut, whore, whatever ... I don't care.* She fell asleep careless of the world, her body molded up against his.

After some time, the dog named Spot came into the room and jumped silently onto the bed. It low-crawled up to where Bill Smith and Angela Maxim's heads lay close together.

"You mind if I do?" asked the dog in a low voice that sounded like a child's.

Bill Smith was only nominally asleep. "Well," he said quietly so as not to awaken Angela, "the question is, would it be ethical?"

"She consented to it," said the dog. "I heard her."

"True," murmured Bill Smith. "But she wasn't told the ramifications. She doesn't know, and in light of that ... is it ethical?"

"It will do no harm," said the dog. "And it's only a precaution. Just in case."

"Hmmm," mused Bill Smith, temporizing.

"Hey," said the dog, "I like her!"

"We haven't done this with a human being before," said Smith, sounding a little worried.

"Details, schmetails," said the dog in a low child's voice. "If it turns out to be unnecessary, unneeded or counterproductive, then no harm, no foul. Anyway, you know I err on the side of caution."

Bill Smith made up his mind. "Okay," he said and shifted a little with the woman in his arms. The dog snuggled up between them, all the way up to their heads. It was sandwiched between them. "Satisfied?" said Bill.

"This will do nicely," said the dog. Angela Maxim didn't stir. She was deeply asleep, unconscious and uncaring. Soon she would be even moreso.

Smith lay still. As always, there were many things in the universe to consider. He settled in to think about them.

Spot moved its muzzle up close to FBI Special Agent Angela Maxim's face, almost touching her nose, then opened its jaws more widely than would seem possible. The dog's jaws appeared to lock in place, wide open as they were, and after a moment they spanned Angela Maxim's face, settling lightly over her.

For several hours the dog did not move. Neither did Angela Maxim, for she had been rendered *totally* unconscious ... for the duration.

CHAPTER 11
Suburban Ugliness, Fear, and Loathing.

Aaron Akron, the hulking lawyer from the Individual Justice Foundation, told Dave and Meghan McLaughlin that an IJF staff attorney would be meeting with the district attorney shortly. But they had no idea when that would be.

So they waited.

It was a painful, interminable wait with their 7-year-old daughter being held at an undisclosed location in a so-called "foster home." In their fear and pain they were numb. Time crawled as it engulfed them. All inquiries with the authorities had been stonewalled: "Sarah is in a foster home for her own good and for her own protection," they were told.

Nothing else.

"Protection from whom?" Dave McLaughlin had demanded at the blank-faced bureaucrats.

From you, was the unspoken reply.

The McLaughlin's had been ordered by the local judge to refrain from even attempting to discover the whereabouts of their daughter, on pain of re-arrest. So all they could do was wait in fear, even after the IJF lawyer had visited them.

"Our child has essentially been kidnapped," Dave McLaughlin told the IJF lawyer as his wife Meghan clung to him crying.

"That is an accurate description of the process," Aaron Akron had replied. "Unfortunately, attempting to free her extra-legally right now would be counterproductive. I'm sorry. There are certain steps that must be taken to break the legal stonewall you're facing." He had smiled sadly at them. "We're essentially trying to unfreeze the wheels of justice here."

"When and how will we hear from you?" Dave McLaughlin asked.

"Pretty soon," Akron told them. "Another IJF attorney named Gwendolyn O'Connell will be meeting with the district attorney as soon as possible. She will immediately report to me thereafter. You will be informed, one way or another."

So David and Meghan McLaughlin waited ... *and waited.*

In the meantime word had spread quickly in the Wilding Oaks neighborhood that both Dave and Meghan McLaughlin had been arrested for abuse and neglect of their daughter ... and that Sarah had been taken by the state Division of Child Protective Services for her own safety. The overwhelming reaction in the neighborhood was one of relief: "No parent should allow a child to break the law like that," said one woman on the local email list, "whether it's a lemonade stand or a bank robbery!" Another said, "Good riddance!" and opined that. "Now we have a safer neighborhood." One other neighbor added that, "While it's too bad police and others were hurt, this shows that Sarah and her parents have to obey the rules just like the rest of us!"

Most of the other neighbors agreed. No voice was raised in defense of the McLaughlins, who had lived in their home for years and personally knew many of the people who were now denouncing them. Nor did anyone object to what had been done to them and their daughter by the authorities. In fact, many openly cheered it.

A narrative had been launched, to be carried and magnified by the local media. It caused some Wilding Oaks residents to begin a petition campaign urging the McLaughlins to sell their home and move out of the neighborhood.

It had been three days since Dave and Meghan McLaughlin were visited by Aaron Akron, so it was unsurprising that they both leaped to answer the front door when the bell rang. David opened it and found a small group of people on their front porch. It included some neighbors that he knew well, and some that he did not. In front was one he did know, Ed Gronski.

Another longtime neighbor and friend named Sam Forman was with them, as well as Patsy Scanlan who Meghan had known as a friend for a number of years. There was an older woman present also; she had a heavily bandaged wrist where her hand was missing.

That's the poor lady who lives down the street, thought Meghan McLaughlin. She had never met Mrs. Newton, but knew about the incident that had occurred a day or two after the explosion. Like all the neighbors, she and her husband had been frightened.

"Hi Ed," said Dave McLaughlin, opening up the door and gesturing to welcome them. "You all want to come in?" Both Sam Forman and Patsy Scanlan seemed to have turned their attention elsewhere. They didn't acknowledge his greeting, and barely looked at him.

"That won't be necessary, Dave," said Ed Gronski. He was apparently the leader of the group, and held a sheaf of papers in his hand. David knew he was a retired teacher, and active in the local zoning enforcement panel. Gronski was also on the "water sprinkling rangers," a volunteer group that searched for and reported homeowners watering their lawns on non-approved days.

"Okay," said Dave McLaughlin, "what's up?"

Ed Gronski held out the sheaf of papers. There were 10 or 15 sheets with writing on them ....

Dave took the papers and looked at the first page: The printing at the top said "WE THE FOLLOWING RESIDENTS OF WILDING OAKS COMMUNITY ASSOCIATION DO HEREBY PETITION AND URGE DAVID AND MEGHAN MCLAUGHLIN TO MOVE OUT OF THE NEIGHBORHOOD."

There was more printing expounding on how Sarah McLaughlin had violated the law and caused a confrontation that resulted in a tragedy with many deaths. It held them and their daughter responsible for the horror that had occurred, as well as for the maiming of Mrs. Harriman Newton III.

Dave McLaughlin was normally an even-tempered person, but his anger rose. "What's the meaning of this?" he demanded, staring the group down "Who is behind this?"

"Many neighbors are behind it," said Ed Gronski. "Look at the signatures. We've only been circulating it for a couple of days. Many have signed, and others will be added."

Dave McLaughlin's anger was increasing: "You must be *shitting* me!" he snapped. "Why would you do this Ed? *Why?*"

The older woman with the bandaged hand spoke up: "Your child has been taken away from you for her own safety!" she barked. "It has been extensively reported in the newspapers."

"So what!" shouted Dave McLaughlin. "Those stories are filled with lies! We're good parents, and you all know that! We've lived here for years!"

"The fact that your daughter was taken from you for her own protection is proof enough," retorted Mrs. Newton.

Ed Gronski spoke up: "Where there's smoke there's fire, Dave."

McLaughlin addressed Sam Forman and Patsy Scanlan: "Sam? Patsy? Are you part of this? Do you support this?" They did not look at him; both were looking down. "Sam, *look at me!*" snarled Dave McLaughlin. Forman didn't look up, he just nodded his head.

Patsy Scanlan responded out loud: "Yes," she said firmly, "you and Meghan are causing problems in the neighborhood. People are scared. We don't feel safe."

"We want you to move out of the neighborhood," said Ed Gronski.

Meghan McLaughlin was standing by her husband, holding his arm. Tears began streaming down her face.

"Are you fucking *insane?*" roared Dave McLaughlin. "*Are you all totally* **INSANE?**" The entire group stepped back, recoiling from his rage.

"Take these papers and *stuff 'em!*" he shouted. He threw the papers in Ed Gronski's face. "I don't *believe* this!" he said incredulously.

"It's for the good of everyone," said Gronski. "Like Patsy said, people are scared."

"*So you turn into a mindless mob?*" McLaughlin accused them. "You join up to get out here and *burn some witches? Is that it?*" He was enraged. "You can all go straight to hell! **Get off my front porch! All of you! Now!**"

"This isn't going to go away," said Gronski. Dave McLaughlin clenched his fists and stepped toward his former friend. He was turning red.

"Sam!" he snapped again at his good friend and neighbor Sam Forman. "Answer me! *Look at me!* Are you going along with this?"

Sam had drifted to the back of the group, and wasn't looking directly at Dave McLaughlin. He was still looking down, but nodded his head quickly. He wouldn't look up.

"GODDAMMIT SAM!" Dave shouted at him. *"Look at me, man! Tell me that you want me and Meghan to move away and not be your neighbors!"*

Sam Forman finally looked up. He looked at the McLaughlins and spoke in a small voice: "People are scared, Dave ... a lot of people were killed. Mrs. Newton has lost a hand." He paused and looked down again, shaking his head. "We've never had anything like this happen in Wilding Oaks before. No one's child has ever been taken away."

Dave McLaughlin *lost it*: **"You low-down, indecent, goddamn cowards!"** he bellowed at them. **"You are nothing more than a mob of fools, every one of you!"** He raised his fists at Ed Gronski and then exploded again: *"GET THE HELL OFF MY FRONT PORCH RIGHT NOW!"* He shook off his wife's hand and shuffled forward, fists up, to smash Ed Gronski in the face. Meghan beseeched him in a small voice, "David, please ...."

The group hurriedly retreated from the front porch with Ed Gronski hastily stumbling backward. They walked away leaving the papers on the ground where they had fallen. Meghan stooped down to pick them up, still crying. Her husband stood, fists clenched, seething with rage.

After Meghan gathered the papers they went inside, closing the front door behind them.

~~~~

Within a day after the Wilding Oaks group invited the McLaughlins to move out, IJF attorney Gwendolyn O'Connell paid a visit to district attorney Nick Alabattis in his downtown office in Winston.

As the elected DA in the judicial district that included the city of Winston, Alabattis was one of the most powerful local politicians. He was young for a prosecutor and very ambitious, keenly aware that a term as an elected DA was often a steppingstone to higher elected office.

Alabattis had risen fast after joining the office right out of law school. In a surprisingly short time he'd maneuvered himself into position to run for District Attorney and won the election handily. He was a physically imposing man, with bulk that had made him a star defensive tackle and offensive guard on his high school football team in Winston. It had also earned him a full-ride college scholarship, and he was still remembered as a local football hero. It didn't hurt either that he was a handsome man, one who still kept in top physical shape, which made him an imposing presence in any courtroom.

Alabattis' face was framed by a thick shock of dark brown curly hair. His face was a brooding olive-tone that threw off a vaguely menacing air. He was seen as both mysterious and irresistible to many of the young ladies in Winston, and it was no surprise that as an eligible bachelor he'd been seen with multiple beautiful women at various events ... including attractive daughters of prominent local families who were part of the political power structure in Winston.

But Alabattis wasn't prepared for the small, shockingly beautiful brunette who walked boldly into his office as his secretary closed the door behind her. Gwendolyn O'Connell was tiny, no more than 5 feet tall, and slim but by no means skinny. There were muscles under her skin that made her both wiry and athletic. Her hair was short, thick and black, cut in a spiked-out, no-bullshit pixie style that suited her just fine. It had some red highlights and framed a beautiful alabaster-white face.

Gwen O'Connell looked like a model off the front cover of a popular woman's magazine. She wore bright red lipstick that complimented the red highlights in her hair, and both were set off against a short black pencil skirt she wore underneath a black leather duster overcoat. She had a simple white-strap tank top on under the duster that showed surprising cleavage on such a small-framed body. With her small size and good looks the IJF lawyer looked elfin, radiating an almost ethereal beauty.

But Alabattis was no fool either. He wasn't about to be wowed by some midget female lawyer for a no-name legal foundation, no matter how good looking she might be. He put himself on guard, wondering if O'Connell was a lipstick lesbian ball-buster. *Bitch better be ready if she is*, he thought. *I rule here.* Even so, he felt a tiny hint of warning in his mind, some inkling of danger even as he felt desire stir at the tiny lawyer's beauty.

Gwendolyn O'Connell shrugged off the black leather duster and dropped it on a chair, then approached Alabattis and shook hands firmly across his desk. Her tiny hand was enveloped in his, but she had a surprisingly strong grip. *Stay aware and on guard, man,* he thought.

The IJF lawyer had come to talk about Sarah McLaughlin. Alabattis knew the case, and knew the kid was being held as a bargaining chip against the parents ... and so the public would know the authorities—*and Nick Alabattis*—were *doing something* at a time of crisis.

As she shook hands with Alabattis, Gwen O'Connell looked at him through a dainty pair of wire-rimmed glasses. She stepped back and put a black briefcase on top of the leather duster, then opened it and took out a single file folder. She held it out to Alabattis, saying in a deliberate voice, *"You are responsible for a 7-year-old girl being taken away from her parents without good cause.* She is being held illegally and incommunicado in a non-disclosed location against her parents' wishes. *What do you have to say for yourself, Mister District Attorney?"*

CHAPTER 12
Office Beatdown: "She's Not Real!"

District Attorney Nick Alabattis considered himself to be a tough man, mentally and physically. And he was. He was also well-aware of the legal and political power he wielded under the law. But he was taken aback by the very hostile and forceful accusation by the tiny female lawyer in his office.

Gwendolyn O'Connell was not smiling. And Alabattis, being a political animal, knew he must tread carefully where a public interest legal foundation was involved, no matter how small and insignificant it might be. But he also reacted instinctively: *Who does this little lesbo bitch think she is, coming in here and challenging me in my own office?*

"I'm sure there must be some kind of misunderstanding," he said smoothly. "Sarah McLaughlin is being protected from suspected abuse and neglect by her parents."

"You and I both know that's bullshit," O'Connell stated flatly. "Her parents are disfavored because they were at the wrong place at the wrong time, and Mr. McLaughlin is being targeted for being part of the local Tea Party movement ... as you well know."

"I know of no such thing," Alabattis lied. "But let's get the players straight first: Who do you purport to represent today, and in what capacity?" A smirk threatened to break out at the edge of his mouth. He would humor the bitch while promising nothing, the standard *something-will-be-done* BS. After all, he didn't get where he was by being politically inept. He also knew he could step on anyone who got in his way, and had done so in the past. So he wasn't scared of the IJF lawyer, but was smart enough to be wary.

"You could say I'm here representing the public interest against abuse of power by your office," said Gwen O'Connell. "But I need you to know that I and my foundation are authorized to represent the entire McLaughlin family, including specifically Sarah McLaughlin."

"Sounds like a potential conflict of interest to me," said Alabattis with a smirk. "The girl is 7 years old. Do you have a court order appointing you as her guardian ad litem?"

"I don't need that," said O'Connell, *and you know it.* "I am retained by her biological parents as her natural guardians. I am empowered by them to represent the interests of their daughter who is being illegally detained. *Kidnapped,* if you will."

"Strong words," said Alabattis, steepling his hands in front of his chin.

"What else would you call it?" retorted O'Connell. "You seized a young girl for no legitimate legal reason and you're holding her at an undisclosed location. She's being held incommunicado, not even allowed to talk to her parents, and your office refuses to tell her parents where she is ... until you squeeze concessions out of them."

Alabattis hesitated. *This could go off the rails ... but he wasn't going to let that happen* "What exactly do you expect me to do, Ms. O'Connell?"

"It's Miss O'Connell," she said, flashing a feral grin that the DA found somehow arousing. "I don't go for the feminist crap, and I'm happy to let you know I'm not married."

Alabattis was taken aback. It was as if she had flipped a switch. Now she seemed ... different. Even flirtatious. "Whatever you say," he said noncommittally. He hesitated, then added, "Are you saying you're *happy* to be unmarried? Or do you just want everyone to *know* you're not married?" *I'll play this game if the bitch wants.*

Gwen O'Connell lost her smile. "Both, as it happens. I'm always open for suggestions."

Alabattis was alarmed in spite of himself. *Better be fuckin' careful. This chick could be outright nuts AND a ball-buster.*

"How can I help you?" he asked flatly, suddenly shifting the conversation. He wasn't smiling.

"I'm here on behalf of the McLaughlin family, including Sarah McLaughlin as I told you. They are a family that lives in the neighborhood where the suicide bomb went off."

"We haven't established that it was a suicide bomb," said Alabattis, correcting her to keep control of the conversation.

"A dozen people are dead, no matter what you want to call it," she responded. "The media presumes a suicide bomb, but what caused it is irrelevant. As you know, the explosion occurred at a child's lemonade stand."

Nick Alabattis nodded, saying nothing. Neither of them were smiling. They watched each other like circling MMA fighters.

The tiny IJF lawyer continued, "Sarah McLaughlin's parents' have made repeated efforts to locate their daughter and speak with her. They have been continuously rebuffed and stonewalled." She stared at Alabattis with a cold look on her face. "We want her released and returned to her parents immediately." The tone of her voice made it a direct challenge to the hulking District Attorney.

Well fuck THAT shit, thought Alabattis, *screw her and the horse she rode in on*.

"Sarah McLaughlin is being cared for at a loving foster home for her own good and safety," he said. It sounded rehearsed. "There are allegations of both abuse and neglect by her parents, and the state has determined that she should temporarily reside in a stable foster home pending the outcome of our investigation."

"That's all bullshit, Nick, and you know it," Gwen O'Connell snarled at him. "There was no reason at all to detain Mr. and Mrs. McLaughlin in the first place, and there was even less justification to kidnap and hold Sarah McLaughlin."

"Kidnap," said Alabattis with emphasis. "There's that strong word again, *Miz* O'Connell." He used *Miz* instead of *Miss* intentionally to goad and shake her off balance ... to show who was boss here.

"It's a word that accurately describes what you have subjected the child to," Gwen O'Connell shot back. "The Individual Justice Foundation has been brought in because of what you are allowing to be done to that child and her family. It is wrong, it is illegal, it is immoral, and it is unjust. We want it ended now."

Nick Alabattis smirked openly now. "You're not exactly in your own hometown making demands here," he said. "The McLaughlins have already hired a lawyer and he's been to court on their behalf. The court backs what my office is doing. It is a matter for the judicial system to resolve, unless you're demanding that I bypass the courts and take the law into my own hands." He smirked at her again.

Gwen O'Connell stared at him silently. "You've already bypassed the courts one time," she said, "and having done so, you can also have Sarah returned to her parents right now with a single phone call. The reason you are holding her is so you can extract some kind of confession of involvement from her parents."

"What makes you so sure that those people were *not* involved?" said Alabattis, struggling to ease the smirk from his face.

Gwen O'Connell barked out a single bitter laugh: "You must be shitting me, little man."

The very large man across from her felt his anger rising. *He* was the District Attorney and *he* was in charge here. He didn't like being insulted, especially by some cunt lawyer, no matter what fly-speck organization she was with. Alabattis was known to have a temper. It was showing. His face started flushing red.

Gwen O'Connell was still standing across the desk from him. She hadn't sat down. "I've got some pictures of the so-called *loving foster home* where Sarah McLaughlin is being held," she said as she reached into the file folder and threw a couple of color eight-by-tens onto his desk. They showed an overgrown yard with trash strewn about fronting a shabby one-story cement block house. There were broken shades hanging in some of the windows. One window in the front of the house was broken. Cardboard covered the hole.

Nick Alabattis struggled to control himself. *What the fuck, who IS this bitch?* He leaned back in his chair and didn't touch the eight-by-ten photographs on his desk.

"What are those supposed to mean?" he said evenly.

"As you can see, what they *mean* is that Sarah McLaughlin is being held at a filthy dump, you *asshole.*"

"That's not my department!" snapped Alabattis angrily. He leaned forward, thrusting his face at her, gritting his teeth in anger.

"Well then," said the petite lawyer. "I guess you'll say the two drunks at the house that you call *foster parents* aren't in your *department* either." She tossed three more color eight-by-tens onto the desk. One showed what appeared to be a pot-bellied bum with a scraggly beard wearing a dirty white wife-beater. He was holding a can of beer in one hand as he stood in a trash-littered yard. Another of the photos showed a similarly dissolute male who was older but also dirty and unkempt. This one also held a beer as he stood in a trash-strewn dirt yard. The pictures had obviously been taken with a telephoto lens. The third photograph showed the two men embracing each other, face-to-face and body-to-body. One held a hand down the front of the other's pants in the genital area.

Alabattis held his temper with difficulty. "Goddammit, where the hell did those pictures come from?" he demanded. "That's a safe-home for abused kids! That location is not to be disclosed unless you want to talk to a judge about it from inside a jail cell!" He was leaning forward at his desk, his face flushing even more red in anger.

She responded in kind: "I'll tell you what, you idiot: *I took these photos, and that's all you need to know."* Alabattis's face was turning scarlet as he gritted his teeth in rage.

The little IJF lawyer continued levelly; sarcasm had crept into her voice: "And since this is about Sarah McLaughlin being held in a *loving foster home, let's see how she's doing there."* She threw down three *more* color photographs on the desk. All were Sarah McLaughlin. In two of them she was in what looked like a back yard, possibly behind the foster home. There was no grass. The ground was dirt. She was dirty and huddling alone on the ground, clearly afraid, holding her arms around her knees. In all three pictures her hair was matted and unbrushed, her face smeared with dirt. Two of them showed that she had visible bruising on at least two places on her body, one on her face and one on an upper arm.

Nick Alabattis's jaw almost dropped open. He was dismayed by the pictures, not so much by the condition of the brat, but at what it could mean politically if those pictures got out.

"Not your department!" barked Gwen O'Connell in his face, leaning forward over his desk. She stabbed a finger at one of the pictures. It showed Sarah McLaughlin looking out of a grimy window at the house, her face twisted and crying. *"Not your fucking department, right asshole?"*

Alabattis held his hands up. "Okay, okay," he said, trying to calm the situation and regain control. He stood up and leaned forward on his desk. "Look, I didn't know about this. The Department of Child Protection handles foster homes and placements. I've never seen the place."

"Well then fucking *do something about it!*" Gwen O'Connell snarled. "Don't sit here on your fat ass and say it's not your fucking department while that little girl suffers!" Her mouth twisted in contempt at the big district attorney. *"How about you put on your big boy pants and get that girl out of there right now and back with her parents. Right now!"* She was leaning over the desk barking directly into his face.

Alabattis cracked. *No one fucks with me in my own office!* He thrust his face out at her, clenching his fists. *"Listen bitch!"* he snarled. "I'll do whatever I goddamned please, and I do it when and how I damned well want, and no cunt from some two-bit law firm comes in here to tell me otherwise! *Got that?"* His face was fully red and twisted in rage.

Gwen O'Connell jammed a finger into his chest as she looked up at him: "Talk about a *cunt*, Mr. DA, it looks like the only *cunt* in this room is you!" Despite her size she obviously wasn't afraid of the huge man, even as he towered over her.

"Fuck you, bitch!" he snarled. "This interview is over! *The girl stays in the goddamn house until I fucking say so!"*

"No," said the little lawyer back at him, speaking in a surprisingly calm voice. "This interview isn't over ... *bitch!"* She came around the desk and spat the last word directly into his face.

Alabattis reached out to push an intercom button on his desk, but she was faster, blindingly so, and slapped his beefy hand away from the intercom. The impact was surprisingly strong. In another split second Gwen

O'Connell hauled off and slapped Alabattis *hard* across his face. The *smack* of the impact reverberated and stunned him.

"God *dammit,*" he roared, losing his volcanic temper. Without thinking, he grabbed the smaller lawyer in front of him by her thin shirt and violently shoved her. The rope-top pullover tore, exposing her breasts as she stumbled backward.

Alabattis was shaken, and instantly moved to hit the intercom again, but the tiny girl lawyer moved blindingly fast. She jumped back to knock his hand away from the intercom again and leaped at him, raking his face with her fingernails, drawing blood. She was unnervingly fast and Alabattis stumbled backward just trying to get away from her slashing nails. Gwen O'Connell pressed him, keeping herself between him and the door to his office. Her pixie-like face was twisted oddly. She didn't show rage, or even anger. She seemed to be ... concentrating.

Alabattis tried to protect himself by trying to shove her away. Again she moved unnervingly fast and with shocking force slapped his hand aside even as she continued raking his face with her nails.

Nick Alabattis was a physically tough man. He'd done some boxing and knew how to throw a punch. His money punch was a left hook that could be devastating. With the girl lawyer slashing at his face he reflexively unleashed the left hook without thinking.

He caught her cleanly on the side of her delicate face with all his weight behind the punch. Her head snapped violently to her left, the impact opening a gash in her right eyebrow. She was knocked entirely off her feet as she slammed into the wall. Blood spurted from her mouth and the gash at her eyebrow.

Alabattis felt his groin turn to ice and wet himself as the petite lawyer hit the wall and fell onto the floor. *Holy shit!* He was terrified at what he had done, sure that he had knocked her out and possibly killed her.

What happened next almost unhinged the former football lineman: Gwendolyn O'Connell wasn't knocked out. In fact, as she hit the floor she seemed to *bounce* back at him, as if some form of energy had thrown her up from a tensile surface. She appeared unconcerned with her bare breasts and the blood streaming down her face. In a flash she launched herself back at Alabattis, her hands flying at him again.

"What the FUCK!" roared Alabattis in terror as she raked at him. His eyes were bugging out as he lunged for the office door. The little female lawyer was faster. She threw herself sideways, blocking him—*like a fuckin' linebacker!*—and grappled with him. The strength of her tiny arms was simply unbelievable. Panicking, Alabattis tried to throw her to the side, but it didn't work. She was both faster and stronger than him. *Jesus H. Christ, what the hell is going on? She can't be so fucking strong!*

Alabattis couldn't get away from the petite lawyer, so he crowded her and threw a side headlock around her neck. He found himself struggling to stay upright as she fought with astonishing strength, screaming at the top of her lungs. In a desperate attempt to escape, Alabattis threw her to the side hard as he could. She flew bodily across the room just as the door of the office flew open, hitting the wall face-on, splattering blood and smashing her petite nose.

"What the hell!" shouted the lawyer in the doorway. It was one of the department heads, a chief division assistant to Alabattis. He stood horrified, frozen in the doorway, staring at the scene with his mouth open. The beautiful little IJF lawyer glanced at the dumbfounded lawyer in the doorway and slid slowly to the floor, her back against the wall. She was wailing and sobbing hysterically, her tears mixing with makeup and blood smeared all over her face. Her blouse had been torn entirely aside and was hanging down, exposing both of her surprisingly substantial but still perky breasts.

Alabattis looked at the lawyer in the doorway, panicking. Gwendolyn O'Connell was down on the floor up against the wall, her face twisted and bloody as she wailed piteously. Alabattis gaped at her as the scratches on his face seeped blood.

The little IJF lawyer turned her bloodied, tear-streaked face toward the doorway and lifted a delicate arm to point directly at a frozen and stunned Alabattis. *"He tried to rape me!"* she wailed, putting her hands over her face and sobbing uncontrollably.

Even at that point, Alabattis might have been able to save himself, not to mention his career. But he was unhinged as his eyes bugged out of his face. All he could do was point at the tiny female lawyer on the floor and shriek at the top of his voice, *"She's not REAL! Goddammit,* **she's not fucking real!"**

CHAPTER 13
Yes, the Dog is Talking ... to You.

FBI Special Agent Angela Maxim came awake slowly as light peeked through a curtained window in Bill Smith's bedroom. She was naked, her body molded up against him. One leg was thrown over his midsection and her head rested on his shoulder as one of his arms cradled her.

Oh shit! The office! She felt panic rising, but a thought came: *Saturday! Oh thank god it's Saturday!* She held herself motionless against Bill Smith, inhaling his scent. *Damn that's nice.* She and her lover were half covered by a colored sheet. Behind her, something wet nudged into her lower back.

"Yikes!" Angela Maxim swung an arm back to pin the wet thing. Her hand came down on a furry body under the sheet. *Spot*, she thought, *Bill's dog Spot*. She sighed and carefully lifted herself from Bill's arm. Turning over, she lifted up the sheet, and there was the dog. It looked happily back at her with the silly doggy grin. She smiled in spite of herself, reached over and scratched him behind the ears. Spot twisted its head to the side, loving it.

"That feel good?" she murmured in a low voice, not wanting to wake up her lover.

"Mmmmm," said the dog in a child's voice. "That feels *really* good."

Angela Maxim screamed, threw off the sheet and scrambled away from the dog, crawling over Bill Smith's body and falling off the other side of the bed in the process. Bill came half awake, groggy. She knelt on the carpeted floor by the bed, shaking his shoulder. *"Bill!"* she whispered urgently, forcing him to wake up. Lying on his back, Bill Smith turned his head to one side to look at her, squinting his eyes.

"What?" he asked hoarsely, eyes half open. Then he smiled. "Good morning ...."

Angela pointed urgently across his chest at the dog lying on the other side of the bed. *"HE TALKED!"*

Bill flopped his head over the other way to look at Spot. "Did you talk?"

"Yes," came the answer in a human child's voice.

He flopped his head back again to look at Angela Maxim. "So?" he asked.

"What the fuck!" exclaimed Maxim in an urgent whisper. She was hyperventilating, staring at him. *"He talked! The dog talked!"*

Bill Smith was still squinting at her. "Yeah? So? He talked." He grabbed an edge of the sheet and tugged at it to cover himself. He pulled it up over his head, then turned away to go back to sleep.

"DON'T YOU TURN OVER! DON'T YOU GO BACK TO SLEEP BILL SMITH!" Angela Maxim squealed urgently from the side of the bed. *"DON'T YOU DARE DO THAT!"*

Bill Smith threw the sheet off and turned his head back to look at her, opening only one eye. "Angela ... it's Saturday morning." He pulled the sheet back over his head.

"No fucking way!" she yelled at him. "I don't care of it's Saturday *night!* There's a goddamn dog talking at me!"

Bill Smith pulled the sheet off his face again. He leaned up on one elbow, sounding resigned: "Angela, get control of yourself. I swear, it's like you're like Atz Lee's wife on that Alaska show on TV when they were fishing and saw the bear nearby." He flopped back on his back, opened his mouth and yawned widely. "Atz Lee said *Jane, get control of yourself!*'"

Angela Maxim stared at him, her mouth open. "Well goddammit Bill there *was* a bear!" she said indignantly.

"Yeah?" he responded. "So?" He turned back to look at the dog. "There's no bear *here*. Besides, I *told* you Spot can talk ...."

Spot watched the interplay with interest, its head swiveling back and forth between them as if watching a tennis match. Now it turned its muzzle back to Angela. It had that shit-eating grin on its snout again.

"Jesus Christ!" Angela exploded. She raised up a little by the bed and peered over Bill Smith's body at the dog. *"Jesus H. Christ!"* Her breathing was fast and shallow.

"PMS," said Spot from the other side of the bed.

"The hell it is!" she screamed back at it.

"Hey, I'm just reporting what I smell," Spot said in a hurt child's voice. "I am a dog after all."

"He's right, you know," said Bill. "You do have PMS. I could tell last night, when we were being ... umm, *amorous.* "

Angela stared back at Bill Smith, keeping an eye on the dog out of a corner of her eye. "Oh great," she said sarcastically. "So you're on the dog's side, and now you've got the ability to sniff like a dog too."

"I really do have an acute sense of smell," he said. "I can detect very faint pheromones and chemicals, that kind of thing. To a certain degree, at least. But we were *very close* last night, you know ... ." He smirked, then leaned over to kiss her on the lips.

Angela Maxim didn't move. She felt Bill Smith's kiss, but her eyes were big. "You've got to be *shitting* me!" she said finally. Her hands were on the edge of the bed and she glanced again at the dog sitting quietly on the other side. "I ought to smack you," she said.

"Me or the dog?" asked Bill Smith.

"Both of you!"

"I'd understand," he said. "But look, we did make delicious love last night, did we not? And, was it not ... *good for you?"*

"What the hell does that have to do with a talking fucking dog!" she shouted at him.

"Plenty," he said. "Spot's my best buddy. We're a package deal."

"Shit!" she exploded, and then narrowed her eyes at him: "Okay ... *yes.* All right? Last night? Yes, it was ... very good."

He propped his head up on one elbow. "Did we not agree to join the very essence of our minds, our bodies and our spirits? I could feel it! Could you?" He reached out to pull her toward him, to kiss her again.

Angela Maxim pulled back. "I can't believe this," she said with exasperation. Her eyes tracked back and forth rapidly between Bill and the dog on the other side of the bed. "If I'd hadn't had goddamned PMS I probably wouldn't have *fallen* for you like that, *Mister William Hamilton Smith!*"

"I think that means she's pissed off at you," said the dog in the child's voice.

"You shut up!" snarled Angela. "Nobody asked you!"

"Uh ... *sorry*," said Spot. It flattened out on the bed on its tummy and put its front paws on top of its head, assuming the classic comedic dog pose.

"Knock that shit off!" Angela Maxim shouted at it. "You're just faking it anyway! You're not sorry!"

"Look," said Bill Smith, bringing her attention back to him. "Last night was real, Angela. It was wonderful." He held a hand out and covered one of hers. "I promise you I've never felt like that before ... or experienced anything like it. It was ... ecstasy."

"Jesus Christ," said Angela Maxim. "You're trying to distract me! There's a damned talking dog on the bed!" She was silent for a moment, then gave up and said, *"Yes, dammit* ... it was the best sex I've ever had in my entire life. Satisfied? *But that's not what we're talking about!"* She glared over at the dog again. It was sitting up now, obviously enjoying the interplay between her and Bill Smith.

"I know what you're thinking, Angela," said Spot. "Being a suspicious type by nature, you probably think *this is some kind of trick! Bill is playing me!'* You know, like hidden microphones and speakers? That kind of thing? *Am-I-right?'*

"If it is, you're both dead meat," she snapped at the dog. "And if that's true, it's gone on long enough! *I'm not fucking amused!"*

"Calm down, would you?" said Bill. *"Geez* Angela." He scooted back to lean up against the bed's headboard. He was entirely naked but the bottom part of his body was still covered by the sheet. He crossed his arms and looked at her almost petulantly.

Angela Maxim gave a long hard look back at him. *He's just adorable.* Angela reached over to Bill and grabbed his arm, shaking it violently: "Bill! Wake up! *Wake ME up!* Tell me there's no talking dog on the bed!"

He looked back at her evenly, then peered across at Spot, then turned back to Angela and tilted his head, raising his eyebrows. He shrugged elaborately. "Okay!" he said. *"There's no talking dog on the bed!"* He looked back at Spot. "Got that?"

"Got it," said the dog.

Angela snatched her hand away from Bill Smith's arm. *"Dammit Bill! Dog's don't talk!"*

"Correction," said Spot, *"most* dogs don't talk."

"Shit," said Angela in a small voice. She was still crouched at the side of the bed. "Bill, please tell me right now that your dog isn't really speaking? Please?"

"Angela," he said gently, reaching out a hand to cradle the side of her face. She leaned into it and put her own hand over his. "I'm sorry if you're a little freaked out ... but I can't say the dog isn't talking." He sounded apologetic. "Spot is my dog, okay? He has the ability to talk. Pretty good at it too."

"Really?" said Angela Maxim in a small voice, finally convinced. "Are you with a circus? Or a TV show?"

"No," said Smith, "not really." He shrugged again. "Spot has the ability to just ... *talk.*"

"Angela, I ..." started Spot.

"You shut up!" she screeched at the dog, snatching her hand away from Bill's. Spot snapped its mouth shut and looked over at him.

"What the FUCK!" yelled Angela Maxim. She leapt up, stark naked, and dashed to one side of the room. She started rummaging in her purse with Bill Smith and Spot-the-dog watching curiously. She came up into a crouch with a gun in her hand. Backing up against the wall next to the doorway, she covered Smith and the dog with the pistol. It was a small-frame Smith & Wesson .38, a hammerless model.

"Geez," said Bill Smith from where he was leaning against the bed's headboard.

"Geez indeed," said the dog, still watching Angela.

"Get out of bed and get down on the floor!" she shouted in her command voice.

"Geez again," said the dog in wonderment. It looked back and forth between Angela Maxim and Bill Smith and sounded chagrined, especially for a dog.

"Are you shitting me?" Spot asked Angela Maxim. It turned to Smith: "This is kind of ... unexpected."

"You can say *that* again," said Bill Smith without taking his eyes off of Angela.

"This is kind of ... unexpected," said the dog again.

"Shut up!" shouted Maxim. She was freaking out, breathing heavily and fast. The gun's aim wavered back and forth between Bill Smith and the dog. "Get on the floor!" she shouted again.

"Him or me?" asked Spot.

"Shuddup!" she yelled. "Both of you!"

Spot looked over at Bill Smith, who was watching Angela Maxim with puzzlement.

"Are you serious, Angela?" he said. "I mean, at least stop waving that gun around."

"I'm not waving it around!" she screeched. "I'm covering you! Both of you!"

"Well I'm not going to crawl around on the floor," Bill said matter-of-factly, "even though it might be fun in another context." He paused for a moment. "But I will get us some coffee! Spot? You want some?"

"Please!" said the dog.

"Don't move!" shouted Angela Maxim.

"Does that mean you'll shoot me?" asked Smith. He casually threw the sheet off and stood up by the side of the bed. He stretched luxuriously, his arms behind his head.

God he's beautiful, thought Angela Maxim. She was still standing against the wall, the gun pointed at him. "Would you like some coffee?" he asked.

"I want some!" said Spot eagerly.

"Heard you the first time," said Smith. "Angela? Coffee?" She stood silently where she was, back against the wall. The gun was still pointed at him.

"Angela, listen," he said. "You've already been checked out by an FBI psychiatrist, and he gave you a clean bill of health."

"How do you know that?" she snapped.

"I know a lot of things," he said. The corners of his mouth lifted slightly in a maybe-grin. "Besides, come on Angela, what are you going to do, shoot me for getting you a cup of coffee? If the psychiatrist thought you were mentally healthy last week, wait until he sees *this*."

He walked around the end of the bed, still naked, and passed in front of the FBI agent. She tracked him with the pistol.

In the doorway Bill turned back to talk to Spot: "You want yours the normal way? Cream only?"

"Please," said the dog in its kid's voice.

Bill looked over at Angela who was still pointing the gun at him. "You?" he inquired. "Cream? Sugar?"

"Both!" she barked.

"Great!" he said happily. "Wait a minute!" He walked out the door and they could hear him moving cups and things around in the kitchen.

Angela Maxim shifted her gun to cover the dog. She sidled sideways up to the doorway, her back against the wall, and nipped a quick glance around the corner. She jerked her head back, the gun in both hands.

"I think he's using Keurig Cups instead of natural roast," said Spot. "Usually he likes to do his own grinding."

Angela Maxim stood with her back to the wall. She was aiming the gun at the dog, but finally started lowering it. She looked sheepish.

"Thank you," said the dog with evident relief.

Maxim didn't say anything. She was still staring. She slid down and ended up sitting on the floor, back against the wall. She seemed to suddenly notice the gun, looking at it curiously. She let it hang slackly from her hands, then looked up at the dog. Spot was still lying on the bed watching her.

It had that stupid dog-grin on its face again.

CHAPTER 14
Elna Bibber to the Rescue!

The Winston, Pennsylvania judicial system was in an uproar over the District Attorney, Nick Alabattis. He was accused of beating up and sexually assaulting an attractive female lawyer who had come to meet in his office. She had been rushed to a hospital where she was being held incommunicado under police guard.

The media loved the whole thing and was having a wonderful time covering "the Alabattis Affair" as they'd quickly dubbed it. Tongues were wagging and rumors were flying in Winston about how many other women Alabattis might have assaulted and intimidated into silence in the past.

It was quickly rumored, then picked up and repeated as true in the press that the DA was known to have a longstanding fear and hatred of women. Local social justice warriors gleefully roared into action, launching a press release within hours demanding that Alabattis step down.

The normal accusations were trundled out and trumpeted, including claims of misogyny, racism, homophobia, sexual harassment, white privilege, islamophobia, transphobia and so forth ... not to mention the attempted rape itself. Within 24 hours it was obvious to everyone that the previously popular district attorney was guilty. Nick Alabattis had been tried and convicted by an online mob of politically correct activists feeding a bogus storyline to smug journalists.

And besides ... *women never lie about rape!*

Almost instantly a critical mass of publicly outraged feminists emerged. They charged that "the DA's Donnybrook" (as it was also labeled) was the result of Alabattis demanding sexual favors from the beautiful lawyer, Gwendolyn O'Connell. Sex was demanded in return for information about the young girl who had been unjustly victimized by a patriarchal system led by the likes of Alabattis.

The press went into overdrive when they discovered that Sarah McLaughlin had been hidden away from her parents at a secret location. That, combined with the *DA's Donnybrook*, established that Alabattis hated *all* women, no matter what their age, including their blameless mothers.

At the scene of the crime the chief assistant district attorney who had opened the door was stunned by the bloody wreckage in the DA's office. *Chaos!* Alabattis, the hulking former football star, had thrown the petite lady lawyer all the way across the room and up against a wall where her dainty nose had been smashed upon impact.

Deep scratches and blood on the DA's face confirmed the ferocity of the petite lawyer's efforts to save herself. For her trouble she'd been slugged in the face, choked, thrown against a wall, and had her nose broken and her blouse ripped off.

An initial police investigation ramped up within hours and interviews began while Alabattis hunkered down. The only thing heard from him since the ... *event* was his protestation that, *"This is a setup! This is a setup!"* That was even as Gwendolyn O'Connell was being rolled out of his office on a gurney, sobbing piteously.

"Bullshit, bullshit, bullshit!" Alabattis screamed as O'Connell accused him of trying to rape her.

That didn't seem to go over so well ... but there it was: The gutsy, bloodied, beat-up little lawyer had given as good as she'd got, even as she was pummeled by the vicious District Attorney, suffering multiple contusions to her delicate body in the process. Since political correctness had long since dispensed with the trifles of investigation, facts, and withholding judgment ... *everyone knew Alabattis was guilty as hell.*

Doughty little lawyer Gwen O'Connell had fought that bastard off! *But just barely!*

And besides ... *women never lie about rape!*

Someone at the office had thrown a coat over Gwen O'Connell's small shoulders to cover her up while police and EMT's were called. She was rushed to the nearest hospital where a rape consultation team was convened to interview and physically examine her.

At the DA's office police sealed off everything prior to bringing in a forensic team to take detailed photographs and blood splatter samples from around the room.

But what *really* got tongues wagging were the large color 8-by-10 photographs found lying on the desk of Nick Alabattis. No one had thought to grab them before police arrived, so they were instantly leaked to the press ... which was how Sarah McLaughlin was identified as the purpose of the meeting.

No one seemed to know where the leaked photos came from, and no one in the media was talking, so the public was soon treated to front-page photos of a little girl huddled crying in the dirt while a couple of deviant foster parents drank beer and fondled each other nearby. The photos also showed hints of a nearly derelict foster home where Sarah McLaughlin was being held.

Not surprisingly, the public went berserk with the mob being egged on by the local press. Alabattis was quickly abandoned by the media even though it normally covered for him as part of the local power-structure. The Department of Child Protection Services in turn lapsed into a full bureaucratic stonewall: "We're-just-following-the-rules," they protested, and blamed everything on the District Attorney's office. But Nick Alabattis wasn't going to take the fall without a fight, so he blamed the Winston police department for demanding that Sarah McLaughlin be held incommunicado. The Winston police department in turn denied everything and blamed the local FBI for the little girl's travails.

The brawl between Alabattis and Gwendolyn O'Connell occurred on a Thursday afternoon. The news media narrative didn't emerge until Friday afternoon ... meaning that the story was in full-throated, scandal-mode-roar as the lead on front pages and TV news reports by Saturday morning. It had taken a day or so for the media narrative to jell, especially since there was conflict between the normal duty to serve the local insiders as opposed to the juicy story about an evil, hulking, hate-filled, predatory, white, cisgender male—*Nick Alabattis*—trying to exert his patriarchal white privilege over a plucky female lawyer who wasn't going to put up with it.

Hear her roar!

In fact, the most delicious part of the storyline was that the physically smaller female lawyer had apparently kicked ass in that room, clearly giving as good as she got.

Hear her roar again!

When the pitiable photos of Sarah McLaughlin were leaked, the media instantly recognized a piggyback narrative: Not only had the predatory, white-privileged, cisgender male district attorney tried to rape the petite lady lawyer in his sealed-up office, but he'd also victimized two *other* innocent females, Sarah McLaughlin *and* her blameless mother!

In the meantime, due to a copyeditor's mistake FBI Special Agent Angela Maxim was initially identified as FBI Special Agent *Angelo* Maxim. That unleashed yet *another* part of the agreed media storyline: *It was Special Agent Angelo Maxim's fault! HE* was responsible for the government kidnapping Sarah McLaughlin! *HE* had schemed for Sarah McLaughlin to be hidden away from her mother! *HE* had accused Sarah's innocent parents of being involved in the terror bombing! *HE* was the cause of the suffering and anguish of Sarah and her mother!

By the time the dolts in the media discovered that Angelo Maxim was *Angela* Maxim, it didn't matter: The growing conflagration was recognized as the stuff that media careers were *made* of ... and that opened a window for a certain plucky girl reporter to ride it to national stardom!

But more about Elna Bibber later ....

There were glitches in the emerging storyline too ... twists that raised the stakes: For one thing, as it unfolded by Saturday morning the FBI had to admit that they weren't quite sure *where* Special Agent Maxim was. Only her *car* could be located, found in a restaurant parking lot that morning.

Unfortunately, Angela Maxim wasn't answering Marge's increasingly frantic calls to her cell phone either. That was because she'd turned it off the night before when she'd gone on her date with an unusually attractive young lawyer named William Hamilton Smith.

So the mystery only added to the growing media-storm that day, ensuring that everyone was having a marvelous time ... except of course for Nick Alabattis.

The problem was that Angela Maxim—*against her better judgment!*—had accepted an invitation to go home with her date on Friday evening. *For coffee only! No funny stuff!* And had subsequently been led to bed by her handsome and alluring date after an amazingly wonderful evening at Imbroglio's restaurant.

That Saturday morning Angela Maxim would have *catapulted* herself out of Bill Smith's bed if she'd been aware of the blooming media frenzy. Instead, she dropped the gun back in her purse, got up off the floor, and nakedly joined Bill and Spot for coffee on the bed-of-love she'd shared with Bill Smith the night before.

Elsewhere in Winston, the police department was protecting itself by holding attorney Gwendolyn O'Connell in a guarded hospital room, denying her any contact with anyone. That caused a problem because reporters were normally part of the police team, not to mention servile *presstitutes* for the local political power structure. They could almost always be depended on as team players, loyally following orders from local political insiders. *Almost* always.

Unfortunately, given the size and ferocity of the emerging scandal, some reporters declined to play their normal role. In fact, they were demanding access to Gwendolyn O'Connell, only to be blocked by the police.

Feed the bonfire!

The Winston city politicians and the police department had closed ranks against the media this time. All that could be determined about the lawyer victimized by Nick Alabattis was that she was a staff attorney for the Individual Justice Foundation headquartered in Manchester, New Hampshire (causing some reporters to consult maps to find out where New Hampshire was).

Further background investigating disclosed that Gwendolyn O'Connell had grown up in Dallas/Ft. Worth as Gwendolyn Smith, gone to college in Texas, and then to law school in the Midwest where she'd met and married a guy named Kevin O'Connell. Then it was off to New Hampshire for the happy couple ... where they'd divorced a few years later.

But today there was no way the Winston political power structure was going to let dimwit reporters get anywhere *near* Gwen O'Connell. She was kept entirely sealed off in that hospital room with a 24-hour police guard.

The department basically told the media to piss off ... for the time being at least, until decisions could be made on how to play the whole crisis.

Enter cub-reporter Elna Bibber! A cute 23-year-old blonde, she'd gone to college in Colorado on a gymnastics scholarship and majored in journalism. Now she was a reporter for a local TV station, having been on the job for less than a year ... and was *aching* to make her mark in the media world.

There was something else interesting about Elna Bibber: While she attended college at Colorado State University, when she wasn't partying or doing gymnastics, she'd taken up rock climbing ... and gotten pretty good at it. Including rappelling.

So on that Friday, after the editors at the local newspapers and TV stations had gotten their orders and told everyone to stay away from the hospital for the time being, ace-cub-reporter Elna Bibber "didn't get the message" (and was disinclined to comply anyway). Why? Probably because she was a beginner and didn't yet understand the media-government-money axis and how it worked in Winston.

Thus, when Elna Bibber was able to sniff out where Gwen O'Connell was being held, she hatched a plan: Simply go up on the hospital roof with a climbing rope, secure it to a sturdy air conditioning compressor frame, toss the line off the building, and rappel down to the window where she knew Gwendolyn O'Connell was being held.

Hanging off the side of the hospital, and arriving at what she was pretty sure was the right window, Elna Bibber started *tap, tap, tapping* on the glass.

Gwen O'Connell was surprised and delighted to hear the noise and to find a girl reporter hanging outside her window! Although Gwen was stark naked—the police had confiscated all her clothes "as evidence" and ordered the hospital not to give her any more, just in case she got any ideas—she rushed over to the window to see Elna Bibber holding up a notepad with a simple message on it: *"WTUK TV news reporter!"* A small digital camcorder hung around her neck.

O'Connell let her in the window by breaking a couple of metal fittings with her hands.

As Elna climbed in, dragging her climbing rope with her, Gwen O'Connell quickly and quietly jammed the room's door with a wedge on the floor and a chair under the door handle.

The intrepid girl reporter scurried to get set up with exciting headlines dancing in her head: *Exclusive videotape interview with attempted-rapee-attorney Gwendolyn O'Connell!*

Modestly wrapping a sheet around herself, Gwen flounced onto the hospital bed and folded a leg under her butt, grinning and ready to record. "Good job!" she said to Elna Bibber, holding out her hand. "I'm Gwen O'Connell."

Fifteen minutes into the interview a nurse tried to enter the room and discovered the door had been barricaded. The cop guarding the door tried unsuccessfully to kick it open (hospital doors are solid), then called for re-inforcements (including a battering ram like the ones SWAT teams use to smash in the front doors of family homes).

The pounding and noise coming from the other side of the door signaled Elna Bibber and Gwen O'Connell that it was time to conclude the interview. Leaning out the window, Gwen saw that Elna had thoughtfully stationed a confederate on the ground below.

Throwing out her rope again, Elna clipped on with her rappelling gear and climbed into the open window. They embraced as Gwen O'Connell kissed her hard on the cheek: *"Mwah kid! Good job!"* Elna Bibber pushed away from the side of the building and smoothly rappelled to the ground with Gwen leaning out to watch.

The helper on the ground unclipped Elna and they sprinted to a nearby van, jumping in and leaving the rope behind. The van squealed out of the parking lot and before it had gone two blocks video footage of the exclusive interview with rape-survivor Gwendolyn O'Connell was being fed to the television station. The feed continued as the van surged through traffic to get Elna to the studio and in front of a camera for the midday news reports.

They made it just in time. Everyone at the station knew it was going to be a smash hit exclusive report. *Elna's breakthrough story as a cub reporter!* She was going to become a big part of the story herself: If there's anything the public loves, it's a fearless girl-journalist who can rappel off a dangerous hospital rooftop and *get the story*, evading police guards and bypassing block-ades to make her escape!

Well done Elna Bibber!!

When the exclusive story hit the airwaves, it caromed off Winston, Pennsylvania and hit the national media like a mini-bombshell. America ate it up! *Brave, plucky cub-reporter Elna Bibber!* It didn't hurt that she was cute as a button and nearly as pretty as a super-model.

And it all fed the growing media bonfire ....

CHAPTER 15
Media Inferno: All Join In!

Elna Bibber broke her story at noon on Saturday: *"Direct from the hospital room! Sexual assault victim Gwendolyn O'Connell held naked and afraid by the Winston Police Department!"*

The story not only fueled the growing media inferno, but caused true liftoff. It also created twin-victims: Not only did Nick Alabattis rape—*or TRY to rape*—public interest lawyer Gwen O'Connell ... he and the police kidnapped 7-year-old Sarah McLaughlin! And when the IJF lawyer tried to help the child she was attacked by rapist Nick Alabattis! Unconfirmed reports indicated that Alabattis demanded sexual favors from attorney O'Connell in return for freeing little Sarah McLaughlin! FREE LITTLE SARAH!

There was a brief struggle at the outset over whether to publish the pictures Gwen O'Connell had presented to Nick Alabattis. Especially those showing the two foster parents drinking beer and fondling each other. There was the uncomfortable fact that they were ... well, *"gay"*. And it might therefore be seen as ... *homophobic* to publish the pictures. *Yikes!* The neutermales in the media didn't know what to do! The conflict raised its ugly head like a gigantic, engorged penis, threatening one and all!

So while the media neutermales and 4th Gen feminists in the local media were initially cock-blocked by their own doubts, the problem was quickly resolved when the Fifth Generation Feminists came on the scene. Normally referred to as Feministas, they were adamant: *No Y-chromosome-damaged patriarchal predators were going to get a pass, no matter HOW many cocks they were willing to suck!* Just being *gay* didn't cut it with the 5th Genners. *All* Y-chrom-damaged humans were predators, up to and including the suck-up neutermales who supported the Feministas.

It was agreed in passing that there was still responsibility to disclaim homophobia, but the fact that a *gyrl* was being held by the patriarchy over-rode the rule. Thus it was easy for the Feministas to swing into action and whip the media neutermales into line to get the pictures published ... *which caused a sensation!*

When the pictures were published—including those showing little Sarah McLaughlin forlorn and huddled in the dirt—the story went viral. That in turn created *another* cultural firestorm, and within hours an interne-cine PC culture war was breaking out.

Genderqueers and other sexually peculiar activists attacked the local media, proclaiming that showing pictures of the two male foster parents fondling each other was driven by—*wait for it*—homophobia!

But radical feminists and other sexactivists quickly concluded the pics were *not* homophobic, and counterattacked. *Sarah McLaughlin must be released to her mother immediately* (with her father having no further contact)! In a counter-counterattack the genderqueers and their supportive homosexuals upped the stakes by claiming that the 5th Gen Feministas were themselves homophobic!

This created conflict among genderqueers and other sexactivists who generally supported the 5th Gen feminists ... and the whole thing quickly degenerated into a zoo-like struggle among a menagerie of genderqueers, homosexuals, lesbians, neutermales, bestiality boosters, men who thought they were women, women who thought they were men, kiddie-porn aficio-nados, and various other sexactivists (the original LGBT movement had morphed into an acronym that had so many letters that no one knew what LGBTGGGGBTTTTQIAAAAAPPOODSSCTB stood for ... including whether pedophile activists from NAMBLA—the North American Man-Boy Boy Love Association—were part of it).

The confusion and infighting teetered for half a day ... until the 5th Gen Feministas launched an overwhelming attack reinforced by several genderqueer subcategories backed up by neutermale allies in the media. The Fifth Gen feminists knew—far better than their chicken-hearted earlier-gen feminists—that *males of any sexual orientation were dangerous evil filth*. To 5th Genners, having the birth defect known as a Y-chromosome was enough to earn fear, loathing, and animus from normal humans … no matter how "*gay*" you might claim to be.

Earlier-generation feminists were still trying to catch up, protesting that *they hated men just as much as anyone!* But it was too little, too late for the 5th Genners. Earlier radical feminists were accused of hiding their hatred of males, cowardly bitches that they were. In fact, to the 5th Genners it was widely understood that the weakness and failure of earlier-generation feminists had made the Feminista movement *necessary*.

So when the 5th Gen feminists counterattacked on behalf of little Sarah McLaughlin, they quickly cleared the battlespace and carried the day. The neutermales and other genderqueers had to get in line and show solidarity with the Feministas, even though the 5th Genners had already announced that neutermales should always and everywhere be rejected as Y-chrom predators in sheep's clothing.

Neutermales? To the 5th Genners neutermales were just Y-chrom pretenders and intruders trying to horn in and ride the Vulva Vanguard!

The support of Sarah McLaughlin by the 5th Gen feminists yielded secondary and tertiary benefits too. It also allowed them to agitate in support of multiple womyn, including Sarah's female mother, female lawyer Gwendolyn O'Connell and female cub reporter Elna Bibber. Not only was it imperative that Sarah McLaughlin be freed from the Y-chrom-damaged foster parents, but also Gwendolyn O'Connell must be freed from the Y-chrom power structure holding her hostage in the hospital.

This was *especially* true since Gwen O'Connell had valiantly challenged the Y-chrom power structure by resisting the sexual assault of Nick Alabattis, who was wickedly trying to force PIV ("penis-in-vagina") sex on her.

By midday on Saturday the 5th Gen feminists were baying like hound dogs: *Womyn don't lie about rape! Gwen O'Connell is a Y-chrom victim! Nick Alabattis is a rapist! Free Sarah McLaughlin!*

Gwen O'Connell watched it all unfold on her hospital room TV with glee. She loved human sexual dimorphism and thought PIV sex was terrifically boffo, even in the absence of the love and comedy that often went along with it. So she found herself clapping delightedly at the TV as sexactivists fed the media frenzy that day.

Sexual dimorphism and sexual reproductive comedy, she thought, *all perched atop an extremely unstable neural substrate giving rise to a shaky consciousness, which supported an equally wobbly sentience on top of it all.* O'Connell found herself dazzled by the antics, thinking ... *is this great or what?*

In the meantime the 5th Gen Feministas and their supporters were pressing ahead: A young female had been kidnapped at the behest of the Y-chrom patriarchy running the Winston police department, which was acting at the behest of Y-chrom sexual predator Nick Alabattis! And now the Y-chrom patriarchy running the state Department of Child Protective Services was abusing Sarah McLaughlin!

It was clear to all that an evil Y-chrome conspiracy by the patriarchy all the way down the line. Young proto-feminist Sarah McLaughlin was being kept from her feminist hero mother Meghan McLaughlin.

Outrage!

And the patriarchy wouldn't even let little Sarah talk to her womyn lawyer.

Outrage again!

Even worse, poor Sarah was being held and abused by two predatory homosexual Y-chrom-damaged foster parents ....

And it all had been approved by yet ANOTHER enemy of the Vulva Vanguard, a corrupt patriarchal judge ... himself a Y-chrom predator.

In the face of the steadily-building media inferno, the local political structure hardly knew what to do, and the narrative was being fed and hardened by both genderqueer and neutermale activists inside the local media.

Heroic womyn lawyer comes all the way from New Hampshire to confront injustice! Is attacked by patriarchal predator! Using the threat of PIV rape to reinforce his patriarchal power! PIV rape! Y-chrom pigs!

Ohhhh, it was delicious all the way around.

Gwen O'Connell watched it avidly on TV, thinking *you go girls!* She especially cheered on the daring young reporter Elna Bibber. The entire show was grand, and everyone was having a wonderful time as the frenzy built.

Until ... *it got even better!* By early Saturday afternoon the leader of the *Vulva Vanguard*, a self-proclaimed Feminista Strike Force, publicly challenged Nick Alabattis to a fistfight in front of the Winston municipal building. That was Aurora Colorado, who shouted into a bullhorn in front of the building as the media avidly covered her: *"Come out and get on your knees Alabattis! You Y-chrom PIV rapist pig!"*

"Who *are* you?" asked a cowering local male reporter.

"I'm the Boss Bitch of the Bull Dyke Brigade!" thundered Aurora Colorado, then turned away and ignored him. *"I'll kick your ass, Alabattis!"* she bullhorned. Her sisterhood leadership had been earned through personal combat ... thus the title *Boss Bitch*. Now she was ready—and quite possibly able—to kick the ever-living shit out of the Y-chrom PIV rapist Nick Alabattis.

Aurora Colorado's entire brigade promised to be at the municipal courthouse for the fight. They were reinforced by a local chapter of Dykes on Bikes who joined up to support them and threatened to roar up the courthouse steps on their mighty Harley Davidson motorcycles to attack Alabattis. *We'll lay treadmarks on his face!* they screamed. And that went for Nick Alabattis or any *other* PIV-demanding Y-chrom pervert!

When Alabattis publicly declined Aurora Colorado's invitation to individual combat on the courthouse steps, the 5th Gen Feministas and their neutermale supporters jeered at him: *Yaaaa!* they all screamed, *Chickenshit wimp! Alabattis is a PIV Lipstick Lesbian!*

That last taunt by the 5th Genners brought the Lipstick Lesbian Legion into the conflict. They had been in a long-running catfight with the 5th Genners, who had made cruel accusations against the LLL, claiming that they were secretly "male-lovers" and "Y-chrom submitters."

The fight between the 5th Genners and the Lipstick Lesbian Legion involved even nastier accusations: The ugly claim was that the lipstick lesbians were crypto-heterosexuals who betrayed their sisters by willingly submitting to the patriarchal oppression of PIV sex ... *even liking it!*

PIV-submitters! the 5th Genners jeered at the lipstick lesbians, causing many in the Lipstick Lesbian Legion to burst into tears and publicly wail that *they hated men just as much as the 5th Genners! Even more!* And they *hated PIV sex just as much as any womyn in the entire world!* The 5th Genners and their neutermale suck-ups sneered back that the Lipstick Legionnaires were sissies, and not even worthy of the title *feminists*.

By Saturday afternoon the viral media conflagration was roaring out of control and everyone was having a terrific time, with local media neutermales feeding the bonfire behind the scenes.

In the midst of the maelstrom, though, problems cropped up: The normal function of the local media was to be toadies to the local government-and-money power structure. But now a powerful mob of sexactivists of all sorts was unsetting that arrangement and attacking the entire structure, from Alabattis and the DA's office, to the Winston police department, to Child Protective Services in the state capitol, to the local patriarchal judge who had condoned it all.

For a time, neutermales in the media were torn. After all, the gay foster parents were, well, "*gay*" ... *and* they were government employees. They *should have been immune* from media criticism! But the journalistic neutermales ultimately took the side of the Feministas, who got fawning publicity along with the *Vulva* Vanguard and the Boss Bitch and her Bull Dyke Brigade.

By midday Saturday all the guilty parties in the firestorm—including Nick Alabattis and the DA's office, the police, the judge, and the CPS bureaucracy—were pointing fingers at the FBI. It was *their* fault for causing Sarah McLaughlin's misery! *The FBI agent in charge of the investigation did it! Angelo Maxim!*

Except some media dolt finally figured out that the FBI agent in charge of the Wilding Oaks bombing investigation was ... *a womyn*.

Specifically, FBI Special Agent Angela Maxim.

But where was she? It was midday on Saturday and a massive media-manhunt was springing into existence. The entire city of Winston, Pennsylvania was being *scoured*. But no one could find Angela Maxim ... mostly because her frantic assistant Marge wouldn't disclose where she suspected Angela was, i.e., still in Bill Smith's bed from the night before. And she couldn't raise Angela on her cell phone.

But Marge was tough: She wasn't going to say *shit* about *shinola* until she heard back from Angela. *Go ahead, media assholes! Make my day all you neutermales! Pull Marge's fingernails out! She ain't talking!*

The conflagration roared higher and hotter.

Elna Bibber? The brave cub reporter who broke the story and ignited the bonfire? It made her a flaming heroine. The media likes nothing more than to pat itself on the back, so the story of the plucky reporter rappelling off the hospital roof to get her story was quickly fed onto the national news wires and went viral along with the rape accusation against the local DA.

The story even appeared at the top of the Drudge Report.

It all made both Elna Bibber and the "fighting little lawyer from New Hampshire" famous. Elna became America's spunky darling in no time, and before long she received an offer she couldn't refuse, ending up at a cable network news desk in New York City where she joined other knock-out blonds yakking about the days' events.

Elna stayed in touch with Gwen O'Connell and nicknamed her *"my Elf Queen friend."* In later years, when Gwen would travel to New York city, she'd always call ahead so they could get together and catch up. They became BFF—*best friends forever*—and would giggle over rumors spread by excitable media neutermales that they were a "lesbian item."

Giggles, in fact, didn't describe it. Whenever one of them spotted a piece about "the famous lipstick lesbians Elna Bibber and Gwen O'Connell"—invariably written by national-level neutermales—they would call each other up and roar with laughter. They also rushed to share such stories with their boyfriends—and eventually husbands and children—so that everyone could enjoy the jokes over the years ... and burst into raucous laughter together.

CHAPTER 16
The Rescue of Sarah McLaughlin.

There were two big mysteries in Winston, Pennsylvania that Saturday as the frenzy exploded: Where was little Sarah McLaughlin being held and where was the FBI agent responsible for her suffering ... Angela Maxim?

When the media demanded information about Sarah McLaughlin's whereabouts, the Child Protective Services bureaucracy went into a stonewall crouch: "We're just protecting Sarah's privacy," they blandly repeated as demands to see the girl multiplied. *"We're just following the rules."*

Ironically, the CPS intransigence turned out to be a great help: Sarah's parents were able to drive unnoticed to the foster home where their daughter was being held. IJF attorney Aaron Akron was waiting for them in the trash-strewn front yard when they arrived. Mr. and Mrs. McLaughlin conferred with him before approaching the front door, then knocked loudly.

When the door opened Aaron Akron flashed a badge and CPS identification card, demanding to see Sarah McLaughlin. The two soon-to-be-famous foster parents were Aye Jensen and Billy Napper. Both looked to be anywhere from their late 40s to mid-60s. Between the two of them, Aye Jensen was the top and Billy Napper the bottom. Groggy and still half drunk from the night before, the two of them stood aside as the IJF lawyer and the McLaughlins shouldered their way into the house.

Sarah's parents found their daughter in a darkened room down the hallway. She was huddled in a corner, her arms around her knees and her face hidden. Three other kids were scattered around the room on the floor on dirty mattresses. When David and Meghan rushed to her, Sarah was afraid to lift her head. She was traumatized, dirty and forlorn, and had multiple bruises on her little body.

As it turned out, one of the kids in the room was a violently mentally ill 14-year-old named Thor Collock. When the visitors entered, he stood up and challenged them. "What the fuck do you want!?!" he screamed. *"I run this room!"* David and Meghan McLaughlin ignored him as they gathered Sarah into their arms. Meghan was crying as she held her daughter close.

Aaron Akron had entered the room also, and now turned to consider Thor Collock, who was quite big for his 14 years. Almost 6 feet tall and fat, he used both his size and psychotic rage to intimidate and abuse others. On this particular morning, Collock also had a weapon, a wooden board about four feet long. Aaron Akron strode briskly toward the boy, who smashed the board down without hesitation on Akron's head using all his strength.

The board shattered. Akron neither flinched nor paused as it happened. Instead, he seized Thor Collock by the throat with one hand and squeezed. It felt like a vise as his air was cut off. The boy gurgled, grabbing and struggling at the single hand holding him like a steel pincer.

"Okay now," said Akron conversationally, his face held up close to the boy's face, "it's time to calm down." Collock immediately stopped struggling. Not able to talk with his air cut off; he nodded his head frantically up and down. His eyes were bulging out of his face. "Good!" said Akron brightly. "Let's sit down, shall we?"

There was a filthy couch up against one of the walls with holes in the lining and a spring sticking out in one spot. Akron dragged the boy onto the couch and sat down, still holding him by the neck. "You're in here because you're violent," he stated matter-of-factly, "and you attack people, right?" Akron eased his grasp on the boy's neck a bit.

"Bullshit," shouted Thor Collock. "I din't do shit!"

"Glad to hear it!" said Akron. "In that case we're going to have a little chat, shall we?" He compressed Collock's neck again, shutting off his air, and looked over to the McLaughlins. "It's time for you to go," he said, "If you're challenged by the two guys up front, tell them I ordered you to take Sarah to the hospital. Send them back here if they object. You know where you're going?"

David McLaughlin nodded his head. "What about you?" he asked as he picked up his daughter in his arms and moved with his wife toward the door.

"Oh, don't worry about me," said Akron, "I'm a lawyer! I'll handle it ... you two do what you've decided. It's time to execute the plan. We'll meet again, I'll be in touch. But in the meantime, wait for things to play out here."

"Bless you!" said Meghan McLaughlin as they walked swiftly out of the room. She held out a hand and gently brushed it across Aaron Akron's face as they exited down the hallway. In the living room they turned toward the front door where foster parents Aye Jensen and Billy Napper were standing around wondering what to do. Jensen was holding a chilled morning beer in one hand.

"Hair of the dog," Aye always told Billy, but Billy didn't buy it. For one thing, he didn't like beer that much, and especially not in the morning. Noontime was the earliest. And for another reason, he liked wine, always in one of the long-stemmed crystal glasses they kept safely in the top cupboard in the kitchen out of the reach of the kids.

"Hey," said Aye Jensen to the McLaughlins as they approached the front door. "You can't take her!"

"The fuck we can't," snarled Dave McLaughlin. His rage was percolating as he closed his right fist, ready for violence. "If you want to keep your fucking jobs, go talk to the CPS regional investigator back there. He *told* us to take her to the hospital!"

Aye and Billy looked at each other with an admixture of dubiousness and fear. "You stay here!" snapped Aye Jensen to Billy Napper and rushed down the hallway. Billy watched him go, looking confused. He glanced at the McLaughlins and their daughter, then followed his boyfriend down the hallway.

The McLaughlins walked out the front door to their vehicle. It was a late-model SUV loaded with their possessions. Dave McLaughlin started it and pulled out of the front yard as his wife sat in the passenger seat holding Sarah tightly in her arms. It was still early morning. Traffic was light.

Sarah rested her head against her mother's chest, then turned slightly to look at her father. "Where are we going?" she asked in a small voice. They were the first words she spoke.

Dave McLaughlin turned and smiled. "We're going for a little vacation, Bubbles," he said.

"Vacation?" repeated Sarah. "Where?"

"A place called New Hampshire," he said. Dave McLaughlin sounded happy. Everything was going to be all right. Sarah could tell that from her father's voice. Meghan McLaughlin slid one hand over on top of her husband's right thigh and smiled at him. She held her daughter to her chest with her other arm. Sarah's head rested on her shoulder.

The McLaughlins knew where they were going and who they would contact when they got there, courtesy of Aaron Akron and the Individual Justice Foundation. They knew they would be meeting with representatives of both the IJF and the Free State Project in New Hampshire. Unknown to them, a number of Freestater families had eagerly volunteered to host the McLaughlins when they arrived.

David and Meghan had been assured that they and their daughter would be safe in New Hampshire and not subject to extradition. Even if accused of kidnapping their own daughter—which they had been told to expect—they would not be rendered up to any state or federal authority. The governor had affirmed this when Aaron Akron contacted him and explained the situation.

The governor of New Hampshire was named Edward Sorensen. He was originally from California, but had left that state to escape the spiraling Third World chaos. He had chosen New Hampshire because of its strong and growing economy, as well as the burgeoning liberty culture being driven by the triumphant Free State Project movement. Before he'd been elected governor some years later, New Hampshire had formed a state militia modeled on the Swiss military. As a result, New Hampshire had its own trained military forces armed with battle rifles, machine guns, hand grenades, rocket-propelled grenades, tanks and other military weaponry, most of which was kept at their private homes.

When the Swiss-modeled state militia was set up the national media and many politicians had called them "crazy." The Washington, DC swamp had huffed and puffed about "the New Hampshire problem," but nothing was done. The 2nd Amendment guaranteed that people could be members of state militias, and it was thought to be up to each state's governor and legislature to implement it.

New Hampshire did so.

In turn, multiple states—including New York, New Jersey, Illinois, Massachusetts, and of course California—brought lawsuits to have "the New Hampshire Model" (as it became known) declared illegal and unconstitutional. The case went to the Supreme Court, which ruled that "well regulated militias are no longer necessary because in our ever-changing modern world with our ever-changing values the security of the states is guaranteed by the federal government."

New Hampshire ignored the Supreme Court decision.

That caused a call for direct federal military intervention, the first against a state since the Civil War. But as the question was being debated in Congress and the President was threatening to take action ... Texas, Oklahoma, Florida, Alaska, Georgia, South Carolina, Wyoming, and Montana all announced that they were adopting the New Hampshire Model and established their own similar state militias.

Despite a national media campaign railing against them all, the issue petered out and no federal action was taken.

So if the governor of New Hampshire said that the McLaughlins would not be turned over to federal or state authorities in Pennsylvania, that was the final word. Of course the family would be entirely free to leave and travel wherever they might desire ... but they would not be arrested and extradited to any other state by authorities in the Free State of New Hampshire.

"Things are going to happen over the next few days," Aaron Akron had told the McLaughlins, "It's best that you and Sarah get out of the state now, before those events occur. You won't be able to come back, for a time at least, until everything sorts out."

"That's fine by us," said David McLaughlin with some heat. "All we want is Sarah back. Everything and everyone else can go to hell as far as we're concerned." Meghan sat next to him holding his arm and nodding her head vigorously: *"Fuckin' A!"* she snarled. He husband turned and looked at her in shock. "Did you just say what I think you said?" he asked.

"Fuckin' A," she snarled again. They both laughed as Aaron Akron smiled and looked on.

Now the reunited family was accelerating onto an Interstate Highway ramp heading north out of Winston. The morning air was cool as Dave McLaughlin opened the windows of the SUV and took a big breath. Meghan snatched a blanket from the back seat and wrapped it around herself and her daughter to stay warm. Their route had already been mapped, and they knew where they were going, with an emphasis on getting out of Pennsylvania as quickly as possible.

Dave McLaughlin began whistling as the cold air hit his face. He was happy. *First time in a long while,* he thought as he merged the SUV onto the Interstate highway.

~~~~

Back at the CPS foster home Aye Jensen and Billy Napper found themselves at the bedroom door where Sarah had been kept. It was closed and locked. Attempts to open it and speak to the CPS investigator failed. They pounded on the door and yelled for him to open it. They made threats. Billy Napper tried to break the door down but hurt his shoulder. Aye Jensen stood back and tried to kick it in. He hurt his ankle.

They called 911.

Inside the room Aaron Akron had jammed the door shut with a chair. He sat with Thor Collock on the filthy couch, still holding the boy by the throat. "I'm going to take a look around inside your brain," he told the psychotic boy, "and you're going to sit tight and be still."

The boy had struggled feebly, then gone limp as Akron squeezed his neck in a certain way. He pulled the boy's face up to his, almost touching, and opened his mouth wide—wider than any human jaws should have been able to—then pulled the boy to him and melded his mouth over Thor Collock's face, sealing the two together.

Impossibly small filaments—essentially a series of linked atoms of certain types—snaked out of Aaron Akron's mouth, wending their way into Thor Collock's brain through his nasal cavities. One set of filaments turned upward, worming their way past his cerebral cortex and penetrating into the cingulate gyrus as billions of branching connections sprouted along the way. Other invisible fibers invaded the boy's brain through the back of his mouth and throat, heading for his hypothalamus and branching billions of times as they extruded. A third set of filaments penetrated into the boy's brain stem and cerebellum, also extruding billions of branching connections along the way.

The invading fibers multiplied in ever-expanding tributaries as they advanced at the approximate speed of electricity. Trillions of connections thus sprang into existence. Monstrous amounts of data were fed at near light-speed from the boy's brain into Aaron Akron. Data was examined, collated, evaluated, interpreted, analyzed, and then reevaluated in a spiraling series of quantum-based recursions occurring in nanoseconds.

Neither Akron nor the boy moved. Loud pounding on the door continued.

Lesions and other abnormalities were located and noted to be in the boy's orbitofrontal cortex. There were further abnormalities in Thor Collock's anterior cingulate cortex and amygdala, the sources of his psychotic rage and violence. Atomic-sized wires that had funneled unmeasurable amounts of data from his brain to that of Aaron Akron became intelligent tools working at near the speed of light, each one operating independently and intelligently, each one excising lesions and rewiring as necessary various areas of the boy's neuroanatomy. Trillions of neuronal connections in Thor Collock's brain were destroyed or disconnected, then repaired, re-wired or re-routed. Neurobiological imbalances arising from a malfunctioning endocrine system acting on his pituitary gland were similarly located, analyzed, diagnosed and repaired.

Thor Collock had been a physically large and dangerous 14-year-old psychopath suffering from major body/brain malfunctions resulting in periodic rage and extreme violence. Now, with IJF attorney Aaron Akron's mouth grotesquely contorted open and clamped over the boy's face, trillions of neurobiological modifications were being made in a cascading flow of instantaneous information exchange.

Whether the boy would be entirely fixed or not would remain to be seen, but Aaron Akron thought it to be an interesting experiment, an opportunity, and took his best shot. For good measure he scanned, rearranged, and added billions of neuronal connections in the boy's brain underlying general intelligence areas of the *homo sapiens* species, many of which could never have been made by normal DNA instructions.

The filaments extruding from Aaron Akron's contorted mouth retracted. He pulled his wide-open jaws back from the boy's face, put a hand up to his jaw and pushed sharply. The jaw cracked audibly as it snapped into place and closed. He stood up and brushed his lawyer's suit off. The boy was unconscious, his head lolling to one side with drool coming out of a corner of his mouth.

Aaron Akron looked down at him with interest. *We'll see*, he thought.

The pounding on the door changed abruptly. It got louder and heavier as a new voice bellowed out, demanding entry: ***"THIS IS THE POLICE! OPEN UP NOW!"***

CHAPTER 17
Chaos at the Foster Home: All Join in Again!

As the pounding and shouting at the door continued, Aaron Akron stepped across the dark room and pulled away the chair. He stood aside as he opened the door.

Two police officers burst into the room brandishing long black metal flashlights. Thor Collock lay on the couch to one side, unmoving. Several children cowered on dirty mattresses on the floor in corners of the room. In the dim light it couldn't be seen whether they were boys or girls. The cops turned on Akron, shining their flashlights into his eyes.

"I'm Thomas Miller," he said, holding up a CPS card. "I'm an attorney with Child Protective Services. I was sent here to check on Sarah McLaughlin, *but she's not here!*"

The two cops looked at each other, then at Billy Napper and Aye Jensen standing in the doorway. They shifted their flashlights, shining them into the eyes of the two men. "Where is she?" demanded one of the cops.

"She's out front!" squealed Billy Napper. "In the living room!"

"Great!" said Aaron Akron happily. "Let's go look. I demand to see her!"

Aye Jensen and Billy Napper led the way down the hallway, followed by Akron and the two cops. The front door stood open. The cops hadn't closed it when they'd rushed inside. Billy Napper looked confused: "Where are they?" he said.

"We just got here," said one of the cops. "There was no one in this room when we came in."

"They were just here!" shrieked Aye Jensen. He turned to Billy. *"I told you to stay here and watch them!"* he screamed.

"You did not!" Billy Napper screamed back.

"Did too!" screamed Aye, and then hauled off and slapped Billy hard across the face. The loud **smack** reverberated in the room. Billy cried out and cowered, holding his face.

One of the cops grabbed Aye Jensen by the arm, tripped him and threw him to the floor. *"Assault!"* he yelled, then shouted at Aye Jensen who was struggling underneath him. *"Do not resist me!"* He jammed a knee into the middle of Aye's back and reached for his handcuffs.

"I don't think they know where the girl is!" Akron said desperately to the other cop. "They've lost her! *She was entrusted to these foster parents by the Division of Child Protective Services!"*

The cop on the floor cuffed Aye Jensen and hauled him up, *"Now where is she?"* he snarled in Jensen's face.

"You leave him alone!" screamed Billy Napper and leapt at the mean police officer.

"Stand aside!" shouted the second cop as Billy threw his arms around Aye Jensen and burst into tears. **"You can't have him!"** screamed Billy, trying to pull Aye Jensen away from the cop. *"He's mine! You leave him alone!"*

The second police officer grabbed Billy Napper from behind, pulled him away from Aye Jensen, and threw him down on the floor. He looked up at the other cop: "Jesus, we need backup. We're gonna have to take this mess downtown to get it sorted out."

"No way!" yelled Aaron Akron at both of them. "I represent the State of Pennsylvania Department of Child Protective Services and there are abused and suffering children here! We can't leave them!" He gestured at Aye Jensen and Billy Napper in their disheveled and dirty clothes. "Children abused by *them!* **Homosexual rape!"**

"Fuck you!" screamed Billy Napper from the floor where he was pinned on his face, a knee jammed into his back. The cop holding him down yelled, "Give me your hands! Put your hands behind your back sir!"

The cop grabbed and tugged on one of Billy's wrists but couldn't pull it out. Billy had twisted it away and tucked it underneath his chest, squealing and screaming the whole time.

"You can't do that!" screeched Aye Jensen from where he was being held. **"You let Billy alone!"** The cop on the floor was struggling to get Billy's hands behind his back. Billy was screaming continuously and incoherently, which caused Aye Jensen to start struggling again with the cop holding him. *"You leave Billy alone!"* he shrieked.

The cop holding Aye Jenson was trying to hold him with one arm while he spoke urgently into a shoulder microphone calling for backup. Aaron Akron sidled to one side to watch the show.

At that point, as if from nowhere—**Whoo hoo!**—*the media arrived in force.* They'd been alerted by multiple phone calls from tipsters about where the child Sarah McLaughlin was being held! Two news vans and a separate SUV with a reporter and camera crew skidded up in the front yard. They slammed to a halt and spilled reporters, talking heads, and camera crews out of the vehicles. All sprinted to the front door and shouldered their way in as the two cops struggled with Aye Jensen and Billy Napper, both screaming their heads off.

Lights were on and cameras rolled, recording the two cops fighting with the two flailing foster parents. Reporters shouted questions and shoved microphones into the faces of Billy Napper and Aye Jensen as well as the cops fighting with them.

One of the reporters kneeled down to put a microphone in front of Billy Napper's face which was being squashed into the floor: *"Where's Sarah McLaughlin!"* demanded the reporter. *"Tell us where Sarah McLaughlin is!"*

"Shegguzragghhooeenah!" screamed Billy Napper as face and mouth were being mashed on the floor. The excited reporter interpreted that as, *"She's right here!"* and jumped up to search for the child.

Camera crews and talking heads fanned out through the house, dashing down the hallway and illuminating filthy interior rooms as Aye Jensen and Billy Napper continued screaming and fighting with the two police officers. The cops were shouting their own commands at the top of *their* lungs as they tried to control Billy and Aye, even as the reporters and camera crews swarmed through the house.

A shoving match broke out between two camera crews from different TV stations as the cops bellowed commands trying to gain control of the situation. But the media crews were having none of it and added to the chaos. They would later insist that they didn't hear the cops say a thing, only the two screeching foster dads.

Aaron Akron raised his own voice to get the attention of a stunning blond talking head rushing by in the midst of the tumult. *"Check the right-hand room at the end of the hallway!"* he shouted helpfully at her. *"Third door on the right! Abused kids!"*

The blond bought it and yelled for her camera crew to follow as she dashed for the hallway. Another camera crew in the living room had heard Akron. They surged in the same direction, led by a male talking head who looked like a Calvin Klein model.

The blond got there first and hit the third door on the right before anyone else. But by the time she threw the door open two more stampeding media crews had arrived and everyone tried to cram themselves through the doorway at the same time.

It was like a Three Stooges routine. They all got stuck shouting and shoving at each other in the doorway. One cameraman swung his shoulder camera violently to one side and caught the gorgeous blond on the side of her head. She went down in a tangle of shapely arms and legs, breaking the logjam in the doorway as they trampled her and surged into the room with lights shining and cameras rolling.

The illuminated scene was awful. Several small, dirty, terrified children cowered on their dirty mattresses on the floor, crying pitiably. The motionless body of a larger boy lay on a ragged couch, unmoving. He appeared to be lifeless.

"It's a dead body! A dead boy!" shrieked a cameraman, zeroing in on the unmoving Thor Collock for a close-up.

Other cameras and lights were shoved into the faces of the terrified children on the floor, causing them to scream in terror at the cameras. One of the reporters shoved a microphone into a child's face on the floor, shouting a question: *"It is true you were raped by your foster parents! How many times were you raped! Which one raped you! Did they take turns raping you!"*

The poor kid cowered into a fetal position in the corner, hiding his face with his hands. The reporters took that to be confirmation that the children indeed *had* been sexually abused by their CPS foster parents as the anonymous tipsters had said. That caused the camera crews to stampede back out of the room and up the hallway to shout questions into the faces of Aye Jensen and Billy Napper: *"Why did you rape those boys!"* shouted one reporter at Aye Jensen. *"How many did you rape!"* Billy Napper was still struggling face-down on the floor with one of the cops on top of him when a female reporter crawled down to shove a microphone into his face: *"Did you rape the boys or the girls or all of them?"* she shrieked at him. *"Why didn't you just rape the boys! Why rape the girls too?"*

This was the first that the cops heard about the two guys being child-rapists, figuring that the screamed questions from the reporters were confirmation of the crimes.

"Fucking faggot!" yelled the cop holding Aye Jensen, slamming a metal flashlight down on his head. *"Tell us which ones you raped! WHICH ONES!"* Jensen howled in pain, adding to the pandemonium.

As the chaos increased in the front room, Aaron Akron happily added to it by shouting as loud as he could and pointing down the hallway where he could see the blond had been knocked to the floor: **"A reporter has been assaulted! Reporter assaulted! Reporter down!"**

Akron's yelling caused a couple of news crews in the living room to surge back down the hallway where they ran into at least one group hustling *out* of the bedroom to come back *up* the dim hallway.

The dazed blond was on her hands and knees the floor in the doorway trying to get up, but she was trampled and flattened again by the crews stampeding into and out of the room.

Blood flowed from a gash in her scalp, splattering her professional white suit jacket and plastering her blond hair down over her bloody head wound. She made another try to get up just as two camera crews collided in the doorway and knocked her flat again as they tried to get video of the dead body on the couch.

In the midst of all this sirens wailed as ambulances and police backup cars slammed into the front yard. EMT's and cops burst out of the vehicles and stampeded into the house themselves. They found Aye Jensen and Billy Napper still squalling and struggling with the two cops trying to hold them.

Aaron Akron stood against a wall by the front door smiling as he surveyed the scene. A police officer rushed up and shouted in his face, **"Who the fuck are you?"**

"I'm a lawyer," Akron said, handing a fake legal business card to the cop. It said he was attorney Averill Smith. "I came here to see Sarah McLaughlin!" he shouted urgently to the cop. "But she's not here! She was lost by these two degenerate rapists!" He pointed dramatically at the two screaming boyfriends still struggling with the two original cops.

The cop looked at the card, then up at Akron. "You stay here!" he snarled, jabbing a finger at Akron's chest. "Don't go anywhere!"

"Okay!" he shouted back happily. "I'll stay right here!" The cop hurried off. Akron surveyed the scene. Screaming, terrified, dirty children were being hustled out by EMT personnel on stretchers to ambulances waiting outside. Some of the children had gone catatonic and collapsed.

An EMT crew rushed a wheeled gurney down the hallway and disappeared into the room where Thor Collock's body lay on the couch. Someone was shouting hysterically **"It's a dead BODY!** *There's a dead BODY in there!"* The gurney reappeared with Thor Collock strapped securely on it. An oxygen mask had been slapped over his face.

As the EMT's wheeled Collock past Aaron Akron, the boy turned his head and opened his eyes. They were clear, sharp and intelligent, and he looked directly at Akron as he was wheeled past. Even in the midst of the chaos, Collock looked ... *aware.* Whereas before there had been rage and anger on his face, now the boy was merely alert.

Only Aaron Akron noticed the boy's awareness. Thor Collock appeared to be *appraising the situation.* As the gurney rolled past, their eyes met. A slight smile tugged at the edge of Thor Collock's mouth. He *winked* at Aaron Akron as he went by, then disappeared as he was rushed out to an ambulance.

Akron smiled to himself. *Well, well, this may turn out okay ... the kid may be all right.* He turned his attention to the ongoing chaos and tumult. *I do believe my work here is done*, he thought happily.

Calmly stepping out the front door, Aaron Akron walked to his car, got in and headed for the hospital where IJF attorney and alleged rape victim Gwendolyn O'Connell was being held.

CHAPTER 18
The Morning After: Two Aliens and a Lady.

While the chaos unfolded at the CPS foster home, FBI Special Agent Angela Maxim was sitting naked on a carpeted floor in Bill Smith's bedroom. She leaned up against a wall with a quizzical look on her face. A hammerless stainless steel Smith & Wesson .38 Special dangled loosely from her hands between her knees. She listened to her lover of the night before moving around in the kitchen.

A small-to-medium-size dog—mostly black, but with some white spots—lounged on the bed not far from her. It had intelligent, alert eyes and watched her with interest.

The jet engine sounds of Keurig cups brewing coffee came from the kitchen. "One cream or two, Spot?" shouted Bill Smith.

The dog opened its mouth. "Two!" came a voice that sounded like a child.

"Coming up!" said Smith.

Presently he walked into the room carrying two coffee cups by the handles in one hand, and a dog's bowl carefully held level in the other. He put the bowl on the bed. The dog crawled over to the bowl and tentatively lapped at it. "Ouch! *Hot!*" it protested.

"Yeah," said Bill. "Watch it. Just came out. He turned and seemed to just notice that Angela Maxim was sitting on the carpeted floor against a wall. "What are you doing down there?" he asked curiously. He handed her one of the coffee cups. She held the gun in her left hand and took the coffee cup in her right.

Spot lapped at the coffee again a couple of times on the bed. "Mmmm," it said, "decent coffee, even if it does come from a Keurig cup."

Bill Smith carefully sat back on the bed holding his own cup and leaned against the headboard. He gestured at Angela, still sitting on the carpet by the doorway. He patted the bed next to him, inquiring politely: "Would you care to come up and join me?"

Angela Maxim stared at him, then at the dog, then back at him.

Jesus H ....

She dropped the .38 revolver into her purse and stood up carefully with the cup of coffee. "You shouldn't play tricks on people!" she said with some heat.

"So far as I know," answered Bill Smith, "no one's playing tricks on anyone here." He sipped at his coffee and looked over at Spot lapping from the dog bowl on the bed. "As I have repeatedly told you," he said patiently, "my dog can talk." He didn't smile ... even sounded a little peeved.

God he's adorable, thought Angela Maxim, *What a body. And that smell ... it's still there.* She came to sit on the edge of the bed and stared at him. "I'm, um ... *freaked out,*" she said, trying to explain.

"Well, I guess you have a right to be," said the dog, looking up from its coffee bowl.

Angela looked suspiciously at her lover: "You don't really expect me to drink whatever's in this cup, do you?" she asked.

"You can, or not, as you please," said Smith with a slight shrug. "I admit, Keurig-brewed coffee isn't like brewing with my own beans ...."

Angela shook her head. *What the hell.* She faced him and folded a leg under her butt, then sipped carefully at the hot coffee. "Now would be a good time for you to pull a gun or a knife or whatever," she said. "That would at least explain some of what's going on."

She sipped at her coffee again.

Bill smiled and reached over to pat her affectionately on her naked thigh. He sipped his own coffee, watching her, but didn't say anything.

"Would you just do me one favor, Bill?" Angela asked. "Just one?"

"Of course," he said.

"Would you just tell me ... *what is that fucking perfume you wear all the time?*"

Bill Smith grinned, his coffee cup halfway up to his mouth" "Oh, that ...."

"Yeah *that*!" said the dog from its spot on the bed.

"We don't need comments from the canine peanut gallery," said Smith, sounding indignant. "It's a pheromone," he said to Angela. "It's not perfume, at least not in the traditional sense. And you can't buy it anywhere."

"A pheromone?" said Maxim. "What kind? And where the hell does it come from?"

"It comes from me," he said. "I can generate it at will. All male human bodies manufacture it at various times and in various amounts ... just not on command and not in the concentrations I can."

"Well fine!" she said sarcastically. "And now you're going to tell me you're not even human." She grimaced at him: "Go ahead then ... tell me I fucked an alien last night."

"No way!" he protested. "I'm a human being just as much as you are! I've got the same basic genotype you have and the same kind of DNA." He paused, smirking: "Except of course I've got a Y-chromosome and you don't. Besides, you're the one who did the big background check on me. Do you want to say I didn't get born to my mom Emily in Dallas? Did I not go to the schools you saw I did? And play the sports I did? Did I not play saxophone in high school and then go to college? You know I did ...."

"How do you know about that!" she said sharply.

"Wouldn't it be the normal thing to do," he responded, "for an FBI agent about to go out on a date with a new beau?"

"Well," she said, "at least I know you're basically human." She sipped her coffee again. *Not all that bad, actually.*

"Yeah," said the dog with an edge of sarcasm. "*Basically* human ...."

Angela Maxim paused with the coffee cup halfway to her lips. Her eyes zeroed in on the dog, then tracked over to Bill Smith.

"You shut up!" Bill Smith snapped at the dog. "Nobody asked you!"

"Bill," asked Angela Maxim, the coffee cup still held motionless in one hand, "will you please tell me what the dog *means* when it says *basically human?*"

Bill Smith looked peevishly at the dog, then back to Angela. "Well ..." he said, hesitating, "I *am* kind of ... special, as humans go."

Angela raised her eyebrows at him questioningly: *"Meaning?"*

"Well, um, I'm ... *enhanced.* I have an extreme level of control over my body. You've heard of karate masters who can punch through wood? Yoga masters who can regulate their heartbeat, body temperature, and so forth? People who can hold their breath for a long time?"

"Yeah," the dog chimed in, "like, an *inhuman* amount of time!" A child's giggle came from the dog's mouth.

"An inhuman amount of time," repeated Angela Maxim slowly. She was staring at Bill Smith.

"Well ... yeah," he said, shrugging his shoulders. "What can I say? I've got superpowers!" He grinned at her and sipped his coffee.

"Superpowers," she said dubiously.

"You seem to be repeating me a lot today," he said.

"Superpowers," she repeated.

"There you go again." He was still grinning.

"Hooo-kay," she said, letting out an exasperated breath. "How about let's see you do something ... *super.*"

Bill Smith smirked at her: "You already did! Don't you remember ... *last night?*"

Angela Maxim could feel her face and chest turning red.

"That was kind of *super,* wasn't it?" he said.

"Wipe that smirk off your face!" she shouted. "I'm trying to be serious here!"

"It was quite serious last night Angela," he said, suddenly solemn. "That wasn't fake ...."

She wondered what she looked like, feeling flushed all over, breathing a little faster.

"Can't I get a straight answer out of you?" she said plaintively.

"You just did," he answered, "even if you want to ignore it."

She felt heat spreading throughout her body, and wanted nothing more than to embrace him, to hold him tightly ... but she felt turmoil inside too.

"How about some *other* demonstration of your supposed super-powers," she suggested.

"It's kind of early in the morning," he said, smirking again. "But we could have an instant replay maybe?" He looked hopeful.

He looks adorable. "Not that, damn you!" Angela burst out. "Show me something else super-powerish!" She was grinning now too, in spite of herself.

Bill Smith paused, his coffee cup in one hand. It was a ceramic cup. The kind marked as microwave-safe. "Really?" he inquired.

"Sure," she said offhandedly. "Show me another trick."

"A super-power trick," said the dog in its babyish voice.

Bill Smith looked resigned. "Okay," he said. He lifted the coffee cup to his mouth, tilted it up and drained it. "See this cup?" he asked her, holding it up. "Normal? White? Ceramic? Coffee cup?"

Maxim looked at him narrowly, trying to spot the trick. He held out the coffee cup to her. "Same as yours," he said. "Check it out."

She took the now-empty cup and turned it in one hand, looking at the sides and bottom. She clinked it against her own coffee cup. It sounded like two ceramic cups being hit together. She shrugged, handing it back. "Okay. One coffee cup, standard issue," she quipped.

He held it in his right hand, his arm held out in front of her as he squeezed the cup without any great effort, watching her as he did so.

The cup shattered, crumbling into shards in his fist.

Angela Maxim jumped, then grinned widely. She put her own cup down on the bed and clapped delightedly. "Good trick!" she said enthusiastically. "I'll bet you're a member of IBM, the International Brotherhood of Magicians, right?"

Bill Smith grinned ruefully and looked over at Spot, his hand still held out, ceramic dust falling from his fist. The dog looked back at him and shrugged its shoulders minutely.

"Damn, Angela," said Bill, "you're going to be hard to convince, aren't you."

"Oh come on," she said. "Give me your hand." He opened his fist, dust and shards of broken ceramic falling from it. She held it in both of hers, turning the hand this way and that. "Not a scratch on you," she said, looking at it closely.

"Well no," he agreed. "So?"

"*So?*" she queried back at him. "*SO?* You don't break a ceramic cup in your damned hand and not suffer some kind of injury unless it's a trick cup."

"It wasn't a trick cup," he said seriously.

"*Riiight!*" she said sarcastically, then seemed to come to a decision. "Let's go back to the cologne."

"Pheromone," said Bill Smith.

"Whatever," said Angela Maxim. "Tell me how it is that only you can generate your ... *pheromone*. I mean, I'm assuming there aren't any other ladykillers out there who smell the same way."

Spot looked like he was watching a tennis match as he followed the conversation, head turning now one way, then the other as each of them spoke.

Bill Smith thought about it a moment. "Well ... there are other people like me," he admitted, "but I guess it's just in our DNA!" He grinned again.

She just wanted to hug him again. *Adorable.*

"Slightly *modified* DNA," said Spot from where he was on the bed.

"Oh shush," said Bill.

Angela Maxim looked back and forth between them. "What's going on here please?"

Bill Smith and Spot looked at each other for a moment. "Tell," said Spot. Bill nodded, then turned back to Angela.

"It appears that my body and brain are somewhat, um, *different* from most people's," he said. "They're kind of ... *modified*. That's what gives me special control over various bodily functions. Such as being able to generate that pheromone like I do."

"You have other tricks up your sleeve, Bill?" she asked.

"Well," he said. "A fair number, I guess ...."

"Actually, a large number of other tricks," said Spot. The dog was looking at Angela now. It looked strikingly intelligent and engaged.

"Stop that!" Angela snapped at the dog. She looked back and forth between them, frowning, then turned to look hard at Bill Smith: "The coffee cup was real?"

"Yes," he said simply.

She regarded him levelly. "Well?"

"Well what?" he said innocently.

"Well how about telling me what the hell is going on," she snapped. She wasn't smiling, and in fact seemed to be holding back anger. "I don't like trickiness."

Bill Smith sighed. "Well, I guess you do deserve a more detailed explanation," he said, "but first I want to give you some bona fides about me." He paused. "I haven't called my mom for *days*."

He reached over to a side table, picked up his cell phone and punched an icon. It gave out a tone. "Call Mom," he said into the phone. He listened to it ring for a few moments, then when someone answered gave a bright greeting: *"Hi Mom!"*

Angela Maxim could hear a woman's voice on the other end of the line. "Yeah," said Bill after a moment, "I'm here with a new friend. Her name's Angela Maxim. I'd like to introduce you to her." He paused, listening, then turned to Angela: "Are you my girlfriend?" he asked with sincerity.

Angela's mouth twisted. She was trying to look severe, but she wanted to smile. Bill spoke to his mother again: "Angela's not going to admit it, Mom, but as a matter of fact I hope she *becomes* my girlfriend ... I really like her." He listened again, and said, "Okay."

He held out the phone to Angela. "My mom!" he said. "Emily Smith." He pointed the phone back at himself and said "Mom, this is Angela Maxim." He held the cell phone out to Angela again.

She took the phone, put it up to her ear: "Hello?" A woman's voice answered and said several things. "Well ... yes, Mrs. Smith .... " She paused, "Okay ... *Emily*. Yes. No, we've just started dating. Yes." She listened again, then smiled in spite of herself: "I really don't know."

Angela Maxim listened for a moment, then said, "No, he hasn't told me anything about that. Was he good in sports?" She listened. "Track and field *and* baseball?" She listened some more. "Saxophone too?" Then she laughed. "Well, he's certainly an interesting fellow, I'll give him that. Very charming, in fact. Was he always that way?" She listened again, then laughed out loud. "Well of course! Every mother says her son is perfect!" She listened some more. "Oh really?"

"Yes," said Emily Smith in Dallas. *"Actually, we call both him and his sister our Miracle Kids."*

"Why's that?" asked Angela.

"*Well, John and I were told by the doctors that it was impossible for us to have children,*" Mrs. Smith said, chatting as if she and Angela were best friends. "*John and I always wanted a family, and we thought about adoption, but we figured we'd leave it in the hands of God.*"

"You didn't try any of the medical procedures?" Angela asked.

"*No,*" said Mrs. Smith. "*And the doctors told us there was no way either of us could ever have children the normal way. We had all the tests done, and both of us were … barren.*"

"Well then where did Bill and his sister come from?" Angela asked curiously.

"*Right out of me, and right on time,*" Mrs. Smith said happily. "*John and I have always said God did it for us. And maybe He did. William and his sister Gwen were always wonderful kids. Never gave us a speck of trouble!*"

"What does Bill's sister do?" asked Angela.

"*Oh she's a lawyer too!*" said Emily Smith. "*Just like William. The doctor told us they would be different, and they were, in lots of ways, but in that way they decided to be alike!*"

"Interesting," said Angela. "Well here, let me give you back to Bill. Good talking with you Mrs. Smith!" She listened for a moment, then handed the phone back to Bill.

"Whaddaya think Mom?" asked Bill with a grin in his voice, looking at Angela. "Sounds great, doesn't she?" He listened for a moment. "She's terrifically beautiful," he said. "She's about five foot ten or so, and has long beautiful dark hair." He listened. "Dark brown," he said, "really dark." He eyeballed Angela's disheveled hair. It framed her beautiful face and cascaded over her shoulders in an unruly mess from their lovemaking the night before. "Yeah," he said to his mother, "almost black. She says she's Black Irish in fact." He paused, then laughed.

"Don't worry Mom," he said, "I'm always a gentleman … I love you too." He paused, then hit the hang up icon.

Angela sat on the bed looking at him. She thought for a moment, then crossed her arms stubbornly under her breasts. "It can all be faked," she said, giving him a gimlet eye.

"Yes it can!" he said brightly. "But you're FBI, so you can check out every inch of my story, all the way back to John and Emily Smith of Dallas, Texas, parents of William and Gwendolyn Smith ... *can't you.*"

Angela nodded. "Yes."

"You'll find it's all real," he said, "and I am what I appear to be ... kind of."

Angela shook her head. "*Kind of.* Then what's the story?"

"The whole story?" said Bill Smith.

"Yes," said Spot from his vantage point on the bed, "the whole fucking story."

Angela looked over at the dog and regarded him evenly. "I do believe I'm getting used to you being able to talk," she said.

"Thank you," said the dog.

Bill snapped his fingers. "Hey, back here you two ... lose the mutual admiration society, would ya?" He paused, grinning. "So you want *the whole story* Angela?"

"Yes," she said. "I do."

"Well then, let's begin," he said. "It may take a little while ... ."

"I'm all ears," she said. Her voice had a studied neutrality to it.

Angela Maxim waited. Her arms were still crossed under her breasts as she waited for Bill Smith to speak.

CHAPTER 19
Insolent Bureaucrats vs. Akron & Laflorrie.

It didn't take long for Aaron Akron to get to the Winston hospital where his staff lawyer Gwendolyn O'Connell was being held. He expected to be stonewalled by the hospital staff, and was, but doggedly plowed through each bureaucratic level as he met it. *Fucking humans,* he thought ... *what power-tripping idiots.* Then he felt bad at the thought.

Several levels up, both literally and figuratively, Akron was confronted by an officious woman at a reception desk. "Hello," he said cheerily as he came through the door. The woman frowned and stared at him, saying nothing. Having been warned that a lawyer was headed up to her desk, she knew it was her job to stall, block, delay, and discourage him.

Akron grinned widely. "I'm here to talk to Amber Crescent!" he said brightly. "Management VP for the Winston County Hospital? Is that correct?"

The receptionist stared at him unsmiling. "I really wouldn't know."

"Gee!" said Akron with enthusiasm. "What a shock! I was told by the head nurse at the west wing nursing station that this is where I could talk to Miss Crescent."

"I'm afraid Ms. Crescent is unavailable at this time," the receptionist lied in a sourly neutral voice.

"Well gee again," said Akron with fake wonder, then leaned forward to stare into her face and speak in a monotone: "I'm shocked. Especially since I was told a few minutes ago that Miss Crescent is in her office right now, and that she *is* available. Quelle *surprise, eh?"*

The woman he faced was a classic bureaucratic office dominatrix. She held power over a tiny domain, delineated mostly by the outlines of her desk, and she defended it zealously. She was also enraptured by her power, little though it was, and was thrilled at feeling it now, even as Aaron Akron spoke. It sent a tingle of gratification up her leg.

"Ms. Crescent is not presently available," she repeated robotically, as if Aaron Akron had not heard her the first time and was an inconsequential interloper in her domain.

Aaron Akron leaned further over the desk as if to conspiratorially whisper into the woman's ear. He spoke in a very low, deliberate voice, almost whispering: "Well then maybe you should … ***MAKE THE FUCKING BITCH AVAILABLE RIGHT NOW!***" He screamed the last words directly into the woman's ear, then stood back and smiled. *I am sooo sick of these petty humans with their power-games.*

The receptionist clapped a hand over her ear and scowled at Akron, then stabbed an emergency button on her desk to summon security. He stood by whistling a little tune through his lips.

This is really cool, he thought, *driving air through prehensile lips generates sound waves that can be varied to make music! How cool is THAT? Maybe they're not entirely worthless after all ….*

Before the security muscle arrived, a professionally dressed woman stepped out of an office behind the desk. Amber Crescent had been on the phone and heard the commotion. Right now she was angry, a sour presence as she eyed Aaron Akron with distaste, even loathing. As it happened, she had just taken a phone call from nowhere … a place called Gorham, New Hampshire.

Now about Gorham, New Hampshire: Although it certainly is in the proverbial "middle of nowhere", it is also famous. Everyone knows about Gorham because there's only one thing there: *The Gorham Arcology.* A monstrous, imposing cube-like structure jutting into and out from the White Mountains granite where it was built, it housed thousands of people. The famous Gorham Arcology is the biggest in the Western hemisphere and was built by a unique individual named Herbert Laflorrie. The establishment media hated and feared Laflorrie. They always referred to him as "that crazy, neo-Nazi extremist," and he gloried in it, laughing in their faces.

The call that Amber Crescent had taken was a direct call from the Gorham Arcology ... and from Herb Laflorrie in person. He had called at the request of his sometime-girlfriend, Gwendolyn O'Connell. She'd been able to get a call him from her sealed hospital room after jiggering the phone wires in the room and routing the call through her office at the IJF headquarters in Manchester, New Hampshire. The call got through to her lover, also sometimes called "America's richest right-wing, extremist, anti-government wacko-bird."

Those were some of the typical epithets thrown at Herb Laflorrie by frustrated fedgov politicians and the media presstitutes that served them. The near-trillionaire was also regularly called "a neo-Nazi" and "racist", as well as "an enemy of the public" by fedgov functionaries and their presstitutes.

Thus it wasn't surprising that Herb Laflorrie was continually investigated, audited, stalked, harassed and threatened by various fedgov agencies, including the IRS, Homeland Security, the FBI, the Treasury Department, and others who used the government agencies as tools at their disposal.

Alas for the federal government and its media servants, Laflorrie was fully capable of mounting his own army of lawyers against the agencies, and was aided by his own stable of politicians who were determined to defend him.

In New Hampshire itself, Herb Laflorrie was revered and celebrated. Fedgov operatives were frowned upon there, and the state government made it clear they were generally unwelcome if they were there to harass New Hampshire's favorite son ... or any other citizen, for that matter.

Herb Laflorrie had been the sole inheritor of a billion-dollar fortune when his father died. He promptly set about turning it into *tens* of billions of dollars, then *scores* of billions, then *hundreds* ... and now he was up in the stratosphere worth nearly a trillion dollars. No one knew the actual amount, only that he'd done it in less than 20 years.

Uncannily, Laflorrie—"wacko-bird" or not—always managed to be on the leading edge of whatever the next-big-thing turned out to be. From previously impossible robotic operating rooms and automated medical procedures, to wide-spectrum cancer treatments including vaccinations; to driverless cars that went over 200 mph on specially-equipped highways, to flying cars that essentially flew themselves ... Herb Laflorrie was on the bleeding edge of everything.

The best thing of all—or *worst*, depending whose side you were on—was that Laflorrie had great fun doing what he did. He was of course roundly hated by Democrat socialists and other people for his success ... but what really drove them crazy was his politically-incorrect sense of humor. With his hundreds of billions of dollars, he gave *nothing* to politicians ... or to the permanent political classes that ran and fed off of the Deep State. Despite continual, fervent, and heartfelt entreaties to do so.

That was the thing about Laflorrie: He didn't pay off *anyone*, from corrupt high-level fedgov operatives in Washington, DC right down to the small-town pols trying to squeeze payola and extra tax money out of local citizens.

And because he wouldn't play the political parasite game, Laflorrie was always spending millions of dollars on lawyers. Their job was to block, blunt, and deflect the attacks of political hacks and bureaucrats at all levels. *You didn't build that!* they would tell him about his business empire.

Oh yeah I did, he would respond without apology. And the people of New Hampshire loved him for it.

Laflorrie was no shrinking violet in the political sphere however: He was known for endorsing and supporting candidates who challenged the entrenched, media-favored Deep State pols at all levels. That *really* pissed them off, so it was no surprise that Herb Laflorrie was Public Enemy Number One in Washington, DC and to the presstitute media. Hence the large lawyers' bills that Mr. Laflorrie incurred every year.

When Laflorrie's cell phone number rang on that particular Saturday morning he was still in his pajamas sipping coffee and scanning Drudge Report and Breitbart News on the Internet. He was ensconced in his private "eagle's nest" (as he called it) at the top of one corner of the Gorham Arcology that jutted out from its White Mountain perch. He'd built the fantastical structure to house his business empire and the thousands of headquarters employees and their families who worked for him.

As noted, the Gorham Arcology was in the proverbial "middle of nowhere," yet even so, in the beginning Laflorrie had to overcome resistance from local politicians as well as small-time political and environmental rent-seekers. With them swept aside—due in no small part to New Hampshire's political and ideological culture—Laflorrie's mammoth construction project supercharged the formerly dead economies in both Gorham and the nearby city of Berlin.

It had taken over five years to complete the initial phases of the mammoth construction project, and it was still growing ten years later.

When the arcology was ready, Laflorrie had moved his entire business empire across the country to get out of the third-world culture and economy of California. He'd chosen New Hampshire because it had developed a reputation for being an economic powerhouse despite its diminutive size. That in turn was because of the long-term success of the Free State Project which had started back in the early 2000s.

The attorney general of California had immediately sued Laflorrie and his business conglomerate for moving out of the state, claiming that it was "racist" and "xenophobic" to move, and that by doing so Laflorrie had "harmed the vibrant, multicultural state of California."

Laflorrie laughed at the lawsuit and mocked it publicly by calling it "the California parasite-ploy!"

The state of New Hampshire gleefully joined the lawsuit on Laflorrie's side, and by the time the case had dragged on for almost a decade with no end in sight, Laflorrie was so popular in New Hampshire that even if California had prevailed they never could have touched him.

As it was, the case eventually collapsed, leaving California to deal with its own political stupidity and poor economic decisions.

When the state of New Hampshire intervened in the California lawsuit, it had also taunted the giant, backward state with the dying economy: "You didn't want Herb Laflorrie and we welcomed him, so now you're The Biggest Losers!" jeered the entrepreneurs who ran public interest advertising campaigns in support of Laflorrie.

Ultimately, just about everyone in New Hampshire felt they were part of the lawsuit, and sneering at "the stupid Californians" became something of a popular pastime in the state.

In the meantime, Herb Laflorrie repeatedly and publicly denounced what he called *the political and economic parasite culture of California,* which "*sucked*," as he put it. "*So fuck them!*" he'd say publicly ... but only in front of audiences of no more than a few thousand.

Even more fun was when California presstitutes would come to New Hampshire to write stories attacking both the little state and its new favorite son. They would ask Laflorrie questions such as "Did you enjoy harming California and its people by moving away? Did it make you feel good to avoid paying your fair share? Are you glad that there are people in California who can't afford to buy *food?*"

Laflorrie would laugh in their faces. *In public!* Then he'd tell the reporters. "I loved California! I really did ... *but science tells us a giant earthquake is coming! Can't argue with science! Millions of people are gonna die in California if they stay there! The science is settled!*"

The presstitutes would repeat Herb Laflorrie's words, thinking to discredit him while trotting out scientists to reassure the populace in California that, "There's nothing at all to worry about! Nothing at all!" But every time Laflorrie would say something along those lines, a certain percentage of people in California would listen, and then move out of the state ... thus further depopulating the state and causing even more problems for California's socialist political leadership.

Herb Laflorrie did it all the time: *"Get out of California while you can!"* he'd proclaim ... and the state's unraveling third-world economy would crumble just a little more. The politicians and tech billionaires in California pretended to grind their teeth, but were actually glad to see the state being depopulated.

"California's no place for anybody with brains!" Laflorrie would chortle, causing political toadies in the media to seethe, along with their ruling class patrons.

"Why New Hampshire?" came to be a ululating cry across North America. First it was whispered, then openly asked, by the richest people in the toniest precincts of San Francisco, Washington, DC, and New York City. In response, Herb Laflorrie would hold press conferences and say outrageous things: "Well, as I always tell the media presstitutes," he would say—they *hated* being called *presstitutes*, even though they deserved it— "there are lots of reasons to be in New Hampshire! I can tell you a bunch of them!"

The hacks would lean forward, shouting insults and challenges at him, hoping he'd say something they could use against him ... whereupon Laflorrie would look at his famous $10 Timex watch—the one he always wore, bragging about how he'd bought it at WalMart—and say *"Whoops, no more time! Sorry I can't tell y'all right now! All outta time!"*

And he'd get up and *walk out! From a press conference! Just like that!*

Ohhhh yeah ... Herb Laflorrie was having a grand old time in his new adopted state of New Hampshire, and the people there just loved him for all his antics.

On this particular Saturday morning when Herb Laflorrie's cell phone rang he saw it was from the IJF headquarters down in Manchester. He immediately answered. "Who the *hell* is in an office on a Saturday morning?" he shouted into the phone.

"I'm not in the damned office, Herbert!" came a mock-exasperated female voice. It was IJF attorney Gwen O'Connell. *"I'm locked up in a damned hospital down in Pennsylvania!"*

"Why a hospital?" Laflorrie asked. "Don't they have jails down there for people like you?" He laughed out loud. "Besides, darling, why would anyone want to go to Pennsylvania when we've got heaven up here in New Hampshire?"

"Knock that shit off, Herb!" the girl yelled at him. "The cops have me under hospital-house-arrest!"

"Really ..." said Laflorrie, enjoying the news enormously.

"Yes *really*!" said Gwen. "But a girl from one of the local news stations got to me yesterday for an interview."

"What the hell have you gotten yourself into honey?" he asked.

"Take a look online and do a search on Winston, Pennsylvania," she said. "A bomb went off, a young girl was kidnapped by the authorities, a DA tried to rape somebody, a TV reporter named Elna Bibber climbed off a hospital roof to get a story, and all hell is breaking loose!"

Herb Laflorrie roared with laughter. "You gotta be shittin' me girl! There's *no way in hell* anyone has a name like *Elna Bibber!*"

"Is too," said Gwen. "She rappelled down the wall of a hospital to get to me!"

Herb Laflorrie laughed uproariously again. *"Rappelled off the damned roof?* I wanna hire that girl!"

"Well do it after you help *me*, Herb!" she yelled. "I need you to make a call to the damned hospital *right now*. Would you?"

"Of course!" said Laflorrie agreeably. "What do you need?"

"Aaron's on his way here," she said. "I just talked to him and he's gonna have a tough time getting to me. The hospital's working with the local police to keep me bottled up."

Laflorrie chuckled. *"Bottled up,* eh? Why are they holding you? What the hell did you do?"

"Oh ... forgot to tell you," she said with a grin in her voice, "I'm the girl the DA tried to rape!"

Laflorrie burst into raucous laughter again. He knew there was no way in hell *any* male was going to be able to do *anything* to Gwen and her nubile little body that she didn't agree to ... and probably not without her own enthusiastic participation. *No way!* he thought, thinking about the time she had jumped his bones: *Damn near ripped all my clothes off!* he thought, smiling to himself.

"Okay honey," he said, grabbing a pad and pen. "Give me the name of the hospital and town again."

Gwendolyn gave it to him. "You're a doll, Herb!" she said, and kissed him over the phone.

"Yeah?" he said back. "If I'm so much of a doll how come you don't spend more time up here with me?"

"I'm a career girl, Herb, you know that. Besides, Aaron won't let me have any time off!" She was laughing as she said it.

"Well then I'll give that foundation of his a few zillion more dollars if he'll let you have some more time off to spend with me, dammit!"

"He might do that," said Gwen. "But you know you're my number one guy, Herb! I'm just not ready to settle down yet."

"Heck," he snorted, I'm not asking you to settle down, I just want you to be my *girlfriend.*"

She laughed. "I *am* your girlfriend Herb! And if you help Aaron get me outta here, I'll be right up there to show you just how much of a girl-friend I can *be!*"

"Atta girl," he said. "You won't hear back from me, but I'll get on the horn with the hospital now. Fear not, baby."

"Knew you would!" she said. "Love you!" She kissed him again over the phone, *MWAH!*

Laflorrie held the cell phone out and looked at it. He grinned thinking about Gwen's predicament, and laughed again.

Then he started speaking instructions into the phone.

CHAPTER 20
Chatting in the Hospital Lockup.

Amber Crescent was a fixture at the Winston City Hospital. She had two prominent characteristics: She was very masculine and she had a very nasty personality. She wielded great power within her realm at the hospital, and few challenged her authority without regretting it.

But this time ... as she came out of her office glaring her spite and hatred at Aaron Akron, she was subdued, even *shaken*.

The big butch bureaucrat had just gotten off the phone with a certain individual named Herbert Laflorrie who had called essentially from "nowhere"... in the state of New Hampshire. While she was speaking with him she'd heard Aaron Akron scream at her receptionist in the outer office.

Dammit! Now she stood silently facing the big IJF lawyer. Her arms were crossed antagonistically across her chest where she'd had her breasts surgically removed some years before. She stood saying nothing, waiting for security to arrive. *Maybe some muscle will wipe the smirk off this asshole's face.*

Ms. Crescent was a career woman in her early 50's. Like many such females, she'd been one tough bitch as she clawed her way up the corporate hierarchy, displaying in the process just who was in charge. She wore her hair clipped very short, almost like a military cut, and was known for abusive outbursts, exploding without warning at subordinates for one reason or another ... or no reason at all.

Ms. Crescent considered herself a fully committed Fifth Generation Feminist. As such, she had no problem just *radiating* hatred. It was usually aimed at males, but anyone with any power rivaling hers could be a target, especially in the hospital hierarchy. Some of the hospital administrators, including doctors and heads of departments—male *and* female—had simply given up and refused to work, or even *interact*, with Amber Crescent. And that suited her just fine: *Pig males and breeder females,* she thought ... *don't any of you even THINK about messing with Amber Crescent.* That's what she was thinking as she tried to stare down the male lawyer in her outer office.

For his part, Aaron Akron knew all about Amber Crescent. He knew her home address, her living situation, her pay rate and financial status, her lipstick lesbian wife's name, the car she drove, where she banked, and so forth. He grinned widely as they eyeballed each other. She strived for a bred-to-kill pit bull look, teeth bared and eyes showing ... *extreme* distaste at him.

For his part, Aaron Akron served up a Labrador Retriever puppy-dog look. He bounced up and down on his toes trying to imitate an eager happy puppy. But in his mind he was reflecting, not for the first time, on just how ugly humans were. *Like some kind of degraded, deteriorating species,* he thought.

Except there were the two things that saved the humans ... at least in the eyes of the Achrons: *Comedy and heterosexual love* (some Achron TI's thought that was just saying the same thing twice, given the way humans are ...).

As he continued bouncing on his toes and smiling happily at Amber Crescent, Akron reflected on how the different subsets of humans could compete in getting so *ugly* ... so filled with hatred. *Fifth Gen Feminists* came to his mind. It was as if human sexual dimorphism, as wonderful as it was, had turned inward, infecting and attacking itself like some kind of pycho-social autoimmune disease.

A plague, thought Aaron Akron, *a plague always seeking enough power to make everyone else miserable.* He cranked his luminous smile up to a thousand watts and exclaimed happily: "You must be Miss Crescent!"

"Ms." she spat at him. "I heard yelling out here. Are you responsible?"

"Not me!" he said, pointing at the woman behind the desk. *"She did it!"* he exclaimed as he tried to keep from bursting into open laughter.

"I think not," said Amber Crescent in a clipped voice.

"Oh *well* then," he said, "let's not get ... *tumescent* about the situation! Your assistant here has apparently been lying to me about your so-called *unavailability.* But *mirabile dictu* ... you appear to be standing right here in front of me!

Amber Crescent glowered at him, radiating her hatred.

"Oh! One other thing," said Akron brightly, as if he had just thought of it: "You happen to be holding my associate counsel Gwendolyn O'Connell in your hospital. She's locked up and being held incommunicado." He paused, as if thinking, then said sharply, *"That's not nice!"* He reached into his coat pocket and pulled out an IJF business card. "Aaron Akron!" he said, holding the card out to her.

Amber Crescent stared at his hand as if he were holding a writhing snake. "I know who you are," she said in a flat hostile tone.

In fact, she had been tracking him for the past 45 minutes as he surmounted or bypassed every attempted bureaucratic blockade, one after another, all of whom had been told to stop him. She had known he was on his way, and knew why he was at the hospital.

And then that goddamned faggot Laflorrie has to call! Shit!

"Excellent!" said Aaron Akron, beaming at her and slipping his business card back into a pocket, "If you know who I am then you must also know that Miss O'Connell is an attorney with the Individual Justice Foundation, and you further know that I'm the executive director of that foundation, and an attorney.

He paused, then went on in a more deliberate tone: "You then ALSO know that my associate is being held *illegally* ... **don't you.**" Akron wasn't smiling anymore. "Do I have that right *Miss* Crescent?"

She stared silent daggers at him as several uniformed security men spilled into the room behind Akron. They milled there, ready to act but waiting for orders.

"Let's talk," she said finally, uncrossing her arms. "Come in." She spun on her feet and strode back into her office.

Aaron Akron turned around to look at the security men behind him. They tried to look fearsome but came off as just guys standing around. Akron gave them an exaggerated shrug—*I don't know what's going on*—and stepped into Amber Crescent's office, shutting the door behind him. She was seated behind her executive-size desk.

"It seems that you are friends with a certain individual named Herbert Laflorrie," she said without preamble.

"Oh!" he said as if pleasantly surprised they had that in common. "Do you know him too?"

"I've just gotten off the phone with him," she said in a flat uninflected voice.

"Well I hope you had a nice conversation!" he said happily.

"He threatened to sue the hospital," said Crescent. "He also threatened to have ... a large amount of money withheld from the hospital's annual funding pledge package next year."

"That would be about $350 million, wouldn't it?" asked Akron innocently. "That Herb ... he's *such* a philanthropist!" He grinned widely at her.

"That's not philanthropy," said Amber Crescent, gritting her teeth. *"It's blackmail!"* She was not used to being challenged in her own domain. But she knew that Herbert Laflorrie could and would do exactly what he had threatened. She also knew that any such action by Laflorrie would negatively impact—no, not "impact," it would *destroy*—her career.

Not to mention her carefully constructed bureaucratic power center in the hospital. *Shit,* she fumed internally, *the fucker could get me fired ... damned patriarchal pig.* Her live-in girlfriend would *kill* her if she screwed up on her career, and she knew that Laflorrie would be sure to inform the hospital board why he was withdrawing a multimillion dollar annual bequest.

She stared across the desk at Aaron Akron and said, "How about if I accuse you of attacking me right here and now if you think you're so funny?"

"Strike one honey," answered Akron. "No one would believe you for one thing. You're too ugly. You look like a pit bull and I don't swing for guys, pit bull or otherwise. So if you make the slightest move toward me I'm out of here, and we'll see who can get into the courts faster, you or me."

The fucker is smiling, she thought as she glared at him. "Fuck you, asshole."

"Strike two, my lovely," he responded. *"I say again ... you're holding my associate, attorney Gwendolyn O'Connell in a locked hospital room. You have cut off the phone service to that room and you are doing the bidding of the Winston Police Department and District attorney ... victimizing my associate when in fact SHE is the victim. All in violation of the law."*

Aaron Akron couldn't help adding to that: *"And you call yourself a feminist?"* He was smirking. *Okay,* he thought, *I admit it: I'm enjoying messing with this human witch.*

"You're a cocky, white-privileged, cisgender, patriarchal male," she said evenly. "Your day is over, just like all you Y-chromosome types. You think you can bend any woman over a desk and have her? Well think again buddy."

"Strike three," said Akron. "I am thinking that a $50 million lawsuit by the IJF against you personally as well as your hospital should get the ball rolling. Would that catch your attention and concentrate your mind? Especially if this conversation has somehow been recorded? Even if Herb Laflorrie didn't yank a good chunk of the hospital's funding, do you want the hospital sued for a few million dollars ... *honey?* Because everyone will know *you caused it.*"

Amber Crescent stood up suddenly and leaned forward on her desk glaring at him. She was visibly grinding her teeth, her jaw moving.

"Stop that, you man-hating witch," said Akron. "Grinding your teeth makes you even uglier. It's unprofessional too."

Without a word Amber Crescent stabbed an intercom button: "Call the nursing station on the west wing, fifth floor," she barked into it. "Tell them to let this asshole go see Gwendolyn O'Connell."

"Thank you!" said Aaron Akron effusively. "I'll find my own way out." He turned and strode out the door, turned left down the hallway and caught an elevator with two of the security guards following along. He nodded amiably at them in the elevator. "Seen any good movies lately?" he asked.

They didn't respond.

When he exited the elevator on the 5th floor Akron found himself facing a nursing station with several people working behind it. Two more uniformed security men stood nearby. Akron nodded and smiled at them as he approached the nursing station.

One of the nurses looked up while the others behind the counter studiously avoided noticing him. "I'm here to visit Gwendolyn O'Connell," he said cordially. "The one I think you had some excitement about yesterday?" He beamed at the nurse, mentally admiring the girl reporter who'd rappelled off the hospital roof to get to Gwen. *I want to meet that kid!*

"Yes sir," said the nurse behind the station. "She's in 434." She nodded toward the two security guys. "These two gentlemen will escort you there."

"Fine!" he said. He turned to face the security men and gestured with one hand: "Lead on fellas!"

The guards didn't say anything as they headed down one of the hallways. Akron tagged along, looking with interest at equipment, nurses and patients along the way.

There was a cop sitting on a chair outside the door of room 434. One of the security guards produced a key ring heavy with keys. He looked at the cop meaningfully, then inserted one.

How the hell does he find the right one? thought Akron.

The guard stood aside as Akron entered the room, then moved to follow him in along with the other guard. Akron spun around.

"Sorry guys!" he said. "I'm a lawyer ...." He jerked a thumb over his shoulder in the direction of Gwen O'Connell sitting on her bed, "and that's my client. *I represent her* ... and as such I'm afraid I'm going to have to ask for privacy."

The guards looked at each other, then at Akron. He stood silently, waiting for them to leave. They were torn between challenging him, calling Amber Crescent, or acceding to his demand.

"It's probably a good idea to leave," said Gwen O'Connell from where she was perched on the bed, "I'm a lawyer too, and you could cause a ruckus if you try to stay while I confer with my attorney. Besides"—she made a cute little moue face at them—*"pretty please?"*

Akron grinned at the guards as they withdrew silently, closing the door behind them. He turned to Gwen O'Connell: "Hey Babe!" he shouted.

"*Hey Babe* yourself!" she squealed, happily jumping up and hugging him. "It took you long enough! How are things going?"

"Oh good," he said. "Sarah McLaughlin is rescued and on her way out of Pennsylvania with her parents. And I do believe I may have been able to help a badly damaged boy who was there ... as good as can be expected on first try at least." He looked at her meaningfully, "*These humans,* you know? They're so ... unstable, even if nominally sentient."

"What a species," agreed O'Connell. "But you know it's not entirely their fault. I swear I love humans ... but I also want to kill'em all!"

Aaron Akron chuckled as he sat in a chair and she sat on the side of the bed. "Yep," he said, "their unstable substrate sabotages their own damned sentience and intelligence, such as it is. What a mishmash they have for a brain." He shrugged his shoulders theatrically, "What are ya gonna do, ya know?"

"Nothing yet," she said. "But remember, Achrons weren't all that hot before we got it together and started Transitioning. We'd be weird too if we evolved in an environment as drastic and ugly as they've had to endure."

"True dat," he said. "But what I don't get is they *know* the right way to act ... yet they just keep on screwing it up, and screwing each other over ... year after year, century after century; eon upon eon."

"Like you said," said Gwen. *"Chemical mishmash.* Given the evolutionary pressures, I'm surprised they even survived, much less gotten this far."

"Assholes that they can be," said Akron.

Gwen grinned. "Not nice!" she remonstrated. "They're not *all* that way: Look at Herb!" She paused. "But I do admit their power-lust is freaking ugly ... and they've got unlimited justifications for it! From socialism, to communism, to fascism, to Nazism, to the so-called *progressives,* to most governments no matter what they're called. Power-mad, all of them."

"It's an exceptionally ugly human characteristic", agreed Aaron Akron. "On the other hand, the good ones are ... very good indeed." He reached into a pocket and pulled out a key ring with a few keys on it:

"This is for you when you get out of here," he said, tossing the keys to her. She deftly snatched them out of the air and looked at the keys, then at Akron, raising her eyebrows.

"Your new home for the time being," he said. "Or at least as long as you need to stay in Winston. It's Mr. and Mrs. McLaughlin's home in Wilding Oaks."

"Where #22 blew up?"

"Yep," said Akron. "The McLaughlins have also been pretty much invited to leave the neighborhood by their friendly neighbors."

"Oh, a group of real peaches, eh?" said O'Connell.

"Appears that way," he said. "The group included some people that Dave and Meghan considered to be friends. So much for human friendship."

"Too bad," said Gwen. "Where are they now?"

"On their way to New Hampshire with Sarah as we speak. People from the Free State Project will meet and take care of them until things calm down here. Herb Laflorrie even invited them to come up to the Arcology and stay there if they wanted."

Gwen smiled. Herb Laflorrie was her lover and marriage suitor. He was a darling. "I just talked to him this morning," Gwen said.

"And he talked to the last bureaucrat I had to get past in order to get to you," he said. "She looks like a pit bull but she backed down easy enough. I guess you asked Herb to call and threaten her?"

"But of course!"

Akron smiled, "I heard all about it."

"Hah," she snorted. "He probably waved a few million dollars in her face ... or the lack thereof."

"The latter," said Akron as he stood up to leave.

"Hey! When do I get out of here?" she asked.

"Beats me," he said, grinning. "Let's see how the whole thing unfolds. You could always wait for the court hearing the judge set for six weeks from now ...."

"*EWWWW*," she said, blowing him a raspberry as he exited the room.

She put the keys aside and went back to watching news reports about the unfolding scandal in Winston.

"These humans! she thought. *Their daytime TV ... it's just the greatest!"*

CHAPTER 21
Angela Comes Unhinged.

Around the same time that Aaron Akron and Gwen O'Connell were chatting in the Winston City Hospital, two other former Achrons were having a chat with FBI agent Angela Maxim. Not unlike Aaron Akron and Gwendolyn O'Connell, Bill Smith and the dog known as "Spot" were Achron *Transitioned Intelligences* or "TI's."

Angela Maxim had made a demand on her lover Bill Smith, asking an entirely understandable question under the circumstances: *What the fuck is going on?*

"Thank you for your attention," said Bill Smith, joking as he sat naked on the bed facing Angela, who was also naked. She was on the end of the bed, while the talking dog Spot was lounging to one side.

Angela Maxim had more than a few questions, and was upset about it. She had, after all, made love to Bill Smith the night before. *At some length,* she reflected, *and more than once.* She wondered if it had been an awful mistake. *He had better come clean,* she thought, *and fast.*

"You could start at the beginning," suggested the dog.

"Just tell me," said Angela Maxim. A tinge of concern colored her voice. She was thinking about the small-frame Smith & Wesson .38 Special lying at the top of her purse on the floor.

"Okay," said Bill Smith. He heaved a big sigh. "Look, you're going to have trouble believing this, okay?"

"Try me," she said, the edge in her voice increasing.

Spot spoke up: "Bill and I are biological manifestations of an alien intelligence secondary to a species that developed in a radically differing environment on a planet elsewhere in this galaxy, in what you call the Milky Way." The dog paused to see how she'd react, then looked over at Bill Smith.

"Right," she said sarcastically.

The dog looked over at Bill Smith: "Told you so," it said in the high-pitched child's voice.

"The truth will out," he replied. "Sooner or later every human's going to know about us, so Angela may as well be among the first."

"If not *the* first," said Spot. It turned to look at Angela Maxim again: "No time like the present!"

"Sure!" said Angela Maxim, sarcasm still in her voice. But an edge of nervousness made her voice fractionally higher. "No time like the present!" she mocked the dog. "I've love to hear all about it! *Now tell me!"*

"Okay ...." said Spot.

"You keep out of this!" she snarled at the dog. "I want it from him. He made love to me last night goddammit! Several times in fact, and now you both tell me he's a fucking *alien! No thank you!"*

"Look Angela," said Bill Smith, "I'm a human being. As Spot just said, I'm a human manifestation of a non-human sentience. But I have the same DNA as you, I feel the same things you do. My consciousness and my sentience are separate from my body, just like *your* consciousness is independent of *your* body. Both are uniquely yours and mine, as with all sentient beings. So in this ... *human* construct, I retain the unique provenance of my original species. We call ourselves Achrons."

Angela Maxim barked out a laugh. *"Achrons!* You're saying you're ... *aliens."* She paused. "And I suppose you injected me with *alien sperm* last night?"

Bill Smith sighed. "Not at all," he said patiently, "that's what I'm trying to tell you: I'm 100% all-natural, all-human being, based on the same type of DNA you are."

Angela looked back and forth between them, then blew out an explosive breath. "I don't believe this shit! So either I was laid by an alien in a human body last night, or I got fucked by someone who's a stark, raving, lunatic nutcase!" Her voice was rising, an edge of hysteria creeping into it.

"Angela, please," said Bill, sounding distressed. "What we shared last night was real, I care for you ... I care for you deeply."

"You're going to have to do something else to convince her," said the dog.

"I don't *need* convincing!" snapped Angela. "And I don't know what the hell I'm dealing with here! I don't even know what I'm *doing* here!"

"You're here because we cared for each other," said Smith. "When that type of thing happens between two humans it is truly ... unique. It is a total sharing ... of feeling, of communication, of spirit, of bodies, of everything we are, of our very *consciousness*. It is incredibly special ...."

"And incredibly rare in this galaxy as far as we know," added the dog.

"Oh fine!" Angela Maxim shot back. "You just forgot to let me know that you *think* you're a goddamned alien last night before taking me into your bed!"

"It's called making love," said Spot.

*"Shut the fuck up you ... **dog!**"* shouted Maxim. *"This is insane!"* She abruptly stood up and stepped over to where her clothes were on the floor. She turned and faced him: "Bill," she said accusingly, "you know something about the explosion case I'm investigating, *don't you.*"

"The one in Wilding Oaks?" he said. "Yes. I do."

"Then spill it for God's sake!" she shouted at him.

Spot spoke up: "The elderly gentleman that the police were beating to death ... the one your media has been referring to as a 'bum', was an Achron TI."

"An Achron TI," she repeated flatly.

"Yes," said Spot.

Angela Maxim looked back and forth between them. "He wasn't a human being?"

"He was fully human," said Bill Smith, "just as I am fully human and just as Spot is fully a member of the family you know as *Canis lupus familiaris.*"

"I think you're nutty as a fruitcake and I'm sorry I came home with you last night," she snapped. She stooped down to grab her panties off the floor.

Bill and the dog looked at each other. Bill was distinctly unhappy. "Angela ... that was real last night," he said plaintively, "I care for you ... I care for you deeply, and I'm as human as you are. I feel the same emotions you do. I may even be ... falling in love with you. It's just that my consciousness is a little bit different, and ... ."

"And what?" snapped Maxim, standing up holding her red panties. "You think you stole some human being's body and then modified it for super-powers? *Huh, is that it?*" An edge of hysteria was definitely rising in her voice.

"Angela, please," said Bill, "it's true that I have certain ... extra abilities with my body, but it wasn't *stolen* from anyone. I've been inhabiting this body since I was born."

"Oh great!" said Angela. "Have you ever told your mother that you think you're an alien?"

"I love my mother and father," he said, "just like you love yours. And if it had not been for me and my sister they would never have had kids. They would have been left barren, alone, unhappy and bereaved in their lives."

"And you think you've been fooling them all this time?" asked Angela Maxim, an incredulous edge in her voice.

"My sister and I have been good, helpful, kind, respectful, dutiful children," he said calmly. "You've seen my entire background, all the things that I have done and experienced and lived. To this day and for the rest of our parents' lives my sister and I will dote upon them just as we do now. We love them just as much as you love your mother and father."

She stooped down suddenly, dropping the panties and scooping up the .38 Special out of her purse. She raised it in a combat stance, aiming with two hands at Bill Smith, speaking deliberately: "You are saying that you and your sister are monsters or that you are a flaming nutcase who needs to be checked out in a mental hospital. What do you know about the bum and the explosion? Tell me *now!*"

Bill Smith sat calmly leaning against the headboard. "The 'bum', as you put it, was a Transitioned Achron, as we told you. We refer to it as #22. That's its instantiation number."

Angela Maxim backed up a step against the wall. She was breathing fast. The barrel of the gun didn't waver from Bill Smith's chest.

He continued talking calmly to her as the dog looked on. "The so-called *bum* saw an injustice, a misuse of power against a blameless 7-year-old girl. He didn't like it." Bill shrugged. "Unfortunately for those present, he had the ability to do something about the abuse of power taking place, and he did. We Achrons don't like power-abusers, and that's an unfortunate characteristic that is endemic to your species."

"Too bad, that ..." said the dog in a somber voice.

"Are you *shitting* me?" said Angela Maxim incredulously. "An alien in the form of an old bum killed nearly a dozen people who were just doing their jobs? *Fuck you!* Lemonade stands are against the law! Someone in the neighborhood called in to complain about it. What do you expect them to do?"

"Ah yes," said Bill Smith. "A deeply concerned citizen; that would be Mrs. Harriman Newton the Third. What I expect her and the police to do is leave the little girl alone. Of course we don't *expect* you humans to act rationally, to cease your constant struggles to accumulate power to be used against others of your species ...."

"But it's the *law*," snapped Angela. "Those dead cops were just doing their job to enforce the law!"

"And now they're dead," said Bill.

"Those were legitimate police doing their legitimate duty!" she screamed at him.

"And they were stomping on the face of an old man, breaking his bones," replied Bill Smith. His voice was acid: "They were *literally* stomping him to death!"

Spot said, "What happened ... it's something of a message from us. You could call it ... a *gift*. A gift from us Achrons.

"Call it a gift as well as a warning," said Smith. "Call it a *kindness* ... an *Achron Kindness* if you want."

"*SHUT UP!*" screamed Angela Maxim. She was coming unhinged, visibly hyperventilating as she swung the .38 Special back and forth between Bill Smith and the dog. "So you're telling me that a friend of yours, a bum who you think was an alien, murdered those police officers the other day?"

Her face was twisted.

"It was not murder," said Bill Smith, "It was self-defense. I'm also saying that you can't expect Achron TI's to put up with that kind of abuse when they come across it." His voice was level.

"Not all of the cops present were killed," said Spot from the bed, "because not all were engaged in beating an elderly human being to death. One of the cops directly involved was spared."

Angela Maxim stared at the dog, then whispered, *"Officer Buster Caisson."*

"Yes," said Bill Smith. "And you know that he was physically thrown over 30 feet through the air *by an elderly bum,* He landed on top of a car and rolled onto the ground behind it ... which happened to protect him from the subsequent blast."

Maxim was horrified: "How do you know this?" she whispered.

Smith answered calmly: "In a certain sense I was there. I experienced it ... after the fact. And there's a reason you can't find any body parts, debris, or even a motorcycle anywhere in the vicinity."

Her eyes narrowed: *"How the fuck do you know about any of that?"*

Bill Smith ignored the question. "The reason you can't find any bodies or debris at the blast locus is because of the type of explosion that occurred. It made physical objects within a small blast radius go ... elsewhere."

Maxim's eyes weren't narrowed anymore. They were nearly bugging out of her face: *"No one knows about that!"*

"It is what happens when that type of explosion is triggered," Bill Smith told her. "You humans are so infatuated with power that you misuse it all the time. You're going to have to learn to act differently now. Call it a form of *vibrant cultural diversity.* We Achrons are entitled to your respect and cooperation just as much as your *other* aliens, right? The ones from south of the border? You don't want to be *xenophobic,* do you?"

Bill Smith's voice was heavy with sarcasm.

Angela Maxim was shaking her head back and forth: "No! No ... you are a *mental case!*"

"Was it so terrible?" asked Spot. "All #22 did was stop a group of cops from stomping an elderly man to death."

Bill Smith's voice was somber: "Humans are going to have to stop loving power so much ... and you're going to have to stop abusing it entirely."

"Especially using it against other human beings," added Spot.

"I realize that's a tall order," said Smith. "Humanity evolved in a very, very tough environment. A certain percentage of you have vicious inherited characteristics that may have been needed in the past to survive and reproduce, but that is twisted and unnecessary in your current environment. The characteristic originally came from severe environmental evolutionary pressures. But now you're going to have to *understand* that fact ... and *stop* it."

"So you think you and your *alien buddies* can tell the whole human race how to act?" she snapped. "How to *behave?*"

"Not everyone," said Smith. "Achron TI's can't be everywhere ... but we are in the good old U.S. of A. And we like you Americans! We've just decided to teach you about civilized behavior ... and even that will only be in a small geographic part of your country."

"You. Are. Crazy," said Angela Maxim, still aiming the gun at him.

"Hey, you don't want to be *xenophobic!*" said Bill Smith sarcastically. "What about the *vibrant tapestry of cultural diversity* your fedgov is always ramming down your throat? The one that insists on importing masses of culturally violent and misogynistic humans from third world countries? And you're saying we *Achrons* are bad? Hah!"

"*Are you shitting me?*" shrieked Angela Maxim. The gun was still trained on his chest.

"No Angela, I'm not," he responded. "And like other aliens—*legal and illegal*—that you've imported into your country, we Achrons have our own culture and our own demands.

"*Those people didn't deserve to die goddammit!*" she screamed.

"They were engaged in a legally-sanctioned act of murder," said Spot. "But it was still *murder*."

"Let's not forget the old witch in Wilding Oaks who lost her hand," said Bill Smith. "She was responsible for initiating the mayhem, and was proud of it. That's why her hand was cut off ... although she was told it might be reattached if she spent some time thinking about her hateful behavior."

"She deserved to lose her hand," said Spot matter-of-factly.

"The old bat did what you humans love to do so much," said Bill Smith. "She was delighted to call the cops and get the thrill of vicariously bringing power to bear upon someone else—*in this case a 7-year-old girl*—so she got a taste of what it feels like from the other side ... and how it will feel to go about her life without one of her hands."

Maxim was twitching the gun back and forth between the dog and Bill Smith, "Are you telling me that you're responsible for cutting off that woman's hand and carrying the goddamned thing off with you?" She was screeching in hysteria now.

"Not me personally," said Bill Smith. "It was another TI. You are also aware that doctors can't explain how the hand was severed with such microscopic efficiency."

"What do you know about that!"

The dog answered matter-of-factly: "The hand was cut off using a prehensile strand of invisibly microscopic fiber consisting of sequentially linked molecules making up a microscopically sharp, flexible, cutting tool with a serrated edge. You humans don't have it yet, but you have imagined it in science fiction. It's called *molywire*."

Angela Maxim's chest was heaving and her eyes were wide. She kept jerking the aim of the pistol switched back and forth between Bill Smith and the dog.

"Angela, please," Bill pleaded. "Can't we discuss this rationally?"

"Fuck THAT shit!" she screamed. "You're either a fucking psychopath or you're a goddamn alien body-snatcher!" She held the pistol's aim on him as she stooped and groped in her purse with one hand, coming up with her cell phone shaking in her hand.

"One way or another, we're going to get to the bottom of this, and it's going to happen in police custody, not in your goddamned bedroom!"

Angela Maxim had come fully unhinged, and in the process had also made up her mind.

Bill Smith and the dog looked at each other, their faces reflecting emotions ranging from chagrin, to sadness, to resignation.

CHAPTER 22
Death over Reason.

"She's made up her mind," said the dog, sadly shaking its head back and forth. It looked oddly human, and the child's voice it used reflected the sadness. "Very unstable chemical substrate."

"Indeed," responded Smith grimly. He was still watching Angela Maxim standing up against the wall with a gun. "Angela, you know calling the authorities will complicate things," he pleaded. "It won't help. And you know we have the ability to self-detonate. Number 22 wasn't the only one. One just happened in California too ... a TI named Murray Berkowitz did the same thing."

"You know about that?" gasped Maxim, pausing as she stabbed at the cell phone keys with her thumb.

"Of course," said Bill Smith. "His instantiation number is 37. He came across a thoroughly corrupt city council in Stanton, California ... and fixed it."

"Fixed it?" she asked him incredulously. "You call blowing up an entire building *'fixing it'*?"

"Number 37 decided to deal with the problem on the spot, so to speak," said Bill. "The local crooks forced his hand, including the police. They've been exploiting taxpayers in Stanton for years, and in the most corrupt way."

"You call killing dozens of goddamned people *dealing with the problem?"* Maxim shouted at him.

"Yes," he stated flatly. "Virtually everyone present was a part of the crooked local machine and were benefiting from it." He shrugged his shoulders, "Number 37 did ask one lady to leave so she wouldn't get hurt."

"*Name her!*" snapped Angela Maxim.

"Her name was Mrs. Angela Guppert," said Spot matter-of-factly. "She was a member of the Stanton city council but she was blameless. She was not part of the group of criminals bleeding the town's finances." He looked over at Bill Smith.

"It's true," said Smith, nodding to Angela.

"*Jesus H. Christ you two!*" she screamed. She had just read a report on The *Stanton Massacre* (as the media was sensationally playing it) which had happened only within the past 48 hours. She also knew that a single woman at the meeting, a member of the city council, had been asked to leave by the madman before he started killing people.

The woman had survived. *She was Stanton city councilman Angela Guppert.* "How the *fuck* do you know about any of that?" Angela screamed at them.

"We have the ability to communicate through what you will eventually come to understand to be *subspace interstices,*" said the dog on the bed. "Think of it as a multi-dimensional Internet. We can connect when we want, just like you humans can call and talk via cell phone. We can also observe in real time if we desire, just like you can Skype on the Internet. It's also possible for us to ... *experience* things that others of us experience."

Maxim was speaking quickly and urgently into her cell phone. "*Connect 911! Connect 911!*" she spoke frantically into her cell phone. Bill Smith and Spot were on the bed looking on. Bill was shaking his head slowly side-to-side. He looked sad.

A voice could be heard answering the phone:

"*Man with a gun!*" screamed Angela Maxim. "*Man with a gun! Request immediate assistance, this is FBI agent Angela Maxim!*"

A voice came on the cell phone again and said something. "*Fuck you, asswipe!*" she shrieked into it. "I don't care if I'm the Angela Maxim you're looking for or not! *I'm telling you get some fucking cops over here RIGHT NOW!*" She threw the phone down and slid along the wall away from the doorway. She ended up standing in a corner, holding the .38 Special two-handed again. It was aimed steadily at Bill Smith's chest.

"Angela, please," said Spot.

She shifted the gun rapidly between the dog and the man on the bed.

Smith heaved a sigh and came to a decision. "Well fuck this," he said, and started to get up off the bed. Angela Maxim shot him twice in the chest. His body was slammed back against the head of the bed by the impact of two .38 Special hollow-point bullets hitting the center of mass. Blood streamed out of the two bullet holes and seeped out of one corner of his mouth.

Bill Smith looked down at the wounds in his chest. He seemed almost curious as he sat up against the headboard. He looked up at his lover of the night before, his eyes clear and aware. Angela Maxim began physically breaking down. She was sobbing with tears streaming down her face. *"No! No! No! No!"* she was screaming over and over as her lover regarded her from the bed.

"Angela, please," he said matter-of-factly.

Angela Maxim wailed out, *"NOOOOO!!!"* and pulled the trigger two more times. Both hollow-point .38 slugs hit their mark cratering two more wounds into Bill Smith's chest. Just as she was pulling the trigger a Winston city police officer named Edward Mason burst through the door, sweeping his 9 millimeter service pistol across the room as he entered. He'd been on the Winston police force for just over a year and his pistol was fully loaded with 15 staggered 9 millimeter rounds in the magazine and one in the chamber. It was a first shot double-action, the hammer was cocked, and the safety was off.

Angela Maxim's third gunshot thundered as the young police officer came through the door. He saw a male on a bed with blood gushing from multiple chest wounds as he swept the room and heard the explosive crash of the gunshots. He had picked up a person in his peripheral vision and was swinging his aim toward that threat as the last gunshot blasted in his ears.

As Officer Mason swung his pistol toward her, Angela Maxim became aware of movement at the door and turned slightly in that direction. In doing so the muzzle of her revolver turned with her body toward Officer Mason.

The young cop saw someone swinging a gun in his direction even as the muzzle of his pistol lined up. He instantly squeezed off two rounds, the roar smashing into his ears. Both shots hit a nude woman in the corner of the room before she could aim her weapon at him.

Hit in the side of her chest by two 9 millimeter rounds, Angela Maxim was slammed against the wall in the corner where she stood. She tried to scream but only blood came from her mouth. Her arms dropped to her side as the .38 Special fell from her hands and she slid toward the floor, her blood smearing the wall.

Officer Mason moved quickly toward the neutralized threat to kick the pistol away. *"MAN DOWN!"* he screamed at the top of his lungs, but no backup had arrived. His arms were outstretched as his pistol continued targeting the naked, bloodied female on the floor.

From the corner of his eyes the cop saw an impossibly quick flash of movement before both of his arms were smashed violently downward. All the bones in both of his forearms broke with audible *cracks* from the impact on them. His hands went numb and his gun fell to the floor as his eyes refused to process what he was seeing.

The naked and obviously dead male on the bed with multiple gunshot wounds to the chest had ... *launched* himself—*faster than any human could move*—and smashed something down on his arms. It felt like a steel bar had hit his forearms as his bones broke and the pistol flew from his hands.

He tried to track the blur that had just smashed his forearms when he felt a violent impact on the side of his head. It felt like he'd been hit with a leather-covered sap. His ears rang and consciousness faltered as *something* rocketed past him toward the woman on the floor.

Officer Mason heard the word *"Asshole!"* hissed at him as something flew by and shoved him violently to the side. Pain flared in his head and both of his broken arms as he bounced off the wall and toppled sideways toward the floor. Darkness was closing in as he heard the ... *thing* shout at him: *"You fucking trigger-happy idiot!"*

Pain exploded as he hit the floor, agony radiating from the broken bones in his arms and from his face and jaw. *It's dead!* his mind shrieked inside his head. It was his last coherent thought before darkness mercifully enveloped Officer Edward Mason of the Winston Police Department.

Bill Smith kneeled on the floor cradling Angela Maxim. Blood poured from the four wounds on his chest, mixing with the blood coming from Angela's body. He slapped one hand hard over the center of her chest, the other over the two holes in her side. "God *dammit!*" he cursed.

"Angela," he said to her, his face close to hers as he pumped on her chest, *"Angela!"*

Her eyes fluttered and opened. "Bill," she said in a barely audible whisper, "I shot you ...."

He ignored her words and spoke urgently: "Listen to me Angela, I need you to tell me now, *tell me quickly!* You're going to die, I can't save you, but I can save your consciousness!"

Her eyes were only half open. She was fading. "Who wants that ..." she whispered.

"I want it, Angela! I want it! But you have to tell me! *I have to hear you say it!* Say you'll let me bring you back! *Say it now!*" His hand on her chest was pumping, pumping, pumping, keeping her brain barely oxygenated. "Let me bring you back Angela!" he pleaded. "I can love you! *I will love you!*"

The hint of a twisted smile came to the dying girl's bloodied lips: "Love me ..." she whispered, wheezing. "You're not even human ...."

"I am too!" Bill Smith snarled. Tears came from eyes, spilling down his cheeks, *"Tell me, Angela! Tell me I can bring you back! Let me love you! I have to hear it!"*

The light was fading now from Angela Maxim's eyes as she drew a last shallow wheezing breath. As she exhaled it she whispered her last words. *"You'd better ... "* she said, and died.

Angela Maxim was trying to say *"You'd better not,"* but her heart stopped and the sentence was never completed.

Sobs wracked Bill Smith's body ... and yet as he wept he *smiled.* He gently lowered her lifeless body to the floor, leaning down to kiss her lips as blood from her mouth mixed with his.

Okay Angela goddammit, you said I could ... so this discussion isn't over! He wiped the back of his hand across his face. *Fucking human beings!* Tears fell from his eyes as he felt the stab of an emotion common to all sentients.

The emotion piercing at the heart of Bill Smith was not sorrow. That emotion is not common to sentients. Rather it was ... *regret*, a universal emotion shared by all known sentient beings.

The body of Bill Smith stood up from the floor as blood continued streaming from the wounds in his chest. *Fucking idiot cop*, he thought, but immediately felt bad about it: *This wasn't his fault. Others probably wouldn't have done any different. Everything that could go wrong ... did go wrong.*

He sighed and stepped over to the bed, sniffling his nose and wiping his eyes with the back of his wrist. His mouth twisted as he lay down on the bed and glanced over at the unconscious police officer on the floor.

Shit, he thought with a touch of bitterness, *these poor, lost, pitiable souls ... trapped in a world of their minds and their own making.*

He lay back up against the head of the bed where he'd been before. Tears still leaked from his eyes. They were not only for Angela Maxim, but for every human being, all of them on this crazy, awful, amazing, maddening world filled with these strange upright bipedal hominids.

They called themselves *homo sapiens*. But the word *sapiens* was related to the word *sapient*, and they weren't really *sapient* ... not in so many ways.

Created by a pitiless process of evolution in a world that doesn't care, he thought, *a world that never cared and never will care.*

What a fucking awful trip.

William Hamilton Smith lay back against the bed's headboard for the last time. *What a fucking trip* echoed again through his mind.

He heard sirens and vehicles slamming to a stop outside the building. *You've got some explaining to do*, he thought toward the unconscious cop on the floor. *Serves you right*. But then he felt bad about it again. It hadn't been the young cop's fault.

Doors were opening and slamming. Men were shouting and boots pounding down the hallway. Those were the last sounds that William Hamilton Smith heard as he allowed his fading human body to die.

From outside the building officers were sprinting from their cars. Watching it all from a sidewalk was a small-to-medium size black dog with some white spots on it. Alone and without a collar, it looked like a stray.

The dog watched for a few moments as the chaos began unfolding, then trotted on down the sidewalk. It looked back once, perhaps with an emotion of regret ... then turned back in the direction it was traveling and continued.

It didn't look back again.

CHAPTER 23
Sorrow, Escape, Healing ... and a New Friend for Spot.

Aaron Akron was driving on an Interstate when Gwendolyn O'Connell called for him requesting access. She was still in the hospital where she was being held, but she was crying.

Oh damn ....

"What is it #217?" Akron asked. Gwen had been the twin human sister of William Hamilton Smith, aka Bill Smith. She had been instantiated first, and thus was #217. Bill Smith had been #218.

"Oh #14," sobbed Gwen, "my brother has been terminated! He was shot and killed by that poor lady, the FBI lady Angela Maxim, and she was killed by a policeman!"

"Oh *fuck* ..." said Akron, "how's #218 handling it?"

"He's distraught," she said, "poor Angela! They were lovers last night, and shared their wonderful human sexual dimorphism. But this morning she *shot him!* And then *she* was shot and killed! I feel so sorry for them!" #217 sobbed, mourning the death of a woman she'd hardly known ... and yet had known intimately.

"Damn," said Aaron Akron. "How could that happen? #218 thought she'd be one to help us make contact. And now this ...." He paused and sighed. "*Dammit*. Every innocent human being harmed by us is a part of our own human hearts gone." He sounded miserable. "What about #78?"

"It left when the shooting started," said #217. "It slipped out of the building. Nobody paid any attention to it." She was still crying. "Oh #14, what am I going to tell my parents? What am I going to *say* to them? They're going to be *heartbroken!*" Her all-too-human sobbing continued.

"They still have you, Gwen," he said gently. "I'm so sorry ...."

"Poor Angela," Gwen sobbed. "And my poor human parents, losing Bill like this."

"Mourn, #217," said #14 somberly. He could feel others connecting in during the conversation. "We all mourn, now and until we can help these poor people and the world they live in," he said.

"Very hard lives," came the whisper of a thought. It was #218, "Very hard world ...."

It said no more.

Aaron Akron sighed again, leaving Gwen O'Connell to her sorrow. He gently disunited from the others and slowed his temporal flow, grieving as he drove. He grieved for Angela Maxim, and for Bill Smith the human being, and for Gwendolyn and Bill's all-too-human parents, John and Emily Smith. He grieved for every human who had ever lived throughout their awful history ... struggling, fighting, suffering, striving, dancing, singing, creating ... and *trying*.

Only to face inevitable death.

Real death ... every one of them. He felt the sorrow of a world engulf him, letting it flow through him in the reduced temporal flow. Tears came from the eyes of his human body and streamed down his face unhindered.

By the time Aaron Akron completed his drive, he had grieved for years.

~~~~

For nearly 24 hours after the death of Bill Smith and Angela Maxim, the Achron TI known as #78 was on the move. It inhabited the body of the canine known as "Spot" as it left the city of Winston, Pennsylvania and traveled into nearby farming country.

It knew what it had to do ... and quickly found and made a new human friend.

Timmy Scott was an 8-year-old boy, one of three siblings in his household. He walked through the door of his house carrying #78. "Dad! Mom!

I found this dog out in the woods and he came up and licked my face!" The dog was nestled happily in his arms.

Timmy's mother and father were in the kitchen. His mother was cooking dinner while his father sat at the kitchen counter chatting with her. Timmy's parents, Homer and Evelyn Scott, were middle class Americans living in the heartland. Mr. Scott worked for the phone company in a nearby town while Evelyn ran the small farm on their 10 acres. "The farm" consisted of several chicken coops that Homer had built and from which they harvested and sold "natural eggs" in their community.

Homer and Evelyn looked at their son, then at the dog in his arms, and then at each other. Timmy was their youngest, so they both had a soft spot for him. "How do you know he doesn't belong to someone else?" asked Timmy's mother.

"No collar!" said Timmy excitedly. The dog sat calmly in the boy's arms. It had a silly-but-winning grin on its muzzle. It turned its head and licked Timmy's face again, then looked back at Mr. and Mrs. Scott.

"Friendly little dude," said Homer. "But look Timmy, you've got to report that you've found the dog. Its real owners may be looking for it. You'll need to report it to animal services and maybe put up some notices in town."

Timmy nodded excitedly in agreement: "Okay! Okay! I can keep him then?"

"And second," said Evelyn Scott, "if no one claims the dog *you* have to take care of him, understood?"

"Sure!" the boy instantly agreed.

"And that means taking him to the vet," said Timmy's father. The boy eagerly nodded his head again. None of the requirements were deal-breakers as far as *he* was concerned.

Besides, this dog was *cool.* "Okay!" said Timmy excitedly. "If I do all that then can I keep him?"

"Well ... for the time being," said his mother dubiously, "let's see how responsible you are in trying to find his owners."

"Oh *real responsible,*" said Timmy, "*real* responsible!" He let the dog down on the floor and said, "Come on Spot, let's go back outside!"

"*Spot?*" asked his father Homer. "You already gave him a name?"

"No!" said Timmy over his shoulder as he trotted out the door. "That's what he *said* his name was!"

Homer and Evelyn watched their son scamper out of the kitchen with the dog at his heels as the boy yelled, "Come on Spot! I'll show you the fort I built!" Homer rolled his eyes as he looked at his wife and smiled.

Outside the house Timmy was trotting along with the dog. They were headed toward some woods in the distance. "You really think we shouldn't tell my mom and dad you can talk?" he asked the dog.

"Not a good idea right now," it answered in its high-pitched voice. "They might not understand."

"Yeah!" said Timmy with exasperation. "*Adults!* They *never* understand!"

The dog barked twice like a normal dog. "See? I can bark like a real dog too!" it said.

"Good!" said Timmy. "Just bark when we're around my parents, okay?"

"Okay!" said the dog. *What nice people.* It also knew there was a place or two on the 10 acres where it could proceed when the time was right. It would need to get #218's help, but that wouldn't be hard now that it had lost its human body. But it still had that intimate connection to the poor dead human girl, Angela Maxim.

Damn. Too bad about Angela, the dog thought to itself, *she was really nice even if she kind of lost it at the end.* At this point it was unknown whether humans could successfully Transition, but Angela Maxim was now on the list to be one of the possible first.

Who knows? the dog thought. *Maybe it'll work out. It would be nice to have a new sentient species join us. It's been a while since we've found any new ones.*

There was no rush, though. To an Achron TI ... time is no object.

~~~~

After leaving the CPS foster home with their daughter, Dave and Meghan McLaughlin drove at a fairly high rate of speed throughout the day. They headed north on Interstate 91 through western Massachusetts and then into New Hampshire by way of Vermont, crossing the Connecticut River just north of Brattleboro.

"The Free State of New Hampshire Welcomes You!" announced a cheery sign on the east side of the river. Below the welcome sign was another that stated, *"New Hampshire is a 2nd Amendment State: All persons may carry personal weapons openly or concealed at all times in all locations."*

Mr. and Mrs. McLaughlin had been told to call someone ... people in New Hampshire who would help them. In fact, many had volunteered to assist, and the choices available to the McLaughlins included staying in one of the state's larger cities, Manchester or Nashua, or with families in suburbs, or in small towns or farms across the state. There was even an invitation to stay at the famous Gorham Arcology, courtesy of the well-known media-villain and near-trillionaire Herb Laflorrie!

Dave and Meghan made their first call soon after entering New Hampshire, before they came into the town of Keene. "Might as well establish contact now," said David as a slightly apprehensive Meghan McLaughlin called the first number they'd been given by Aaron Akron. It was almost immediately answered. The voice on the line was a happy-sounding woman.

"Hello," said Meghan a little shyly, "this is Meghan McLaughlin and we were told to call this number?"

"Meghan!" said a delighted bubbly voice. "Aaron told us all about you and David! He said you might be calling. Wonderful to hear from you! This is Mary Patterson. Are you in town? Are you nearby?"

"Well, not exactly, not yet at least," said Meghan, charmed by the friendliness of the lady, "But we are headed your way on ... Highway 9?" Dave nodded his head at his wife as their daughter Sarah unbuckled her seat belt and climbed onto the front seat console between them.

"How far out are you?" asked Mary. "Andrew and I have a room specially set aside for you. And I understand you have a daughter? Sarah?"

"Yes," said Meghan, warmed by the woman's enthusiasm.

"Well she'll want to meet our kids too!" said Mary. "We've got six, and a few of 'em are near her age!"

"That's wonderful," said Meghan, then added, "we don't want to impose or anything ...."

"Impose?" said the voice on the phone. "We've been *waiting* for you to call ever since we heard from Aaron Akron. We were hoping you'd come see us first!"

"Thank you," said Meghan with a growing sense of relief. Tears of happiness were creeping into her eyes. "You're very kind and we appreciate it."

"Not at all," said Mary Patterson. "This is the Free State, darling. People who live here came here for a reason! It's called liberty and freedom, and some of us are here because of injustice in our home states."

"Well that would include David and me I guess," said Meghan.

"It's all good!" enthused Mary Patterson. "Anyone who's a friend of that shyster Aaron Akron is a personal friend of ours! Get a piece of paper and let me tell you how to get here. Our kids can't wait to meet Sarah!"

When Meghan hung up, she turned and looked at her husband. Tears were in her eyes. "It's a little overwhelming," she said.

"I know," he responded. "If this is what everyone is like in New Hampshire, we may want to think about staying here permanently."

"I think I'm gonna like it here too!" said Sarah. "Can't wait, can't wait!"

"Well, we're only here for a little vacation," said her mother. "We'll have to see how things go ...." She and her husband smiled at their daughter as Meghan hugged her and they continued into Keene on state Highway 9.

~~~~

Winston police officer Buster Caisson rested in his hospital bed. His shoulder was broken and held immobile in some kind of weighted contraption over the bed. His head was still woozy, his thoughts jumbled from a concussion. The doctor had told him he probably wouldn't remember their talk, but he did.

A nurse came into the room. "Your sister is here to see you!" she said brightly.

Caisson turned his head toward the nurse. He knew his thoughts were fuzzy, but wondered if he should tell her he didn't *have* a sister. He said nothing.

The nurse left the room as a young woman came in and stepped up to the bed. She was tall and lithe and stunningly beautiful with straight blond hair that cascaded down her back. She wore a dark businesslike pencil skirt with a simple white blouse. She looked young to Buster, thinking she couldn't be more than 19 or 20 years old.

The girl leaned over the bed and kissed him on the cheek. "Are you doing okay?"

Buster Caisson was befuddled. He knew he had been concussed, and knew that his brains might be a little scrambled ... but for the life of him he couldn't place this girl.

"Do I know you?" he asked stupidly.

She smiled widely at the question, showing perfectly aligned white teeth and dancing blue eyes. "Apparently not," she said, putting one of her hands gently on his uninjured shoulder. He felt her radiating a kind of calm, pure energy, a tranquility that needed no words. Feeling the light touch of her hand on his shoulder, he smiled.

"I just wanted to come by and make sure you were okay," she said. "I'm sorry you got hurt."

"Thank you," he said numbly, "I'm ... I'm ...."

"I know," she said, "you're a little confused right now, right?" She had a wonderful smile. "You banged your head when you hit that car, and then you landed on it again on the other side," she said.

"I landed on a car twice?" he asked, confused.

"No, silly," she said, beaming at him. "Your head ... you landed on your *head* again." Her hand was still on his shoulder and felt wonderful.

"You ... know about what happened?" he said.

"I do," she said in a kind voice. "Much badness occurred, but it was necessary."

"Necessary?" he asked dumbly.

"Yes," she answered. "It was a type of ... kindness. An Achron kindness."

"Who are you?" he asked again.

"My name is Sara Valencia," she said. "You are Buster Caisson."

"What ..." he asked, pausing and trying to frame a question, but she silenced him by leaning over and kissing him on the lips. She molded her mouth warmly against his, and as she kissed him she opened her mouth and expelled her breath into Buster Caisson, filling his lungs.

"You'll be fine now," she said, pulling back and still smiling. "We will meet again, Buster Caisson." She smoothed the sheet that covered him and he suddenly felt tired. He closed his eyes ... just for a moment.

When he opened them again, she was gone.

But he felt ... something had changed. He thought about it and realized ... he felt *better*. All over. A *lot* better, in fact.

~~~~

In the same hospital where Officer Buster Caisson was recuperating, the formerly psychotic boy Thor Collock lay in another room. He'd been awake, thinking continuously since they'd brought him in. Presently an official-looking man came in ... maybe a plainclothes police detective or CPS investigator from his looks. He had a thin, hard-angled face. "You're awake," he said.

"Yes," the boy answered. "What can I do for you?"

"Your name is Thor Collock," said the man.

"Yes I am," he answered again. "Who are you?"

"I'm asking the questions here," said the man.

Collock didn't respond. His new ability to think hadn't extinguished his memories. He remembered the things he had done, and shrank at the thoughts. But he also knew something had happened to him ... that he'd been *changed* somehow. It had happened in that dark room at the foster home.

That lawyer had something to do with it.

Thor Collock knew these things ... and his knowledge, together with a new clarity of thought, made him go silent. The man was an apparent government official of some kind. He held power ... power that could be used against Thor Collock, as it had been in the past. He lay silently, gazing up at the man.

"What happened back there in the house?" the man asked.

"Who are you?" Collock asked again.

"I said I was asking the questions."

Collock considered his next words: "Let me put it to you this way: You can tell me who you represent, or what police department or state agency you work for, or you can talk to my lawyer. Pick one."

"You haven't got a lawyer," said the man.

"Not now," said Collock. "But I will have if you don't tell me who you are."

"Department of Child Protective Services," said the thin man.

"CPS," said Thor Collock reflectively. He looked away from the investigator out the window, thinking of the pain, the suffering, the havoc and even death caused to so many children ....

"What happened back there?" said the man again.

"I don't know," Collock lied, "I don't remember. I was unconscious and woke up here."

The thin man with the hard-edged face stared at him: "You don't sound like what your file says you should."

"What does my file say I should sound like?"

"Mean," said the man. "Mean and psycho. Violent and potentially dangerous."

Thor Collock cringed inside. "I'm ... changing," he said.

"I doubt that," said the man, almost sneering.

"Have you ever met me before?" asked Collock.

"I know who you are," he said. "I've read your file."

The boy felt tired as a pervasive sense of shame enveloped him. He closed his eyes at the memories ... memories of bad things he had done. A tear came to the edge of one eye but did not spill onto his cheek.

The CPS investigator stood silently, staring down at him for a long time. Collock allowed himself to drift toward sleep, knowing the man was still there staring ... but didn't care.

The enormity of the things that I have done, the boy thought miserably. *But now ... so much hope. So many things to learn ... good things. And so many people ... people to meet, to know, to help, to love ... and even to teach.*

Presently the man turned and left the room. Collock opened his eyes and heaved a sigh. He put his hands behind his head on the pillow and continued thinking. It was his new favorite thing, *thinking.* He found that he really enjoyed it. In fact, he delighted in it.

He took another deep breath and looked out the hospital window.
The world awaits.

EPILOGUE
A Funeral, a Love, and a Proposal.

The air in Dallas was chill, hinting at the bite to come as fall wended its way toward winter. Gwendolyn Smith O'Connell stood with her parents John and Emily Smith at the gravesite of her brother on the outskirts of the city. Gwendolyn's mother held her arm, weeping softly. Her father on the other side held his arm protectively around his wife's shoulders, his face stoic in the face of tragedy.

They stood silently. A few family members and friends stood with them under the darkening sky as a Baptist minister intoned words of finality. At the end some of the people came to them, awkwardly giving condolences, saying their goodbyes. John and Emily Smith thanked them and stayed, standing silently at the graveside with their sole surviving child Gwendolyn at their side.

As the casket was lowered into the grave Emily Smith sobbed openly. Tears also fell from the set face of her husband, as they did from Gwen's eyes. When it was finished, they held each other as they bade goodbye to Gwendolyn's twin brother Bill, laid forever to rest.

Later, at the home where Bill and Gwendolyn Smith had grown up, Mrs. Smith worked in the kitchen preparing a meal. She still cried quietly, occasionally swiping at her eyes with an apron.

When they sat down at the dining room table that Gwendolyn remembered well from her youth, Mrs. Smith had stopped crying, but her eyes were red from weeping. They tried to chat normally, but the chair where Gwen's brother Bill had sat was glaringly empty.

"I'm sorry," said Mrs. Smith, apologizing for her tears as she wiped at her eyes again.

Gwen reached over and put her hand over her mother's. "There's no reason to be sorry for sorrow," she said quietly, squeezing the hand.

"At least we've still got you," said Emily Smith, sniffling and trying to smile.

"Yes you absolutely do," said Gwen.

"Yes *we* do," said Gwendolyn's father John. "Don't forget about me." He was also trying to smile through his sorrow.

They ate quietly, trying to converse normally: "Did they ever figure out what happened in that small town in Texas?" asked Mr. Smith.

"The news said it was some kind of terrorism," said Gwen. "But then they always say everything is terrorism."

"Well, with that big a bomb going off and a whole SWAT team being wiped out, I don't see how it could be anything else," said her father.

"Yes," agreed Gwendolyn, "but if terrorists are going to blow something up, I don't see why they'd aim at someone's farm house in the middle of nowhere."

"Maybe they were making a bomb there for somewhere else," suggested her mother.

"That sounds more like it," said John.

Gwen O'Connell stayed silent, then leaned back in her chair. She seemed to have come to a decision: "Mom? Dad?" she said. "I know it's terrible what happened to Bill and that poor girl he was with. I don't understand it and I'm sure you don't either. I don't think anyone ever will."

"Amen," murmured her father.

"Life is for the living," said Gwen's mother, holding back tears again. She knew she would never recover from the loss of her son. "So we just have to carry on."

"And we will," said Gwen, holding her mother's hand again. "In fact, there's something I want to tell you both."

"Oh?" said Emily.

"Yes," said Gwen, "I want you to know that I have been proposed to ... by a man I've been dating for some time. He's in New Hampshire."

"And we've never met him?" asked Mrs. Smith, sounding nonplussed. "You've never mentioned him to us?" She shook her head in reproach, then added, "I mean, it's wonderful if you like him ... but *who is he*? And how do you intend to respond to the proposal?"

"I haven't responded yet," said Gwen with a crooked grin, "but I'm going to. And I haven't told you about him and I'm sorry ... but there's a reason for it."

"We're all ears," said her father, sounding dubious.

"Well, first of all *he's a wonderful guy*," said Gwendolyn, "but he's kind of ... famous. And you know I've been concentrating on my legal career ...."

"Oh that's all right," said Emily Smith, squeezing her daughter's hand back. "Tell us about him!"

"Well, like I said, he's kind of ... famous," Gwen repeated.

"A movie star or something?" asked her father.

Gwen smiled. "No, nothing like that ... but you do know who he is—everyone does—and I didn't want to alarm you by telling you we were dating ... until I knew for sure. So he and I agreed to keep our romance a secret ... for several years in fact."

"Well don't keep us in suspense!" said her father with exasperation. "Tell us who the lucky famous guy is!"

"Herbert Laflorrie," said Gwen, looking guilty. "The kind-of-wealthy businessman ... the one who moved all his companies from California to New Hampshire?"

Gwen's father froze. Her mother's mouth dropped open.

"*The* Herbert Laflorrie?" her father asked. "The near-*trillionaire*? The one who built that giant ... *thing*, in New Hampshire?"

"The crazy rich man who lives in the mountains in New Hampshire?" said her mother. "In the middle of nowhere? *That* Herbert Laflorrie ... has asked you to marry him?"

"Yes indeed," said Gwen, "*that* Herb Laflorrie." She paused, grinning at both her mother and father: "So I guess you *do* know who he is ... and that kind of explains why we wanted to keep our relationship under wraps ...."

"What are you going to do?" asked her father.

Gwen grinned happily across the table at her father: "I'm going to accept! But only if Herb comes and asks for your approval first. I've been thinking of making a life with him, and now ... losing Bill, it has made up my mind. My career is important to me ... but what's it worth without love, family and children?"

"Well I don't care who he is," said Gwen's father sternly. "You can't accept until he comes and talks to me first! He has to ask me for your hand in marriage! I *am* your father, after all, and I don't care how many billions of dollars he has!" He grinned in mirth as he spoke.

Gwen smiled back: "Of *course* dad! I'll insist on it! Besides, Herb has wanted to meet you both for some time. It was me who made him wait."

Her father beamed while her mother asked, "Just to be clear, is this the Mr. Laflorrie we see on the news all the time? The one always being attacked by the TV networks and newspapers? And the politicians?"

"Yep," said her daughter with a chuckle, "that's my boyfriend Herb!"

Mr. and Mrs. Smith looked sideways at each other. Her father appeared on the verge of bursting into laughter, but his wife still looked uncertain. "Well," she asked, "will you and Mr. Laflorrie want to have children?"

"*Herb,* Mom, just call him Herb. And yes, absolutely, *definitely* we're going to have children! *Lots of them.* He and I have already talked about it!"

"Well, at least there'll be plenty of money to raise them with," said her father wryly.

"You'll be part of it too, mom and dad ... if you want to that is. Grandparents are important!"

"You must bring him here so we can meet him," said Gwen's mother.

"I will, and soon!" she said. She didn't mention that Herb Laflorrie had proposed to her several times over several years, and she had turned him down each time. She smiled in her own mind: *Herb, you're about to get lucky.* She giggled. "I'll bring him here so you can see if he's acceptable!"

The next day, Gwendolyn O'Connell, staff attorney with the Individual Justice Foundation, said goodbye to her parents outside of Dallas She promised to call often, and to bring her boyfriend home to meet them soon, then headed for the airport where she would catch a flight back to Pennsylvania. She would stay in the home of David and Meghan

McLaughlin until the charges of attempted rape against the local district attorney played out. That was a detail she had decided not to worry her parents about.

On the way to the airport Gwen rang up Herb Laflorrie. He was at the Gorham Arcology in New Hampshire.

"Hello darling," said Herb, somewhat subdued. He knew about the death of Gwen's brother, and about the funeral. "How can I be of help to you?"

"I'm on the freeway in Dallas heading for the airport, Herb. I've just buried my poor brother, and I'm headed back to Winston this afternoon. I'll be staying there while the legal situation plays out. But I'm okay."

"Good," he said. "I'm sorry about your brother ...."

"Thank you," she said somberly. "However, there is one more thing you could do for me ...."

She left it hanging in the air, but Herb Laflorrie jumped in immediately: "Whatever you need or want! You know I'll do it and you know I'm yours when you want me!"

"Hah!" she scoffed. "Don't say you will until you hear this."

"Your wish is my command, babe, I'm all ears."

"Well then," she said, sounding shy. "Do you mind if ... I mean could you ... like ... would you consider ...."

"Holy Spanish Mackerel," said Herb Laflorrie in mock exasperation. "Would you spit it out girl?"

"Uh ... will you marry me, Herb?"

Silence came from the other end of the phone. "You're toying with my heart, Gwen," he said. "That's not nice ...." But she knew better, she could hear mirth in his voice.

"No," she answered, "not this time, Herb. And when I get back into your arms, I'll prove it ... by toying with something other than your heart." She giggled as she said it.

The famous and unpredictable Herbert Laflorrie burst into laughter. "Really?" he asked. "You mean it? I mean, of *course* I'll marry you! But you know how many times you turned me down when I asked ...."

"I understand, my love," she said. "And I'm sorry ... but how about now?"

"You know you don't have to marry me to have my love," he said seriously. "You know you've already got it."

"Knock that shit off Herb!" she snarled, teasing him. "If you don't say yes right now, I'll come up there and *force* you to!"

He laughed out loud again: "*Yes* is the answer, Gwen, and you knew it would be! But why now? The last time I asked ... which was about the fifth time if I remember correctly, you told me *fuck off!*"

"I did not!" Gwen protested. "I never said that! I just said ... um, *not right then*. But now ...."

"Yeah?" prompted Herb. "But? Now? *What?*"

"Well, my twin brother's passing has concentrated my mind for one thing," she said. "But there's other stuff too, and you need to know you're part of it ... because I love you." She paused. "We've got a lot to talk about, Herb, and I want you holding me in your arms when we do."

"I'm all for that," said Laflorrie, "but if I'm holding you in my arms I might not be able to control myself!" He made himself sound plaintive.

Gwen laughed: "*Oh you big oaf!* When I get there I'm gonna *gobble you up*! And there are lots of things I want to tell you too. Things about ... me."

"Serious time together and serious talk?" Herb said. "I'm still all for it. We can do it in bed I hope. Can we snuggle?"

"Yes, that for sure!" she said, giggling again. "But lots of talking too ... if we can pause from whatever else we're doing ...." She snickered. "I have lots of things to share with you, my love."

"I know you do!" he said happily. "So when will you be up?"

"Can't tell yet," she said. "But I'll call you every day. I'm fighting with the local political goons in Winston and it's not clear how long it's going to take. But I'll *come* to you, one way or another, every night."

"Your body!" he said with mock eagerness. "I want your body not your voice on a phone!"

"You may get more than what you're asking for," she said meaningfully. "And don't forget my mind. I have a mind too ... but, oh what the hell! You can have all of me. I'm yours! We'll drink wine and champagne!"

"I'm up for all of that!" he said. "You are my love Gwendolyn. You know that."

Gwen grinned into her phone: "Well I just decided I want you just as much as you want me," she said. "I want you, I need you, and I don't want to lose you. The question I have is *do you still want me?*"

"Of course I do, Gwen, you *know* that and you've always known it," he said. "And when you *come* up here we'll talk about whatever you want ... in great, intimate detail."

"Agreed," she said. "And I can't wait ...."

"Bye then, Love," he said.

"Bye yourself," she said. "I love you," and smooched into the phone before cutting the call.

A voice came into her brain. It was #218, the Achron TI formerly known in its human incarnation as ... William Hamilton Smith.

"*So,* it said, *are you going to have some human kids?*"

"*Absolutely yes,*" she responded.

"*It's about time,*" came the voice. "*What brought you to it ... finally?*"

"*Oh Bill,*" she said, "*you know perfectly well. Mom and Dad are so sad, they're just devastated.*"

"*I know,*" the voice answered somberly, "*but it doesn't mean you ... have to get married, or have human children.*"

"*True,*" she answered, "*but Mom and Dad aren't getting any younger, and we owe them; they're such kind and generous people, and they've been such good parents to us ....*"

"*All true,*" #218 agreed. "*So ... you will give them grandchildren?*"

"*Yes, absolutely,*" she thought. "*A bunch of them in fact. It's a part of life that some humans are neglecting ... as you may have noticed.*"

"*Mom and Dad will be over the moon,*" it thought back to her.

"*Yes,*" she thought. "*And you could be one of them, Mister number 218.*"

"*Unsure,*" it thought back, "*I need to spend some time thinking. But I do like being human ... and it will be a great kindness to John and Emily.*"

"*Yes it will*"

"*Does Herb know?*" came the question. "*Uh ... about you?*"

"*Not sure,*" she thought back. "*I haven't said so, not explicitly. He may suspect, but he's definitely going to find out. It wouldn't be fair to him any other way ... and besides, he's a good guy. He'll be fine. It's part of my allure I think, him suspecting but not knowing.*"

"Be hard for him not to suspect, given all the time you two have spent together," #218 responded, *"including those umm ... compromising positions."*

"ALL positions," she sent back emanating human mirth. *"I just hope he takes it okay and doesn't freak out."*

"Acknowledged," came the final thought. A tinge of amusement leaked through from #218 as it broke off.

Gwen O'Connell smiled as she drove: *I'm very, very lucky,* she thought, *and I'm very, very happy.*

And that is the end of the story—for now.

AFTERWORD:
Remarks from Algerine Onyx
ABOUT US ACHRONS
NOW ... ABOUT YOU HUMANS
THE ACHRON WAY
ABOUT EVERYTHING ELSE

Okay, look ... I know you're wondering: *What about the ...* **thing**, *the one that wrote this?* Among my own kind, I'm known as "Number 5" (because that's my instantiation number), but I have taken the pen-name of *Algerine Onyx* ... and I'm a storyteller!

Sooo ... let's talk.

To start off, let me tell you that like some of the characters in this book, I'm a Transitioned Intelligence, formerly of the species *Achron*. We come from a star located near what you humans call the *Pleiades Cluster,* which is about 420 light years from earth.

After giving it a lot of thought and watching you humans, I decided I want to be a storyteller. It's a pastime you all seem to love, both in the telling and listening. Think about it: Storytelling for humans goes right back to your *beginning*, probably back to the invention of language itself. (And who knows? Maybe even *before* that.)

I mean, what do you think proto-humans did as they sat in caves around their protective fires? (A tool your species learned to use early-on, and *well done!*) Back then there were dinosaurs and pterodactyls and shit outside your cave with real bad *juju* ... right outside your cave! And they wanted to *eat* you! (That's a joke by the way: Humans weren't around when the dinosaurs roamed ... but there *were* animals that could and WOULD eat you ... *they were* on the scene.)

So in order to survive, you sat around cavefires! And while you were, what do you think you did to pass the time? You told *stories* of course! (As in, *duh!*) That's one of the reasons I want to be a storyteller: I grok the fact that you love stories ... it's in your DNA so-to-speak. It also just so happens that I've got some pretty good stories to tell (which is why I got in touch with my human friend Mr. Condon and hired him to help me with my writing career).

More about me: Like I said, my instantiation number is "5," so I came into existence here on earth pretty early-on after #1 got here. (That also means that I've never visited my home planet, but *whatever*, you know?)

My man Condon has advised me to take a peek out of the closet and talk directly to you a little about myself. So here I am: Permit me to run my non-existent mouth for a moment or two. After all, "you've probably got questions," and I've probably got answers.

ABOUT US ACHRONS

Your first questions are probably about my species. (Hopefully the questions won't be like the half-bright President in the movie *Independence Day*: *"Why are you here? What do you want from us?"* Oh please, that is *so* Hollywood.)

Nevertheless, the answers to *those* questions are, in order, *"One of us happened to stumble into your galactic neighborhood"* and *"not much."*

That is, we don't want anything *in particular* from you. It's just that ... well, *damn! You exist!* Not only that, but you're *sentient!* That's *more* than cool! And I'll tell you why in a minute.

First, let me give you, some background information: Understand that there's a fair amount of life in our galaxy—you *do* know that the Pleiades Cluster is part of the Milky Way, *right?*—and consciousness is pretty rare. Sentient consciousness is rarer still ... and the distances in our galaxy (and space in general) are so huge that discovery of a new, full-blown (not partial) sentience is a *big* deal.

That would be you.

All of which means we Achrons are inclined to ... well, really be *curious* about you humans. We want to be your friends! (Okay, you could say *that* is part of "what we want from you." ... but it's not that much different from "not much".)

On the other hand, as you may have noticed from the story you just read—you *did* read the *story*, didn't you?—Achrons are *quite different* from humans. And *differenter still* (invented-word joke) in our Transitioned Intelligence format.

All this means there can be, um, *misunderstandings* between us ... ones that can result in damage and *deaths*, of humans at least, including lopping off appendages, blowing shit up, and so forth. Of course, those only happen on occasion ... and when they do, they occur because, *after all*, humans and Achrons are two different species!

So naturally we're gonna differ (like *duh again*)!

Our differences arise not only because we're different species, evolved on different planets—and were thus subject to radically differing evolutionary processes—but also because we unavoidably come from different *cultures*.

Or, to put it differently: "Aliens can be really, uh ... *alien.*" (That's the way one of your science fiction writers put it, and it's true.)

In any event, since the idiots in Hollywood got it all wrong in *Independence Day*, let me help out now: A better first question to put to us would be *"WHO are you?"* rather than *"Why are you here?"* (I mean, why is anyone anywhere, you know? Everybody's got to be *somewhere*, even if it's someplace like *Haiti* or *Nigeria* or *California* (to name three places you don't want to be).

So with the correct question asked—*"Who are you?"*—I'm glad to respond like this: *We are Transitioned Intelligences, i.e. reformatted sentient beings, formerly of the biologic species Achron, from a planet in a star system somewhat over 400 light years from earth.*

When (and if) you humans go spacefaring (interstellar stuff, not hanging out nearby in LEO or on your moon), you'll find that virtually all sentients you encounter will be TI's. Why? Because the end result of evolving at or near the bottom of planetary gravity wells—as almost all of us did—doesn't lend itself to living in the deadly, lightless, weightless, gravityless vacuum of the unfriendly skies of space (another joke; this one was a play on words from one of your old TV ads).

Take Achrons, for instance: We evolved in the atmospheric envelope of a gas giant planet in the area of the Pleiades Cluster where there are thousands of stars. And while our stars tend to be quite a bit younger than your own sun, we were fortunate enough to have evolved really fast once we got to a certain point. That is once ... we became conscious and sentient. (*"Got sentience?"* Another play on words from another of your advertising campaigns ... *great fun!*)

However, unfortunately for you humans, attaining sentience wasn't enough. In fact, things not only didn't speed up (evolutionarily speaking) for you, they got more ... *complicated,* more *restricted,* more *ugly* when you got conscious and sentient. It actually *slowed down* your development (which truly sucks). Why? Because you have an unfortunate evolutionary history, and that process caused you to use your newfound sentience to start quarreling, fighting, conquering, enslaving, stealing and killing ... and when language came along, *lying.*

In short, getting conscious and sentient caused you humans to start acting like a planet-sized bucket of crabs. (And you know what *that* means.)

But back to us Achrons. You probably also want to ask this: *What did Achrons look like?* In our natural pre-transition state. (On our home planet and "*in the wild*" so to speak.)

Well, this is kind of interesting: I'd have to say that Achrons mostly resemble giant versions of ... *jellyfish* on earth. Except we floated in a planetary atmosphere instead of in liquid oceans like yours do. The fact that we're atmosphere-dwellers means it was comparatively easy for us to figure out how to move around and link up with each other.

In addition, the resources Achrons needed to survive and thrive were pretty much, uh, *utterly abundant, and* easily accessible. So we didn't have to engage in any kind of struggle for survival as we evolved ... like you humans did. Nor did we have anything trying to *eat* us. So that was nice.

All those facts were key to quickly accelerating our evolutionary process once we got our bodily bells and tentacles—think *jellyfish* again—up to speed with the phenomenon of sentience (it happened rather quickly, as those things go).

When that happened, it didn't take much time to figure out how to physically link multiples of our kind together to multiply our newfound intelligence. How? Well, in human terms think of a computer that can link up with any number of *other* computers, each running its own *millions* of chips, with each chip having *zillions* of cores. I kid you not ... it was as easy as that. (Humans are beginning to engage in a primitive form the same process ... it's called *the Internet).*

So once we figured out how to cooperate and link up to boost our IQ, which was pretty quick, we started addressing and figuring out the normal issues that rapidly evolving species generally do: *What is consciousness, and what is its nature? What is matter, and how does it relate to light and gravity? How do you bypass the speed limitations inherent in light? What is gravity, and how do you control it? How do you manipulate matter down to the quantum level and below? How do you discover, access and utilize different dimensions? And how do you model, manipulate, replicate, and extend intelligence?* (Just to name a few.)

More importantly, once we Achrons started to link, replicate and expand our intelligence, we also learned how to copy, accelerate and encapsulate sentience and intelligence in new substrates (e.g. a virtually indestructible subatomic structure).

What does all this mean? It means Achrons eventually mastered the incredibly cool realm of *subspace interstices* ... and once *that* happened, it was Katy-bar-the-door for our species (the same might have happened for you humans too except for your ugly inherent nature which seems to have prevented it ... no offense intended).

Keep in mind that even though Achrons didn't evolve at the bottom of a planetary gravity well, we were still woefully ill-equipped to head out into space. But once "all of the above" occurred, and Transitioning became possible, we had a species-wide discussion about whether we really needed or wanted to "do that."

Thanks to our environment, evolutionary history, and resulting biology, the logic was clear and consensus was easy: The solution was for any Achron who wanted to Transition to *go ahead and do* so ... and for those who didn't want to, they didn't!

The result? A minor but significant percentage of our planetary population opted to "re-format" into the TI state, and that was hunky-dory with everyone else (which is a typical Achron outcome).

You've got another question, I can tell: You're wondering, *What's Transitioning?* The answer is that it's a fundamental physical transformation of a sentient life-form (as if that made any sense).

In other words, when you Transition, you *don't look like what you looked like before.* The process involves "transitioning" (*duh* again!*) so as to take advantage of a different, um ... *format* to host your consciousness and sentience ... and thus intelligence.

Put another way, your *consciousness* (which is created, or "hosted" by your "mind")—and which is the foundation of sentience—gets re-formatted in a manner that allows it to reside on/in a different substrate ... different from the one that evolution provided.

Which is a pretty good deal if you can pull it off.

As a side-observation, you humans might *really* benefit from the Transitioning process, as it might afford you a far superior substrate to house your sentience ... which isn't hard to imagine, since your current consciousness results from a sloppy, sloshing, messy soup of largely randomly interacting chemicals.

But that's another story. In the meantime, let's just say humans are saddled with both an unfortunate biology and an unfortunate evolutionary history.

What? You have another question? You want to know what it's like? To *Transition*? It's no big secret, once you understand it (*nothing's* a big secret once a species gets to a level where it can do Transitions). You'll see ... *maybe.* Those of you who decide to try it out ... and those of you who are *invited*, of course. (If any of you *are* invited.)

Now, one more thing about Transitioning: At this point no human has Transitioned, so we don't *really* know how it will, ahem, *work out* ... if at all. However, it's reasonable to expect that the process will ... *probably* work (for some of you anyway).

If the TI process works out as advertised (as it has for other successful species), you won't lose knowledge, memory, personality or any of the other stuff you carry in your current brains ... and that's something that worries us. The process preserves what we call an individual's ... *essence*, and there are some facets of you humans that aren't so great (*more about that below*).

It's possible also that once humans have the ability to Transition, they may be able to surmount their evolutionary history and the ... mindset that goes with it.

But since no human has done one yet, we'll have to find out for sure in the future. (Would *you* care to *volunteer? Hmmm?*)

My own opinion? I think you may be happily shocked by the Transitioning process. True, you may find that it results in humans changing to the point where they're ... not exactly human anymore—at least not in the way you are now—meaning that you may turn out to be *more human* and *better human* than before.

That's a paradox, I know. It's kinda complicated.

But not to worry! Once we Achron TI's help you humans do a few proof-of-concept Transitions—*if* we do, that is, and ... *if it works*—the lucky individuals who do it will *love* being freed from your current unstable form of consciousness (in some ways, think *"mental illness"*).

Another thing I want to emphasize: *No one ever gets Transitioned*—at least not by us Achrons—*without agreeing to it.* To do otherwise would be unethical by our lights, no matter how much of a gift we think it might be. (That's the way we roll ... it's part of *"The Achron Way."*) In fact, there are records of species who were *offered* the gift of Transitioning ... and they declined. Which is fine. You humans can make the same choice if you want.

But I digress. All you need to know right now about us Achrons is this: *We come in comedy! And also kinda come in peace!*

Oh. You're wondering about the people we've already maimed and killed. Like, *what's up with that,* right? Understandable. Well, the fact is you're a really ugly species in several ways. We don't like those nasty parts of you, and when faced with egregious examples of it, we tend to react ... sometimes violently.

Now be aware ... we don't *blame* humans for being the way you are (and a couple of your imperfections are real *doozies*). It's just an unfortunate part of your evolutionary history, and we can't blame you for *that* ... right?

On the other hand, though, Achrons aren't inclined to give you a pass just because of that history. It doesn't stop us from seizing upon ... um, *teachable moments* so to speak.

Think of *Amos Tucklee* ... exploding as he was being beaten to death. Or Mrs. Newton losing her hand (the missing hand, by the way, is in a stasis field for safekeeping, and may even be returned to her in the future ... if she's smart enough to reflect, learn and change).

The takeaway here is that we Achrons have a strongly held moral code, and crossing it tends to offend us. You can think of us as just another type of "cultural diversity" coming into your country ... which *is never a bad thing,* right?

And like some other minorities, Achron TI's also don't care to "assimilate", and we sure as hell aren't "multicultural" in our outlook. We like our own values—aka *The Achron Way*—and we won't hesitate to let you know about it.

So while we may be just another set of "illegal aliens" (that's a joke) who came across your border, we're no more interested in adopting your ways than any other, uh, *illegal aliens.* Besides, like some of the others, we may want to point out to you that *our* culture is a healthy *alternative* or *replacement* for yours.

That's diversity for ya!

On the other hand, relax: Our "Achron Way" isn't as alien as you might think. In fact, it can be pretty much summed up in an old human adage: *"Live and let live"* (honored mostly in the breach throughout your history, but still ...).

Anyhow, back to the mass-Transition that occurred on the Achron home planet after we had that planet-wide discussion. After it was resolved that a certain number of Achrons wanted to Transition, the next question was ... *anybody wanna go exploring?* You know, as in "out there"?

Not everyone who chose to become a TI also chose to go exploring in space. For one thing, it gets *really* lonely out there, partly because the distances are so damned big. In fact, they're outright *humongous.* So only some Achron TI's chose to "head out there"... while many others did not.

As it happens, one Achron TI who *did* decide to explore is the one we refer to here on earth as "#1" (it has a name, but not one translatable into any sound you humans can detect ... and you wouldn't be able to understand it if you could).

Yes, it was #1 who happened to detect human light, radio, electronic and other emissions a number of light years out.

Just by chance!

The rest, as they say, is going to become history.

So don't mind us. We'll try not to be too obtrusive, and will even eschew contact in many instances. However, I've got to be honest here too: Be careful how you act around us, *including* how you treat your fellow human beings. (We happen to agree with what a small but not insignificant percentage of humans believe, so they won't be in danger ... but the others, well, they need to think about the *do unto others* rule, you know?)

To sum up, none of the Achrons on earth (there are a few hundred of us running around at this point) are in our original biological format. Because spacefaring originally made it necessary, and because the process of *instantiation* requires it also ... we're all TI's.

Even though we're not giant floating jellyfishes anymore, we're still, like ... *rah rah* for the home team (or *species*, if you will)! You know how you tend to root for your home sports team even after you've moved away? Well that's what I'm talking about from an Achron species perspective.

As for our original home planet ... you are wondering: *Are there still "original format" Achrons there?* Oh sure! Lots of 'em! And if you humans play your cards right—that is, if you don't blow yourselves up and don't offend us enough to drop you like a bunch of hot-ass potatoes—you may eventually get to meet them.

Of course, that would be well after you learn to do Transitioning yourselves.

If you do.

NOW ... ABOUT YOU HUMANS

Enough about us Achrons! Let's talk about you humans. Which bring us to ....

Your FIRST Big Problem as a Species

I want you to understand that I want to be ... *diplomatic* in this discussion. But I also want to speak frankly. These words aren't intended to offend, but we do need to face one big-ass *fact:* Human beings as a species are ... well, *assholes* (to put it in vulgar but common parlance).

Oh! Did I offend? Have you been *"triggered"?* Well don't bother asking for a safe space and a teddy bear to hug. I'm just trying to talk straight with you, and honesty is usually the best policy. (See? I *told* you we were like you ... well, *some* of you and in *some* ways at least.)

Achrons are like that: We deal with the truth in a straightforward manner as we see it, with as much accuracy and clarity as we can muster.

What about *Achrons in the TI format?* Even more so.

So here's what's up with you humans from our perspective: You are saddled with an extremely unfortunate evolutionary history, one that made you into what you are. It is characterized by short lifespans, ubiquitous confusion, continuous turmoil, lots of pain, abundant suffering ... *and then you die.*

But that's only the beginning: Like Tom Hobbes said, throughout history your lives have tended to be "solitary, poor, nasty, brutish and short." (That's still the case in many parts of the world ... and what you'd expect from a species with some very ugly predilections.)

Why is that? It results from an evolutionary process that featured a perpetual shortage of resources and thus an unending vicious competition to survive. That coupled with striking biological fragility (thus making you pretty easy to kill and eat) made life for early humans ... *pretty damned tough.*

Physically at least. Mentally it's even worse.

The fact that you have to die at all, *and you know it*—much less that you often have to suffer before doing so—is terribly sad. We Achron TI's sorrow for you over that reality. It makes us ... not *pity* you exactly, but it does impel us to give you, well, *allowances* in light of your species' biological history and current reality.

Because of the evolutionary process you suffered, humans tend to be vile, grasping, violent, ignorant, envious, murderous, lying, backward, close-minded ... and just plain *savage.* Even now! The tough evolutionary process you were subjected to made you that way (some would quip, "it sucks to be you" ... but that would be harsh).

The reality of you humans—where you came from and what you are—is one reason your religions generally feature a promise of some type of eventual surcease. That is, either an end to suffering while you're still alive (if you can make the cut to nirvana), or maybe after you're dead (and can make the cut to heaven).

This is also why so many religions teach that human beings are fundamentally "flawed," or just plain *evil* in one way or another. They're right. The concept of "original sin." The wheel of suffering. The path to nirvana. The way to enlightenment. *"All are sinners."*

The list goes on and on ... and for good reason.

Put succinctly, for humans "life sucks." (*Sorry about that. Am I being too frank?*)

The good news is this: *It doesn't have to be that way* (more later on this).

So as we Achron TI's see it, your tough evolutionary history is the reason for your burden of suffering. That process bequeathed you two astonishingly ugly characteristics that we find truly appalling. The first is that ... *you crave power.* You just really *lust* after it! Many humans spend their entire *lives* seeking to accumulate it ... and when you get power, boy do you just *love using it on other people.*

More specifically, *you love using power against your fellow human beings.* You tend to ceaselessly seek *power over others* in virtually every context and environment. You love that power far, *far* too much, and the situation is made worse by what you use it for, i.e. to kick around your fellow humans.

Think about it: What does human history consist of? What is the story of your species, going right back to the beginning? It's about a ceaseless struggle to survive and prevail which shows up as strife, war, lies, betrayal, violence, struggle, death and ubiquitous destruction (aka lives that were overwhelmingly "solitary, poor, nasty, brutish and short").

All because of the limited-resource environment you evolved in.

It got even worse when you figured out how to turn your vicious nature toward the formation of entities that enabled *really* large-scale accumulation and projection of power: You invented *governments!* And *empires!* And organized *militaries!*

When it came to power-accumulation and power-projection, the *State* became the name of your game.

We know this because your history shows that from the very beginning of "modern man" you were scurrying about creating all types of "governing structures" to exert power over others. That's why so much of your ancient history is taken up with stories about wars, states, governments, dictators, kings, and empires.

To review, consider the squabbling Sumerian city-states (c. 4,000 B.C.); the Sun God hydraulic dictatorships of ancient Egypt (c. 3,000 B.C.), the Hittites, the Assyrians and the Mitannis at around the same time; the Akkadian Empire (peaking between 2,400 and 2,200 B.C.); Alexander the Great and the Greek Imperium; the Roman Empire and its subsequent collapse into the Middle Ages; the subsequent European monarchical "divine right of kings"; the Ottoman Empire; Napoleon and the French Empire; the British Empire; the Russian Empire (aka the U.S.S.R.)... and more recently the American Empire (although it generally isn't called that).

All of which is just the *Westen* part of humanity's story. Let's not forget the East, from Ankor Wat in Cambodia (whoever they were, and however they built that astonishing city), the earliest Chinese Xia Dynasty (c. 2,070 to 1,600 B.C.), and right up to communist China in the 20th century and the government that emerged in the late 20th and early 21st century. Not to mention the largely *unknown* civilizations and empires ... including the Aztecs, the Mayans, the Incas and others.

War, war, war. Blood, blood, blood. Savagery, savagery, savagery.

And what do all those ancient-to-modern historical examples have in common? *Organized power*, expanded through political campaigns utilizing martial power—organized violence in the form of *militaries*.

It's what you humans have always been *about*.

Throughout your history you've always seized on the most efficient way to aggregate power, and then used the results against other peoples. This human psychopathy has led to an absolute *panoply* of autocratic tyrannies. Each had a hand in killing part of the *millions*—no *billions*—of fellow human beings across the centuries.

As I say, we Achrons find you in many ways to be ... *appalling*. But it's your world, and it's what you are. We're just visiting for the time being.

The above historical facts mean that the most expert and aggressive— can we stipulate *"psychopathic"?*—human beings generally ended up being your greatest leaders. The number of words you have to describe apex human power-aggregators are endless: Kings, Queens, Pharaohs, Potentates, Masters, Barons, Dictators, Dukes, Shoguns, Counts, Kaisers, Overlords,

Caliphs, Fuhrers, Emperors, Countesses, Sultans, Princes, Khans, Czars and Czarinas. *The list goes on and on.*

So from our standpoint, you kinda suck.

Worse yet, human power-seeking and power-wielding isn't limited to any given time or locale, and it's not limited in *magnitude.* Your abusive power-seekers appear in *every single human era, in every single institution,* not just in politics, governments and empires.

Consider every human institution, no matter how small, from neighborhoods (like the one the McLaughlins lived in), to towns and cities (like Winston), to business organizations (ever heard of "office politics"?), to educational institutions (academic power struggles are among the most vicious), to the military (no explanation needed), to even *religious* institutions (think about the *huge* list of religious wars, right up to and including the present).

In contrast to the psychopaths who devote their lives to gaining and exercising power over others ... there are always people who just want to be left alone. But historically, in human terms *"that ain't gonna happen."*

Most of you won't let other people alone!

Even in the smallest groups of humans, you manage to conjure up conflict through your endless power-seeking and endless dick-measuring (uh ... sorry). Do you know what a "busybody" is? Or a "gossip" (you were warned about them even in the Bible)? They're ubiquitous among humans.

In today's world? Have you ever heard of "condo commandos"? If you ever lived in a condominium, you'd know about them. How about infighting and power-struggles in *church* congregations? But of course! Children's sports teams? It gets *ugly,* especially when parents muscle their way in (as they always do) and get in fights (as they often do) ... *over nothing.*

The result? A very substantial percentage of humans loudly and proudly exhibit quite ugly characteristics, like *pointless aggression, antagonistic arrogance, abject dishonesty, belligerent cynicism, bald-faced lying,* and plenty of other forms of *hubris, hypocrisy, bellicose ignorance, belligerent narcissism, aggressive stupidity, abject venality and ... just, plain, viciousness.*

All in the name of *power.*

It's in your biology, I'm sorry to say ... and *biology is destiny* (to coin another phrase). Short answer? You humans got the short end of an evolutionary stick ... even if you *have* become nominally conscious and sentient.

All of the above is in large part why humans—besides being a considerably older species than Achrons—haven't advanced very much or very quickly as a species. If you weren't burdened with the ugly propensities outlined above, you probably would have landed on the moon several thousand years ago, learned to Transition by then or even earlier, and spread throughout your part of the galaxy by now ... like some of the more, um, *civilized* species have done.

On the other hand, how could you be expected to have accomplished much, given your ... peculiar situation? In the face of natural limitations mandated by your evolutionary biology, including your blind aggression and viciousness, you haven't really done all that bad. Especially considering that your ugliest characteristics have almost always been put in the service of destructive power (i.e. war, strife, violence and mandated ignorance)... and you have accordingly suffered for it.

Your SECOND Big Problem as a Species

But wait! There's another *Bad Thang*, something almost as bad as what I explained above (read "ranted about"): As if your inherent power-lust isn't enough, there's a *second* ugly characteristic you humans abundantly display. Simply put, **The truth is not in you** (to coin yet another phrase). Or put another way, "*humans lie all the time.*"

In our view, this is your Second Major Shortcoming. Again, there's a reason why most of your great religions and religious leaders have addressed the question. They've told you *don't lie* or *stop lying*! (Why? They all knew that *lying and other forms of untruth hold you back*!)

But did you listen? As a species? Do you even listen now? *Of course not!*

When species attain consciousness and sentience, most of them quickly invent language and start communicating with one another. All the better to share information and thus *advance* together as a species. It often happens pretty quickly, as it did for us Achrons.

But you humans? When some lucky pre-hominids enjoyed a fortuitous mutation or two (like those that increased your brain size and allowed your neocortex to expand, or the one that changed the shape of your neck anatomy to allow *speech*), the evolutionary (and revolutionary) result was not only dawning sentience but also the invention of language.

So what did you do with language once you invented it? *You used it to more efficiently seek and seize power over others!* You used it to organize aggressive exclusionary *tribes, clans, troops, gangs, squads, mobs, factions, sects, denominations, etc.*

Again, that is why you have so many words to describe those kinds of things. And when you got *really good at it* you established "the nation state"… which perforce included governments, bureaucracies, and militaries. Why? So you could better gather, accumulate, organize, maintain and project *power* … so as to better seize, monopolize, utilize and defend scarce resources, including the resources which exist where other peoples live.

Arguably the greatest invention in the entire history of your species, languages have been used by humans almost from the beginning as a way to lie, cheat, deceive, con, scam, dissimulate and bullshit … mainly in the service of your unending power-hunger.

Does that suck or *what?* I mean, why would anyone turn such a nifty, crucial, empowering invention like language toward such ugly ends?

Okay, okay: In your defense, language was bound to be recognized and used as an advantageous weapon in your unfortunate-but-never-ending struggle over always-limited resources.

That's your best excuse, and if that wasn't available to explain your egregious behavior as a species, the Achron TI who discovered you (#1) might have passed you by. Who wants to interface with a hopelessly vicious, unthinking, unreasoning, savage species?

Those two awful shortcomings *would have been* a deal-breaker for us Achrons, *except* …..

Your FIRST BIG Saving Grace as a Species

Except you have two *other* ubiquitous characteristics as a species … and they're simply *wonderful!* They rescue you from being little more than a planetary nest of scorpions. And because of these two saving graces, humans are getting something of a *high-level pass* from us Achrons.

What am I talking about? The first of your saving-grace characteristics as a species is ... *you've got humor! Comedy!* (No, it's not "you've got mail".) It's nothing short of *amazing* (as the French would say, *incroyable!*)

"Big deal," you say?

Au contraire (again as the Frogs say), because *get this*: Interstellar aliens aren't (necessarily) dour and humorless, not at all! Not like those low-class Romulans in *Star Trek* (that's wry humor aimed at the Romulans by the way). Or the big-mouthed, trash-talking Klingons (also a humor-jab). Or the imposing but lovable Wookies in *Star Wars* (who never seem to laugh).

Or even the *truly* scary body-snatchers in the movie ... well, *Body Snatchers*. (Talk about aliens who have no flipping sense of *humor* ...).

And that is the first reason the *Achron TI* known as #1, the one that discovered you and your planet, *didn't pass you by*. You humans are like us! Well, the good parts of you at least. You've got the super-cool, super-rare characteristic of ... *comedy!* Call it *divine comedy* (joke again).

Here's what #1 thought: "*Damned if these silly savages don't have the capacity to laugh! How cool is that!*"

So from Achron TI #1 onward we Achrons have been drawn—to the point of *love!*—*to yo*ur comedy! From Buster Keaton to the Three Stooges to Steve Martin to Jack Benny to John Belushi, to Johnny Carson to Abbott & Costello, to Mel Brooks and *Blazing Saddles* ... *we love it all!*

And that means we're drawn to kinda love you humans too ... in spite of everything. (Wait, I feel a song coming on! It's Ray Charles, crooning, *"We can't stop loooving you ... we've made up our minds .... "*)

You'll find, by the way—when and if you get straight with yourselves and learn a few things—that while life in the galaxy is somewhat hard to find, and real sentience is rarer still ... *a sentient species with a sense of humor is a flippin' JACKPOT! Bonanza!*

Thus our excitement—or rather #1's excitement—when it stumbled on you and saw stuff like *Amos N' Andy, I Love Lucy, Cheers, The Little Rascals,* and *Seinfeld.* From our standpoint, it is to *swoon* ... and #1 just about *did* swoon when he got a load of human comedy.

But get this: Even with your sense of humor and ability to laugh—astonishing for a species as vicious as you—*that's not all!*

There's yet *another* human characteristic that makes you just ... *wonderful* as a species. It's something—as far as Achron TI's are concerned—that puts humans up to the level of a *damned* DOUBLE *jackpot!*

What is this strange thing? Ah! That brings us to ....

Your SECOND BIG Saving Grace as a Species

You have ... *intersexual love!* (Or, as you tend to refer to it, *"heterosexual love".*)

Now, you wouldn't think that a crazy little thing called *LOVE* (I resist breaking into another song) would be that big a thing, right? But when you consider how humans *are* ... how you *act*—and the evolutionary processes that *formed* you ... making you *be* and *do* the things you do (and, I have to add, *doobie, doobie doo*)—well, it's kind of, like *impossible.*

And yet there it is: *You've got love,* humans! And it's the craziest imaginable *kind* of love: What makes it truly astonishing is the existence of human *sexual dimorphism.* Yep. Two sexes, males and females, that appear to be essentially ... *two different species* (except different species can't successfully have babies and you humans *can*).

You've recognized this fact yourselves: One set of you is from *Mars,* while the other is clearly from ... *Venus.*

We Achrons see human sexual dimorphism to be like two repelling ends of two magnets: Biologically, human males and females *should repel each other* (and let's face it, you do so in *sooo* many ways). And yet ... in the face of such a total deal-killer, you *still* manage to talk to each other ... to interact, play nice together, and find love! It's crazy!

Human intersexual love is so incredible that we Achron TI's really stand agog *looking* at you! How the *hell* can you take males and females—again, two different species (figuratively), living on different ends of the galaxy (figuratively)—throw them together, and end up with the incredibly astounding, tender, limitlessly beautiful phenomenon of intersexual *love?*

I mean ... *it's impossible.* And yet, from those improbable facts comes the survival of your species ... which itself is kind of surprising (although it could be worse: Think about the love between a male and female Praying Mantis ... *or don't*).

So I'll say it again: To us Achrons ... *incroyable!* The phenomenon of love between a human male and female puts humans into the galactic *record book* as far as we're concerned.

Look, all this probably sounds sappy to you humans. You live with sexual dimorphism from the day you're born. But Achrons know that love of the type you have is vanishingly rare in the known galaxy. And we honor and ... well, *love* you for it. Not every species is so gifted (or saddled, if you will) with something so precious, rare and incredible.

How have *humans*—vicious and nasty as you are—been given this priceless, impossible gift?

Go. Figure.

We Achrons? What we have is "love" in the sense of *agape* in the ancient Greeks (look it up). But we don't feel anything that even approaches the astounding entwinement between a man and a woman, the awesome explosion of ... *feeling* that accompanies intersexual love (which not infrequently approaches *insanity*).

I gotta say, it almost makes us Achrons *jealous* of you, even with all your rather *glaring* shortcomings. (Achrons don't have sexual dimorphism, by the way; in our original form we reproduced through a process that you would characterize as "budding" or "branching".)

You want to marvel some more over this thing you have? Go read the poem *"Black Marigolds"* (said to have been translated from Sanskrit by an Englishman named E. Powys Mathers).

Go on, go read it now! It's on the Internet and much of it is quoted in John Steinbeck's novel *Cannery Row* (which you should also read ... because it might give you some insight into us Achrons). The fact that a human was able to write such poetry *a thousand years ago* in the 11th century? It blows our Achron TI minds.

The Entwinement of Human Comedy and Love

There's something else I want to take note of (because this just keeps getting better and better): There's a *very* close link between intersexual love and—wait for it—*comedy*.

Oh yes there is! And don't give me any of this "there's nothing funny about love." Can you say *RomCom?* Can you repeat *The Taming of the Shrew?* Can you go back a few thousand years and consider *Lysistrata?* Or classical Chinese and Persian literature and poetry that examine love and comedy? Do you know what Shakespeare called "the beast with two backs"? *Hmmm?*

Comedy has been entwined with heterosexual sex for thousands of years, and suffuses your entire history! *Thousands of years!*

And that's not surprising, given how central and important love and sexual dimorphism are to the survival of your species. So don't try to bull-shit the Achron bullshitter!

Love and sex are wonderful ... and they're also just *funny as can be!*

And we love you for it.

THE ACHRON WAY

But enough about you humans. It's clear to Achrons that you have an un-fortunately ugly, flawed nature. But it's also true that you're an incredibly gifted and wonderful species, especially in view of your humor, laughter and comedy ... not to mention the impossible combination of sexual di-morphism and intersexual love.

Because of the wonderfully positive things about you, we Achrons want to hang out for a time ... despite your, um, *ugliness.* The question is ... can we "help" you? Do we *want* to help you? Do *you* want *us* to "help" you? Or would our "help" be no help at all?

And ... would you rather just be left alone?

Big questions, but I've gotta admit—maybe with some unearned grandiosity—that we may be able to pass on a few helpful truisms to you ... truths that could help nudge you in the right direction. Such as help you become a better species? Help you overcome the shortcomings that have kept you so confined, limited, backward and screwed up for thousands of years?

I'd like to think that Achrons *have something valuable to offer humans.* Of course, whether that turns out to be truly true or not will be up to you to decide. If you think endlessly competing for power is a good way to spend your time—if you even think it's still *necessary* after you have learned some things—and if you find *using* that power *gratifyingly enjoyable* ... you may not be a candidate for *The Achron Way*.

Your power-lust, your incessant lying, your endless obscurantism, your denying, ignoring and even obliterating the truth, it's ... *unnerving*.

And yet ... I'm going to proffer some things that are just natural and commonsensical to Achrons. It's called *The Achron Way*. My hope is that it will help you humans overcome much of your very problematical evolutionary biology and resulting history.

In short, there's something *better* out there.

"The Achron Way" is a series of ... *values*, if you will. Or you might want to call them *steps* or *levels* by which humans can be guided away from their base and ugly propensities.

Have you ever heard of the acronym KGTOKUWE? Of course not. We've just prepared it to help us communicate our ideas to humans. Pronounced as a word, it would probably sound like some North American Indian name, maybe for a lake or river: *Kigtokooway*.

Except it encompasses *The Achron Way*.

The eight letters in the acronym KGTOKUWE consist of what you might call *four couplets*. Call them *"Achron couplets for humans."*

The four *couplets* constitute eight steps "upward" or "forward" designed to help you understand, avoid, and even *end* the two natural negative proclivities which have caused unhappiness and suffering throughout your history. That is, we want to help you address and overcome (1) your lust for power and (2) your natural propensity for avoiding and denying reality (otherwise known as "lying").

The FIRST of the four couplets, the "K" and the "G," consist of the step-values *Kindness* and *Generosity*. More accurately and completely, they mean, *"Kindness and Generosity of Spirit."* The two values, like all that follow, relate largely to your interior world ... to the quality and experiential *mental* reality of being a human being.

Kindness of Spirit comes first, because it is a necessary first step calculated to lead you toward the next step, the emergence of *Generosity of Spirit*. The two are linked (that's why I'm referring to them as "couplets").

The SECOND couplet after *Kindness and Generosity* in *The Achron Way* of KGTOKUWE ... is *Trust* and *Openness*. Like *Kindness* in the first couplet,

Trust is meant as a precursor to *Openness*. Learning and practicing *Trust* will lead you to the value of *Openness*.

But wait! You ask this: *Trust of what? Trust of whom? And why should anyone "trust" anyone else or anything else anyway?* (Especially a bunch of aliens like us Achrons!) The same questions apply when the second step-value emerges in the couplet: When Trust leads one to *Openness ... Openness to what? To whom? And for what reason?* (Aka *"Why should we embrace Openness at all? It's dangerous!"*)

Nebbermind all that (word joke alert). For now at least (more information will be provided with other stories I'll be telling).

The THIRD couplet? After *Trust* and *Openness*? *K* and *U* stand for *Knowledge* and *Understanding*. The same human thought-mechanics apply as with the earlier two couplets: The attainment of *Knowledge* (which naturally follows the attainment of *Trust and Openness)* leads to the second step-value in this third couplet of *Understanding*.

FOURTH couplet? Achrons believe that once a human ascends to the level of *Knowledge and Understanding*—made possible by understanding, appreciating, *knowing* and *living* the first three couplets—it may *(MAY)* be possible to attain the fourth and final set of values in *The Achron Way*, the *W* and the *E*.

The final set of KGTOKUWE step-values is *Wisdom and Enlightenment*. If humans can get there—and at this point we don't really know if you can—it may be possible to rise to a form of human fulfillment that will "transcend" or "fix" the worst parts of your human condition.

If you are able to understand, appreciate, and act/live at the "higher levels" of *Wisdom* and *Enlightenment*, you might—*might*—be able to get past the unfortunate and painful human biological roots bequeathed to you by a tough evolutionary process.

Note, by the way, that the fourth couplet works the same as the first three: The first value of *Wisdom* will enable and lead to *Enlightenment*. Without *Wisdom*, there can be no *Enlightenment*, and only from *Wisdom* does *Enlightenment* emerge.

What do those two words mean? We Achrons see them in a certain way and from a certain perspective. You humans, on the other hand, have been debating and struggling over both concepts for centuries, even millennia. What is *wisdom?* How do you *gain* "wisdom"? What does it mean to be *enlightened?* How do you *attain* "enlightenment"?

My storytelling, both here and in future books, will touch on all these questions in different ways, and will be intended to help answer such questions about each of the step-values along *The Achron Way.*

Understand one thing, however: I'm not here primarily to be a didact. I want to be a good storyteller, that's all. And if some of my stories—all of which touch on the human condition ... well, actually *wallow* in it—explain things about the step-values of *The Achron Way?*

So much the better.

ABOUT KINDNESS

The story I've told here is entitled *Achron Kindness,* so it's logical that I give you some more information about *kindness* ... from an Achron perspective.

Humans define *Kindness* variously, but generally this way: *Of or relating to the status or quality of being "kind."* And you define "kind" through a series of statuses or qualities, e.g. having a nice, considerate, indulgent, mild, gentle, humane or helpful disposition.

From the standpoint of *The Achron Way,* almost all of that is *wrong.* I'm not saying that the human definition of "kind" *opposes* or *contradicts* the Achron notion of *Kindness.* However, *Achron kindness* is something else, something both different and *additional* to your human definitions.

From the Achron TI perspective, *Kindness* is meant to reflect the first step in the process of *changing your outlook* as a human being. It is intended to be the beginning of a journey toward *Enlightenment* (and throughout your history many religions have included the concept of *striving for enlightenment*). So we're hardly at odds there.

But the first step in *The Achron Way* from the perspective of us Achrons is not "kindness" in the sense of "being nice to people" or "giving to the poor" or such. Rather it is mainly an internal psychological orientation *toward oneself and toward others.*

This is one reason we emphasize it as being *"Kindness of Spirit."* It means something more along the lines of: *Fighting against and surmounting the two ugliest characteristics of humanity,* i.e. (1) *the lust for power* and (2) *lying or otherwise rejecting the truth.*

Thus, *Kindness of Spirit* in *The Achron Way* means first and foremost *"Don't seek power over others and don't reject the truth when you see it."* (I know you want to ask, *"How do you know what the 'truth' is?"* That's another subject. It has been debated and discussed *also* for thousands of years by humans.)

Do you need a simpler explanation? Maybe from a *human* perspective? Sure! These aren't exactly *alien* concepts (joke!) ... so how about *"live and let live."* Or *"do unto others as you would have them do unto you."* Or *"mind your own business."* Or even *"the inalienable right to life, liberty, and the pursuit of happiness."*

Do those sayings seem so radical?

Actually, given your history, the concept of *kindness* as we're discussing it—including the aphorisms above—have been *quite* radical at most times (including *today* in many places). Why? Because *most humans just won't leave other people alone* ... and refusing to do so is the *opposite* of *Achron Kindness.*

There's something else I want to point out, so just to be clear: *The Achron Way* has nothing to do with passivity or pacifism. Our values neither suggest nor endorse nor even *contemplate* pacifism in the face of unjust exercise of power.

Nor does it matter whether the power being unjustly exercised is "justly held" or "unjustly held". *It's not the power being held*—i.e. the basis or justification for possessing it—but rather *how that power is used and exercised.*

In this respect, you humans have a hell of a lot to answer for—a *huge* amount to answer for in fact—due to your long and ugly history. So don't think embracing *The Achron Way* means becoming a patsy or a pushover: *Power is power.* You exercise it rightly or you exercise it wrongly.

It just so happens that humans have often—or *usually*, or *almost always*—exercised it wrongfully.

Thus, it is inevitable that good people must always be ready and able to resist unjust exercises of power. This is laid out specifically in America's own Declaration of Independence, and the alternative is to become enslaved and abused (which is the norm throughout most of human history).

So when violence becomes necessary—when it is appropriate and just—it is not contrary to *The Achron Way,* including the opening value of *Kindness of Spirit.* You humans have been resorting to violence for millennia ... it's in your evolutionary bones. So it is inevitable that people will move to counter *unjust* power with the exercise of *just power* if at all possible.

To sum up: *The Achron Way* sanctions neither passivity nor pacifism, much less the acceptances of unjust domination or slavery (which is what happens when pacifism confronts savagery). Even in your ancient history—in ancient Greece for instance—the notion of "pacifism" does not seem to have existed, and since then wise men have warned about the danger of pacifism, from Lord Acton to George Orwell.

The Achron Way agrees, and neither requires nor sanctions the trap of pacifism.

Speaking of *Kindness of Spirit,* consider the story you just read (or at least I *hope* you did): Does it seem to illustrate anything about the Achron conception of *kindness* as presented in *The Achron Way*? Remember Mrs. Harriman Newton III? The elderly woman who called the cops on a little girl's "Lemoade stand"?

Mrs. Newton was acting like a typical human in doing what she did. She *loved* the idea of summoning "force", to be used against someone else (it did not matter who). *That's human nature.* It even gives a dose of *pleasure* to do something like this for many of you.

Mrs. Newton called the police because she derived *pleasure* at the prospect of having formalized police *power* exercised *on her behalf* against the little girl Sarah McLaughlin (although Mrs. Newton did get a little more than she expected in this case). Unfortunately, there was an Achron TI who happened on the scene and get pissed off at what it saw happening.

Will Mrs. Newton ever get her hand back? We Achron TI's have the capability to make that happen ... but it depends: Will Mrs. Newton reflect on what she did? Will she come to understand what she has become in her embittered old age? Will she realize why she did what she did? Will she recognize how and why she interacts with her fellow human beings in the way she does?

Who knows? We may have to wait for a future story to find out ....

Also, let's also not forget that other tragic aspect of human nature, the utter, repeated, confounding rejection of the truth when confronted by it.

One of the first steps in learning *Kindness of Spirit* is to "embrace the truth" and "become truthful ... no matter where it may lead."

Be aware: This doesn't mean using "the truth" (as you see it) as a weapon to attack or hurt other people (which is typically human). It means that you need to recognize and accept the truth when it is presented to you ... including understanding and explaining it where appropriate. It also means changing your *own* outlook when new evidence suggests the truth lays otherwise than you thought it to be.

Got that?

So *Kindness of Spirit* for humans means, first, refraining from lusting after power and the opportunity to exercise it over other people. And second, refraining from ignoring and rejecting (or lying about) the truth, whatever the *truth* may turn out to be.

Actually taking those two steps ... *should it be so hard?* Well, for you humans ... yes, because it means ignoring crucial negative portions of your own nature. It means turning your back on your worst instincts. Your human world is suffused with unjust use of power ... and lies are always put into its service.

This is largely how you ... *exist*.

So take the opportunity to look within yourself ... and take note of what you find there. Then think on it, and consider making some changes for the better.

ABOUT EVERYTHING ELSE

Lest you doubt how much we Achron TI's really like ... well, *some* of you humans, I want to highlight our favorite types. We think they're *terrific!* Who? Well, the kinds of people who like the idea of us Achrons being here.

That would include people who like the unconventional (not to mention *the bizarre*), and who tend to agree with our Achron moral code. (It is a fact that some humans were already several step-values into *The Achron Way* ... even before we got here).

These people will probably want to visit a place we're going to set up in the future. Maybe they'll even want to live there permanently (*fine by us*). The venue will be modeled as a type of *refuge*, and will be available for any humans who want to live according to *The Achron Way* (as well as for Achrons inhabiting humanlike bodies).

Why have an Achron refuge for humans as well as TI's? Well ... how about because of how you live and what you humans face every day? How about because of the way so many of you *act*? Although you're used to it, we're not.

So this kinda *theme park* will be a place for anyone to visit if they want, and for anyone to live permanently also if they want ... so long as they're willing to accept *The Achron Way* and abide by our rules. (No problem *there* ... right? Um ... *right?*)

The Achron refuge, by the way, will be in the United States, and will take up only a tiny corner of it. So not to worry ... *we come in peace!*)

How about the small, sparsely populated, inconsequential state of New Hampshire? (It's way up there in the upper right on the map.) Not even 10,000 square miles, it's a sliver compared to the almost four *million* square miles in the rest of America ... and it already has a pretty good culture (thanks in no small measure to the pioneers of the Free State Project).

But all that is a subject for a future dissertation.

So let's end it with this, my human friends: Because I've always liked your political advertisements—false though they all may be!—let me say this: *My human name is Algerine Onyx and I'm not running for anything. Nevertheless, I told this story and I approved this message.*

Is that my final *anseh*? (As Regis Philbin used to say in his Irish-Italian-Bronx accent on *Who Wants to be a Millionaire?*) No ... not by a long shot it's not.

But it's a good start. :-)

ENDNOTE BY ALIEN LITERARY REPRESENTATIVE

I'm Tim Condon, literary representative of the alien entity known as #5 (also known as Algerine Onyx). I'm much obliged to my alien friend for giving me this opportunity to speak directly to you.

What I want to do—here and at the end of other stories by Onyx that will follow—is share some vignettes from my own all-too-human life. All are true, and all are meaningful to me.

So here's my own story ... .

In late 1977 I was driving across the country from California toward Florida on Interstate 10. I was in an old red Volkswagen bug and all my worldly possessions were in it.

At the close of one day during the trip, I ended up in mid-Texas ... and it was cold as hell. Nine degrees above zero as I remember, and the West Texas wind was blowing. It was the coldest temperature I'd ever be in up to that time.

As the night got darker I pulled off the Interstate and entered a rest area, pulling the VW up close against a concrete curb. There were only a few inches between the side of the car and the top of the curb, so I stuffed some of my clothes and jackets into the gap to block the wind ... and went to sleep in a sleeping bag on that concrete sidewalk. Right next to my VW bug.

It was so cold that night that only a part of my nose stuck out of the sleeping bag ... and then only once in a while to get some extra air.

I slept pretty well too.

In the morning I prayed that the car would start ... and it did. *Barely.* God was with me.

After stuffing my clothes and sleeping bag back into the VW—keeping the front passenger seat clear so I could pick up a hitchhiker if the opportunity arose—I turned on the heater and continued east across Texas.

The West Texas temperature warmed up pretty quick that day—into the low 20's at least—as I drove at a top speed of about 67 miles an hour down the highway. I was in the middle of the proverbial *nowhere* (as great stretches of Texas tend to be) ... when I spotted something at the side of the highway:

In the fog of the early morning, struggling up out of a ditch was an old man. He had a full head of long white hair and a large pure-white beard. It made him look Santa Claus-like. He was dragging an old battered suitcase and a duffle bag with him as he climbed up to the road.

I stopped immediately to give him a ride.

Somehow we got his suitcase and duffle bag into the back of my VW and headed off, continuing east.

(Understand, this was the 1970's, a time of ubiquitous cross-country hitchhikers across America. I'd done it myself several times, and didn't hesitate to pick up riders when and where I could. After all, in those days a hitchhiker always had a story ... and I liked storytellers. Still do ... which is why #5 may have gotten in touch with me).

The old man looked to be at least 70, maybe older. It turned out he was a "fruit-picker" who followed the harvests, traveling across America, hitchhiking to where he needed to be, and living in migrant camps. On that day he was headed east toward the winter harvests in Florida.

We talked, that old man and I, for hours as we drove across Texas. I asked him if he wasn't scared, being as old as he was and staying in migrant labor camps and shelters. "Naw," he said, "not at all. They're the nicest people you could ever meet."

"Really!" I exclaimed, shocked.

"Oh sure," he said with a twinkle in his eye. "Sometimes they'll get in fights and might land on top of me, but it's only by accident and they always apologize later."

I was fascinated. Did he have any children, and if so why didn't he just settle down and live close to them? Wasn't it hard, living on the road and doing the work he did?

The old man was matter-of-fact about it. "I've got kids," he said, and told me where they lived in different parts of America. "But I don't want to be a burden on them. And besides, I have all I need with me."

"Everything?" I questioned.

"Yes indeed," he answered. "I've got my clothes in my suitcase and my sleeping bag and a tent in my duffle bag. I carry with me the only two books I need. They have all the answers to any question anyone would want to ask."

I treated the old man with deference (as I tended to do both then and now with the elderly, for there is a reason for the 5th Commandment, and it refers not only to our own parents but to other elders also).

I asked the old guy what the two books were.

"*The Bible* and *Moby Dick*," he said without hesitation.

"All questions answered?" I asked him, echoing what he had told me.

"Oh yeah," he said, "I read those two books over and over. They're my constant companions on the road ... and all the companionship I need."

We talked throughout the day as we hurried across Texas at the VW's roaring top speed of 60-something-miles-per-hour. The old fellow was both thoughtful and learned, and I was happy to have him as a companion. He answered my questions without hesitation or quibble, and I think our ongoing conversation entertained both of us over the long drive.

Toward the end of the day he asked if I'd drop him at an exit before Louisiana so he could go to ground in Texas (it might have even been west of Houston, I'm not sure). I told him that was fine and insisted in carrying him all the way off the Interstate to drop him right where he wanted to be ... at a small convenience store.

He thanked me for the long ride, but I told him I wanted to thank *him* for the long and enlightening conversations as I bade him farewell and headed back onto the Interstate.

That was over 40 years ago. I still think of the white-haired old gentleman on occasion, and wonder what became of him as he traveled the highways, following the harvests with his two constant companions, *The Bible* and *Moby Dick*.

I like to think that in his remaining years on this earth, *kindness and generosity* followed him and graced his life repeatedly. I reminisce and think of this because the whisper of the years tells me that I should. So even now I feel gratitude for the stories we shared as we traveled across the state of Texas that day.

Life is a journey, for all of us. Maybe we don't tend to understand that in our youth, but age will teach us if we make it that far. As for the old man, even now I recite these words for him some 40-odd years later:

May the road have risen up to meet you, may the wind have been at your back, may the sun have shined warmly upon your face, and may God have held you in the palm of his hand for all the rest of the days of your life.

All of this is true, and I now share it with you.

—Tim Condon, ALR.

Please visit the author's web page at:
www.algerineonyx.com

You can contact the author's representative at:
TCalr@protonmail.com

Achron Kindness is a work of fiction.
However, the Free State Project and people moving to live in New Hampshire are real. You can read about it–and them–at FSP.ORG on the Internet.

THE ALIEN TALE CONTINUES: A serving from ACHRON GENEROSITY

CHAPTER 1

The downtown San Diego lounge feels good to Abigale Godwin.

It always does: Smooth jazz plays unobtrusively in the background and subdued lighting glints off polished mahogany and brass fixtures as she rests her arms on brown leather padding at the bar. She sits there alone, and wonders ... .

At age 57 Abigale is retired. She used to have a high-flying, high-profile, high-pressure—and very highly-paid—position in a San Francisco industrial-tech company. She was suddenly (and unwillingly) "retired" from the job she had held (and gloried in) for nearly 30 years.

Now Abigale Godwin lives in San Diego.

Alone.

Oh, she's nicely dressed as she sits at the bar (very ... *professional*) and sips her Tanqueray Gin and tonic with a touch of ginger and Bay leaf (always the same). But she wonders ... is she on the verge of becoming a *regular* at the lounge? A *lonely* regular?

She hates the thought.

That's why Abigale Godwin only lets herself come here three nights a week.

No more than that.

Usually.

Still trying to figure out this retirement thing, she thinks with a hint of bitterness in the thought. It would be one thing if she'd been eased out of her position in her 60s—or maybe even her 70s—but it was entirely another to be outmaneuvered, outgunned, politically isolated, squashed and ejected … *by her own damned protege!*

Ungrateful bitch, she thinks furiously (and not for the first time). Even now she recalls the shock and dismay at being summarily sacked. *I took her under my wing! I mentored her!*

So now the professional Ms. Godwin has become the private Miss Godwin … a lady learning how to live a different life. She has plenty of money—more than she'll ever need—thanks to her expert stewardship of the company for nearly three decades. In fact, the money that came with her defenestration was more than she'd expected … a gesture of *goodwill.*

Nevertheless … *out with the goddamned garbage.* She chokes at the thought.

Now Abigale Godwin is learning there are other things in life outside of business … beyond money, beyond status, beyond power and beyond the exhilarating cut-and-thrust of corporate politics. Worse yet, she has come to realize something: *An impressive office? It's just a bigger cubicle … and still a cubicle.*

Alone at night she sometimes finds herself wondering … *what do I do now?* In those years of working 70-and-80-hour weeks, she had neither the time nor the inclination to enter into a romantic relationship with a man … much less fall in *love.*

The very thought was anathema.

But now Abigale Godwin has abundant time to think about her future … and her past: *I needed a man like a fish needs a bicycle.* She shrugs uneasily at the thought. *Never had time for that.* And besides, it was all traded for what she'd been told would be an exciting and fulfilling life in the world of business.

Far more exciting and fulfilling than mere marriage, motherhood and family.

Regret is what Abigale Godwin feels now. She recoils from the thought and does not share it with anyone. So she dresses up for no one in particular two or three nights a week—*oh, all right, sometimes four … or five*—to visit this lounge that she likes with its muted lighting and piped-in music. Except she also sees candles flickering on small tables, across which young couples share yearning, loving gazes.

Abigale Godwin? Her makeup is perfect, her clothes are perfect, her hair is perfectly coiffed … and a speck of perfume at her clavicles gives off a teasing hint, wafting a subtle invitation.

Gag me, she thinks as she sits unaccompanied at the bar. She winces at what she is becoming … and what she worries she might become for the rest of her life. Motioning to the bartender for another Tanqueray with ginger and Bay leaf, she mulls over what she will do when she goes home to her expensive high-rise apartment with its commanding view of the city skyline.

It will be empty.

Down beyond the end of the elongated bar the lounge door opens and a man steps in. He's a pedestrian-looking fellow of average height, middle-aged with dark hair. *Make that a dark hairpiece*, she smirks to herself as she looks him over. Even worse, he's wearing a stupid off-green polyester suit with an ugly brown striped tie loosened at the neck after a full day at work.

The new arrival pauses inside the door, his eyes adjusting to the light of the lounge, surveying the space and the people as they appear at 8:00 p.m. on a midweek night.

Oddly contrasting feelings well up within Abigale Godwin. She wants to continue her internal smirking at the new arrival, to enjoy a feeling of … not *contempt* exactly, but perhaps a sliver of *superiority*.

And yet … Abigale hopes the man will approach her—*him, someone, anyone*—to help break the aloneness she fears she will feel for the rest of her life. Her sense of superiority, of borderline contempt … it fades as the fellow walks straight up to where she sits at the bar.

He places a hand on the back of the chair next to Abigale and inquires: "*Buy you a drink?*" There's an impish grin on his face. She is charmed, despite what she was thinking about him only moments earlier.

"I'm sorry," she says, "I just ordered a drink." She pauses, then forges ahead: "But I'll buy *you* a drink."

The grin is still on his face as he responds: "I'm elated … and you're too kind! *May I sit next to you?*"

She doesn't know if his request is simple banter or a genuine gentlemanly gesture, but she smiles and nods toward the chair next to her. "Please do," she says.

He tells the hovering bartender, "Makers Mark and water on the rocks, please," then turns to Abigale Godwin, formerly CEO of a major high-tech industrial company, and says … "*So, what's a nice girl like you doing in a place like this?*" His grin is far wider, and he's resisting laughter.

"Well, well," says Abigale in a saucy voice, "*a sense of humor!* Do you mind if I fall in love?" She's grinning at him from ear-to-ear in spite of herself.

He switches to diffidence: "Well, um, I … *try.*" There's a hint of self-deprecation as he slides into the seat next to her and holds out a hand: "Darnell Swann," he tells her.

She takes his hand and is immediately embarrassed by the words that pop out of her mouth: "*Like the bird?*"

"Hey!" he says with mock-excitement. "*There's* a question I've never heard before!" They both laugh as Abigale tries to cover her embarrassment.

"Two N's," he says. "Not the bird … but maybe an ugly duckling."

There's that self-mocking humor again, thinks Abigale. She is delighted. "Not at all," she says, "you look perfectly presentable to me!" *I want him to like me,* she realizes with a start. The normal dose of internal sarcasm, a form of self-contempt, doesn't flow through her now like it usually does.

Someone to talk to!

And talk they do. Darnell Swann, it turns out, is "in insurance." It's not clear to Abigale whether he *sells* insurance or helps manage a company in one of the glass buildings that litter downtown San Diego.

It doesn't matter what he is, she thinks with some surprise. *He's making me laugh. He's real … an antidote, right here and now, to the loneliness that I'll never admit that I feel, every day of my life.*

It turns out he has a degree in sociology from a college in Oklahoma. Minored in business. "Didn't do me a whole lot of good," he says ruefully.

"Gotta major in *something*," she says reassuringly. "I majored in something even worse."

"That's not possible," he responds with a grin. "What's worse than sociology?"

For some reason Abigale is reluctant to say it. She hesitates ... then comes clean: "Um ... *gender studies?*"

Darnell Swann is a gentleman. He keeps a studiously neutral look on his face. "Gender studies," he repeats, sounding dubious in spite of himself.

"Yeah," says Abigale Godwin, sounding apologetic. "Thank God I minored in business."

Darnell Swann laughs. "Well, we do have *that* in common," he says, taking a sip of his depleted drink and gesturing to the bartender for another. "Can I buy *you* one now?" he asks.

"Of course," she nods happily. "Tanqueray and tonic. The bartender knows." Then she blanches at what she just revealed: *Does he think I come here alone all the time? Every night? Oh god I hope not!*

The drinks are set on the bar and they pick them up to toast each other.

Over the course of the next two hours they talk incessantly. He turns out to be an excellent conversationalist and Abigale feels herself relaxing, often laughing with him. She discovers that he's a car buff.

"Check this out," Darnell says furtively, leaning in as if to impart her a secret: "Guess what kind of car I'm driving tonight?"

"I'll bet I'm going to find out," she responds, grinning.

He raises his thick eyebrows comically at her: "Have you ever heard of ... *an Aston Martin DB5?*"

"No," she responds, "but can I find out?" He laughs again, and she's shocked to feel how much she enjoys the sound of his mannish chuckle.

"Think James Bond," he says with a wide grin on his face.

"James Bond?" she repeats, hesitating. Then ... "*James Bond!* The movies! Where he always drove cool cars, right?"

"One of them," he affirms. "I like famous old cars that have been on the big screen."

Abigale eyes him closely: "*Really*," she says with evident interest. "Does it have machine guns and flame throwers and an ejection seat and all that?"

He grins wider. "You've seen the movie!"

"Well, some of them," she says, "but that first one with all the gadgets stuck in my head especially the passenger side ejection seat to get rid of the bad guy."

He laughs out loud now: "No machine guns I'm afraid. No ejection seat either." He looks abashed at not having them, and just adorable. "Sorry … ."

"That's quite a hobby," she says, a hint of interest in her voice.

He rises to the bait: "Well this may be your lucky day! If you liked those old James Bond movies, this is your chance to look over the Aston Martin he drove in *Doctor No*." He pauses, then says, "I could give you a … *ride*." His eyes crinkle at her and she feels a flutter in her tummy as she gazes at him. Their faces are close together … closer than normal for a conversation.

"You promise not to … *eject me*?" she breathes at him in a low suggestive voice.

He holds up a hand, palm toward her with two fingers held up together: "Scouts Honor! No ejection seats in *my* Aston Martin!"

Abigale Godwin and Darnell Swann close out their check—Darnell insists on paying the whole thing—and they exit the soft light and sounds of the urban lounge, trading it for the lights and chaos of the city street. The bar is in a posh part of the city, and side streets radiate away, beckoning toward urban residential areas.

Once outside, Abigale asks him, "Okay, where are you hiding it?" She's looking up and down the street for the distinctive car but can't spot anything like it.

"It's in the lounge parking lot behind the building," he says.

"Then let's go see it!" she responds.

They walk down the sidewalk to the end of the block, take a left and go around back of the building. A small parking lot is tucked away there for regulars. Sure enough, Darnell points out the distinctive car, his beloved James Bond Aston Martin DB5.

"Wow," she says. "That is some *ride*!"

They walk together into the small parking area. The air is heavier back here, the city light attenuated. In fact it's dark, but Abigale Godwin feels secure as she always has in her ability to take care of herself.

"Take a look at *this*," he says, putting on a driving glove as he walks toward the back of the vehicle and gestures. "Machine gun ports!"

Abigale Godwin barks out a laugh, then scurries over, bending down to search out the *faux* machine gun portals. As she does so Darnell Swann swings a short, vicious punch with his gloved hand straight into her temple. She doesn't see it coming and collapses heavily to the ground, unconscious. In the darkness she looks like a "knockout game" victim.

Darnell Swann looks around furtively. No one else is in the darkened parking area. He stays stooped down, out of sight behind the car, puts on the other driving glove and pushes a button on the back of the Aston Martin. The trunk lid releases and he reaches in, coming out with a roll of duct tape and some black nylon cable-ties, the kind that police use to immobilize people under arrest.

Pulling Abigale's unresisting arms behind her back, he loops her wrists together with a cable tie and pulls it tight, then rolls her body onto its side. He loops another cable-tie around her ankles and yanks it tight, then bends her legs at the knees and uses another to secure her bound wrists to her bound ankles. She is effectively "hog-tied." He wraps duct tape repeatedly and tightly around her head and over her mouth, a gag she cannot reach.

Darnell Swann is not the man's name. He is sometimes known as Perry Lichter, at other times as Robert Luther, and still other times as Raoul Jennings … as well as other names. His real name is *Eldon Chandler* and he easily rolls Abigale Godwin's inert body into the low trunk of the Aston Martin, quietly snapping it shut. He stands and walks to the driver's seat on the right side of the car, gets in and starts it. He pulls out of the dimly lit parking area and turns onto the street, joining the flow of traffic.

Abigale Godwin won't be missed for days, he thinks … *maybe even a week*. Eldon Chandler knows this because he knows about her. He's done this before, and is well-prepared. Tonight … well *tonight*: He swells with anticipation at what the hours ahead will bring to him … and to her.

A commercial rental car location looms in a deserted industrial area. This time of night it is closed and empty, but he pulls in and drives into unlit shadows behind a building adjacent to the car lot. His four-wheel-drive truck is parked in the darkness there. Opening the narrow passenger door of his truck next to the back of the Aston Martin, Eldon Chandler drags Abigale Godwin from the trunk and shoves her into the passenger space behind the truck's driver's seat. She's only semi-conscious and doesn't resist as he slams the narrow door.

The keys to the Aston Martin are put under its door mat and the doors locked. Eldon Chandler knows the rental agency will find the car that was rented by a man named Perry Lichter. They'll have the keys to get into the vehicle and will think nothing of it.

Because he has worn gloves every moment he has touched the car, there are no fingerprints on it. None of his, at least.

Chandler starts the truck and drives out of the darkness behind the building. He pulls onto the late-night thoroughfare and accelerates, knowing exactly where he's going. He soon turns onto Interstate ramp, merging into the fast-moving night traffic heading east ... into the vast Southern California desert. He will take Abigale Godwin to a prearranged location, one already prepared for this night, a spot so solitary that no one will happen upon it by accident, and wouldn't know even if they did.

As he drives east on the Interstate Eldon Chandler rubs his chin, thinking about how long it will take to grow another thick beard as he has in the past. He removes his black hairpiece and opens the truck's windows to shake his long brownish hair out to fly in the wind. The thick eyebrows he's glued above his eyes are peeled off, and from his mouth he pulls out the cheek implants that changed the structure—and therefore the look— of his face.

His colored contact lenses will come out later, at his convenience.

Eldon Chandler is a psychopath. And because he is a psychopath he has no conscience or concept of right and wrong beyond what he desires, and therefore demands. He does not and cannot empathize with others ... or even fathom their distress, pain or terror. Those things are irrelevant to him, and thus unworthy of consideration. He doesn't think about them.

But he does know what he likes to do ... which is kidnap, rape, and kill women. He has done this 18 times before. This will be his 19th kill.

I kill dogs, he recites to himself inside his viciously twisted mind. Because women are his chosen prey, he refers to himself as ... *"dog-killer."*

Why? Because inside the blackened soul of Eldon Chandler, women are bitches. *And bitches are dogs.*

The gruesome, horrifying reality that Eldon Chandler lives in is reptilian. Tonight the reptile whispers to him as he drives through the onrushing darkness, deeper into the desert. He is pleased to hear its affirmation:

You are … Killer-of-dogs.

CHAPTER 2

At some point as he speeds through the southern California desert Eldon Chandler starts paying close attention to the flowing mile markers. He's looking for a certain place known only to him. It is well east and somewhat north of San Diego, in the wilderness.

At this place there is a break in the fencing bordering the Interstate highway. It cannot be seen, even if one is looking for it, because it is designed not to be seen. But it is there, and can be reached by pulling off the Interstate at a certain mile marker, then driving over rough ground to where brushy desert plants and trees happen to obscure the fence line from sight.

This is where the man who calls himself Darnell Swann pulls off the highway, douses his truck lights and drives through the grassy verge by moonlight only. He stops at a spot behind the screening vegetation next to the fence, a place where he cannot be seen from the highway.

Swann wields a tiny LED flashlight as he gets out of the truck and approaches a certain fence post behind the concealing shrubbery. He unhurriedly unhooks the fence at three spots on the post and pulls it aside just enough to drive the truck through. On the other side he stops and gets out to re-close the fence, then drives away from the highway in a northerly direction, guided only by moonlight over the unmarked terrain. He has been here before, and thus knows both what he is looking for and how far he must go.

In time the truck crests a sandy abutment and half-slides down the other side. There is no sound to be heard, for it is far enough away from the highway that not even the growling of distant 18-wheelers drift in the night air. At the bottom of the declivity the driver stops the truck and turns on its parking lights only. No one can see the lights because the truck is at the bottom of sandy abyss … a deserted desert ravine with sloping sandy sides.

Darnell Swann, whose real name is Eldon Chandler, recently found this spot with the help of a geolocation application on a burner smart phone. Now he moves the truck so that the dim lights reveal a place on the ground he has previously prepared. He steps out and opens the truck's small passenger compartment door, reaching in and dragging out Abigale Godwin. He drops her bound body roughly to the ground.

She is fully conscious, and guttural noises of fear issue from her as she struggles, trying to scream through the duct tape wrapped tightly around her head and mouth. Her knees are still bent with ankles secured to her wrists pulled tightly behind her back.

Yes, Eldon Chandler has recently visited this place. In fact, within the past few days he dug a hole close to where the truck is parked. The digging was easy in the sandy ground, and the pit is perhaps six feet long by three and a half feet wide. It is a few feet deep and is covered by a lightweight sheet of brown fiberglass sheathing that matches the color of the desiccated ground. He turns the truck's parking lights off and uses the small LED flashlight to walk to the plastic panel and pull it aside and reveal the hole.

From the ground nearby Abigale Godwin can see what has been uncovered. She is sobbing and crying in terror as she tries to wail through the duct tape over her mouth. Because there is moonlight, Eldon Chandler douses the flashlight after uncovering the hole. He can see well enough for what he intends to do.

There are no humans here for miles. The closest ones are those speeding down the Interstate highway heading west into the southern California conurbation that includes the San Diego-Los Angeles urban matrix. Others head east toward Phoenix or Tucson farther south, and then maybe El Paso. Almost all of them travel in vehicles nearly hermetically sealed against the desert air.

The man retrieves a shovel from the pickup truck bed. It has a peculiar round-point head that is flat. There is no angle to the end of the shovel where the metal slots into the wooden shaft. He pulls a folding knife out of one pocket as he walks over to Abigale Godwin lying trussed and sobbing on the ground. Opening the lock-blade knife he moves it toward her face as she tries to recoil in abject terror.

"Here you go," he says in a kindly voice, and cuts through the duct tape wrapped around her head, ripping it from her face and hair. He also cuts the cable-tie linking her wrists to her ankles and pulls roughly on her bound feet to straighten her body out. She lies on her back now, her hands still bound behind her. Eldon Chandler stands silently, as if watching to see what she will do.

Abigale Godwin thrashes about, shrieking and wailing for help—*help from anyone!*—when Eldon Chandler suddenly swings the flat metal bottom of the shovel down on her face. She continues screaming for help, so he hefts the shovel and brings the flat metal end down again on her unprotected face. Blood is spurting from her nose and mouth as she still cries out, but not so loudly.

Again, and then another time, Chandler raises the shovel and smashes it down. Her forehead is cut and her eyes will soon be blackened and swollen shut. Blood is all over her face.

Abigale Godwin abruptly rolls over to lie face down on the ground in a desperate effort to escape the pounding shovel. She is sobbing into the dirt but no longer crying out for help.

"That's a good girl," says Eldon Chandler. "Your yelling ... it *bothers* me."

Through her sobs Abigale begs for her life. She'll do anything. She'll never tell anyone. She cries in terror, begging for her life. Eldon Chandler leans down and grabs a handful of her long blond hair, dragging her onto the brown fiberglass panel lying next to the hole in the ground.

"I don't like to get dirt on myself," he explains to the battered, terrorized woman. She is still face down, still sobbing and begging him. He kicks her sharply in the ribs once, twice, three times. It feels like his shoe has a steel toe. She cries out in pain as he kicks her. He walks around to her other side and viciously kicks her several times in the ribs there.

"Maybe you should be quiet," he says. He waits. She is sobbing on the ground. He kicks her sharply in the ribs again. "Keep the noise up and I'll keep cracking ribs," he says in a conversational voice. She falls silent, her body shaking.

"Ahhh … that's better," he says gently.

Now he leans down with the knife, holding the shovel in the other hand, and cuts the cable tie binding her ankles. She is lying on her stomach on the fiberglass panel. "Pants off!" he says cheerily as he inserts his pocket knife under her slacks at the small of her back to tear them off. Because she screams as he does it, he stands up and smashes the flat side of the shovel down again, this time on the back of her head.

She cries out, then quiets, sobbing silently in terror.

"Better," he says again in a low voice as he leans the shovel against the side of his truck. He reaches down, grabs her shredded pants and pulls them violently off her body. Her shoes come off with the slacks and only a pair of pantyhose covers her backside. He grasps the elastic band of the hose at her waist, pulls it upward and slices through the fabric with his knife. Yanking the hose roughly down and off her legs, Chandler tosses them into the hole.

Abigale Godwin is on her face, naked from the waist down, her hands still cable-tied behind her back. She trembles in terror.

Chandler reaches down, grasps a handful of her hair and pulls her face up from the ground. "See this?" he says, holding the knife blade in front of her face. "Nod if you see it, or you'll get more of the shovel." She nods quickly, her eyes wide in terror.

"I'm going to use this to cut your hands loose," he says. "Won't that be great?" Abigale Godwin is frozen in shock.

"If you try to get away, I'll cut you like this … ." He inserts the end of the knife into one of her nostrils and moves the sharp edge of the blade experimentally against the flesh on the inside of her nose.

"No, no, no, no I won't," she begs, "I won't try to get away!"

"Good," he says, and removes the blade from her nose. "If you act like a good girl now you might have an interesting story to tell. If you try to get away or attack me, you will die from multiple stab wounds … starting with your *face*."

Abigale Godwin shakes her head violently back and forth. "I won't do anything!" she pleads.

Chandler releases her hair, reaches down and slices through the plastic cable tie binding her hands behind her back. She is too terrorized to move as he stands over her.

"Roll over," he commands. She complies with difficulty, rolling onto her back. Her face is bloody and swelling and she groans in pain from the ribs his kicks have cracked. Above her, Eldon Chandler smiles widely.

"Would you like to fuck me?" he asks conversationally. Frozen in terror, she does not respond.

Chandler sighs heavily and shakes his head. "Whores," he says sadly, "you're all whores." He hefts the shovel again, this time slowly, and lazily swings it down at her face so she can raise her arms to take the force of the impact. Chandler hefts the shovel again and again, bringing it down harder on her arms covering her face. One elbow appears to be dislocated or broken as she cries out in horror and pain.

Finally, in desperation Abigale Godwin rolls back onto her stomach, groaning in pain as she does so. Now Chandler turns the shovel head sideways and slashes it down on the back of her naked, unprotected legs. The edge of the shovel is sharpened to a knife-like edge and it cuts deeply as blood gushes from the wounds. He does the same to her buttocks. Several times. She rolls on the ground screaming as she tries to escape the slashing knife-blade of the shovel cutting into her flesh.

Chandler stops and stands silently, as if surveying his work. "Bitch," he says to her. "I kill dogs. *I kill them.*" Abigale Godwin is lapsing into shock, losing blood both internally and externally.

Because this is the 19th time he has done this, Eldon Chandler has left a trail of dead bodies strewn randomly across North America. Police authorities have tried to find a geographic pattern in the case, but failed. In fact, police throughout the country have been coordinating information about the uniquely gruesome murders. But so far there has been no breakthrough.

The psychopath apparently works alone, and follows no geographic trajectory. The frustrated authorities have even given the string of unsolved cases a name: They are called *The Ditchdigger Murders* because of the identical shallow graves prepared for the victims.

"Roll over," Eldon Chandler orders Abigale Godwin lying on the ground below him. He viciously kicks her again in the side. "I said *roll onto your back!*" She is barely able to roll onto her back, groaning in pain. "That's better," he says as he kicks her naked legs apart. Shock is taking its toll on the abused woman, and her consciousness is mercifully fading.

As the woman lapses into unconsciousness, Eldon Chandler pauses. He is breathing heavily, as if from physical exertion. He feels *very* good now, very *alive* as he stands, admiring the demonic damage he has done to the tortured woman lying beneath him. Her mouth sags open, blond hair plastered across her face, disheveled and soaked with blood. His penis inside his pants is fully engorged, his sexual excitement rising.

Off to one side, unnoticed in the darkness ... another set of eyes watches the unfolding scene. The eyes are slit vertically, the eyes of a *reptile*. They belong to a large adult rattlesnake. This location, like virtually everywhere else in North America, is rattlesnake country, and the unmoving eyes are those of a fully grown Western Diamondback Rattler. It has been drawn from its den by the sounds of the man and his victim, by vibrations in the ground and by the cries of anguish from the woman.

The snake is huge, easily in excess of 7 feet long, and weighs well over 25 pounds. It uncoils and slides silently across the sandy ground as it approaches the man standing over the bloodied woman.

Eldon Chandler begins pulling his trousers down, exposing his thighs and knees. The woman lying at his feet on the fiberglass panel is unconscious. *Like a corpse*, he thinks with excitement, anticipating the bloody rape to come. *Like a warm corpse!*

His pants down to his ankles, Chandler bends over, preparing to kneel between the naked spread legs of his unmoving victim ... when he is violently struck on the side of his thigh. The impact is so hard that it feels like he's been hit there with a club.

The rattlesnake strike brings instant pain, like a sharp knife slashing into his leg. Agony lances out from the load of injected venom as the man reflexively reaches down to where he has been bitten, blind to the cause of the pain. Even now Eldon Chandler does not see the well-camouflaged reptile coiled next to him on the ground. As his arm drops to his thigh the snake strikes again, this time injecting a load of poison into his arm.

New pain explodes, radiating up his arm and into Eldon Chandler's upper body. He shrieks in terror, trying to back away from the body on the ground, but stumbles with his pants down around his ankles. The poison that has been injected into him is not normal rattlesnake venom. It has been modified. It will still kill, but does so more slowly and more painfully. An additional chemical compound has been added, one similar to the paralyzing agent curare.

Thus, Eldon Chandler is losing control of his body as he cries out in agony, wobbles and keels over into the dirt. Paralysis is setting in even as radiating pain consumes his consciousness. He tries to cry out, but only manages to whimper in terror as he lies on the ground.

The man has fallen in such a way that he lies exposed, sprawled in the dirt with his pants down around his ankles. He finally sees the snake coiled next to him, ready to strike again, the rattles buzzing loudly at the end of an upraised tail. But as he lies frozen the rattling suddenly stops ... and the huge snake uncoils and slithers directly toward him.

He can see the snake coming and tries to scream in terror, but only a squeak emerges as the huge reptile glides in between his bare legs, then up over his exposed crotch. It continues up, crossing his belly and chest to approach his *face*.

My FACE! The snake is on my FACE! Eldon Chandler releases his bladder onto the ground in terror. He is about to shit himself in horror as he lies unable to move with the terrible reptile *slithering on his face*. It loops under his chin, moving languidly, then nudges at the opening to an ear. He is gibbering inside his head, barely human in his fear and horror.

The snake is trying to enter my body! Through my ear!

But the snake's head is huge. It won't fit.

As he lies whimpering and paralyzed, Eldon Chandler maintains only a tenuous hold on his sanity. Dread panic and horror consume him as the huge snake's head nudges again at his ear, and he ... *hears something.*

Something is ... *speaking* to him. Speaking *AT him!*

Dear God it's in my EAR! he whimpers in terror, trying to cry out, but cannot. *The snake! The goddamned SNAKE at my ear! It's TALKING!*

And indeed it is.

Eldon Chandler hears it speaking directly into his auditory canal. The voice is tiny. It has a tinny sound too, like a mechanical device put into a doll to captivate and charm a young girl. As his veins turn to ice and his tenuous grip on sanity dwindles, Eldon Chandler hears an admonition:

Looks like you've got a problem, asshole.

~~~~

Achron Generosity is expected to be released in late 2019 or early 2020 …depending on public demand and the work habits of Algerine Onyx (also known as #5).